"*Don't Skip Out on Me* is going to make your heart crumple into a little wad of paper and then open it back up into a perfect paper airplane sailing the skies from the hand of a boy. No one anywhere writes as beautifully about people whose stories stay close to the dirt. Willy Vlautin is a secular—and thus real and profoundly useful—saint."
— Lidia Yuknavitch, author of *The Book of Joan*

"Vlautin writes with patience, tenderness, and a sharp eye toward the subtle things that can wear a person down—the fights we don't know we're losing until it's already too late."
— *Los Angeles Review of Books*

"Willy Vlautin is now one of America's great writers."
— Roddy Doyle

"Willy Vlautin will break your heart with his hardscrabble characters. He's the champion of the marginalized, the traumatized, the lonely, and the bereft, ennobling and imbuing the most unlikely characters with a pathos and generosity generally reserved for saints. The world needs more Willy Vlautin, and *Don't Skip Out on Me* is his best novel yet."
— Jonathan Evison, author of *This is Your Life, Harriet Chance!* and *The Revised Fundamentals of Caregiving*

"In [*Don't Skip Out on Me*] Vlautin writes about characters whose big dreams and plans are often stunted by fate and circumstance, but who've managed to find a way to push through, bruised but with hard-won wisdom. . . . Excellent. . . . Vlautin's reverence for the land recalls writers such as Jim Harrison and John Steinbeck."
— *Publishers Weekly* (starred review)

"Vlautin excels in gritty narratives of the American West and has earned a reputation for his economy of words and the courage with which he tells the stories of his working-class characters."

—*San Francisco Chronicle*

"*Don't Skip Out on Me* is riveting. . . . Vlautin's colorful characters inhabit both lonely Nevada ranch landscapes and gritty city scenes. Their world is painted with unflinching reality and raw emotion, yet also with compassion and heart, creating a compelling read."

—*Christian Science Monitor*

"Vlautin's prose is deceptively simple, his clipped descriptions loaded with meaning. The narrative is as unsparing as Hopper's fights, but what stays standing is a profound sense of hope, a hope that drives society's downtrodden and provides the theme for much of Vlautin's work."

—*Financial Times*

"In this climate, a writer like Willy Vlautin seems like one of the last souls left standing on trad-narrative's working-class battlements. He's the literary version of a Neil Young or a Tom Petty, bearing a ragged standard for empathy, compassion and decency, defending notions of the story as a sorting office for the soul. In other words, he's a throwback to a generation of novelists who still championed the underclass and promoted socialist values in fiction: everyone from John Steinbeck to Nelson Algren, or, more latterly, William Kennedy or Annie Proulx."

—*Irish Times*

"Willy Vlautin is the poet laureate of the downtrodden and disenfranchised underclass of American society, detailing with real empathy and insight the daily struggle of his characters in modern society. [*Don't Skip Out on Me*] is just as touching and hard-bitten as his previous work, telling the story of Horace Hopper, a young farm hand in rural Nevada who leaves the farm and heads for the city to try to fulfill his dream to be a professional boxer. Brutal and tender in equal measure, this is exemplary storytelling."

—*The Big Issue*

"Vlautin is on to something about what's wrong with America and many Americans. There is something self-defeating in Horace's personality that exemplifies an unfortunate tendency among certain Americans, corporate managers, and factory workers alike: even though they boast about rugged independence, they're all too willing to take abuse. . . . The tension over whose sensibility will prevail makes this book worth reading — but it infuses it with a peculiarly American sort of pain."

—The Spectator (London)

"Vlautin's sparse, plain sentences are well matched to the brusque world he depicts. At the same time, his compassion for his characters never wavers." *—Sunday Times* (London)

"In *The Free*, Willy Vlautin gives us a portrait of American life that is so hard and so heartbreaking that it should be unbearable, but it isn't. The straightforward beauty of Vlautin's writing, and the tender care he shows his characters, turns a story of struggle into indispensable reading. I couldn't recommend it more highly."

—Ann Patchett

"Few contemporary western writers tell the truth with the unerring eye of Willy Vlautin, a literary realist whose emotionally charged characters achieve that rarest of goals in fiction—to tell a great story."

—Craig Johnson, author of the Walt Longmire Mystery series

"Willy Vlautin is one of the bravest novelists writing. Murderers, cheats, sadists, showy examples of the banality of evil are easy, but it takes real courage to write a novel about ordinary good people—common people, the ones who never get the breaks, the ones who need, and know, compassion. An unsentimental Steinbeck, a heartbroken Haruf, Willy Vlautin tells us who really lives now in our America, our city in ruins."

—Ursula K. Le Guin

"Willy Vlautin writes novels about people all alone in the wind. His prose is direct and complex in its simplicity, and his stories are sturdy and bighearted and full of lives so shattered they shimmer. . . . His prose is strong, his storytelling is honest, and he sticks to it scene by scene. . . . *Lean on Pete* riveted me. Reading it, I was heartbroken and moved; enthralled and convinced. This is serious American literature."   —Cheryl Strayed, *Oregonian*

"If you want an unadorned portrait of American life (at least in some places) at the beginning of the twenty-first century, this is the book for you. . . . Vlautin's eye for detail is sharp: every character is distinctly drawn and memorable. . . . For sheer cinema-verité detailing of American life right now, *Lean on Pete* is a good place to start."
—Jane Smiley, *The Guardian* (London)

"*Northline* shines with naked honesty and unsentimental humanity. The character of Allison Johnson, and the wounded-but-still-walking people she encounters on her journey, will stay with me for a long while. Vlautin has written the American novel that I've been hoping to find."   —George Pelecanos

"Reading Willy Vlautin is like jumping into a clear, cold lake in the middle of summer. His prose is beautifully sparse and clean, but underneath the surface lies an incredible depth, with all kinds of hidden stories and emotions resting in the shadows"
—Hannah Tinti

"I love Willy Vlautin's novels. Downbeat and plaintive as they are, the tenderness holds on like the everlasting arms. . . . Willy's voice is pure and his stories universal. He never loses hope or heart, and I believe every word he's written."   —Barry Gifford

DON'T SKIP OUT ON ME

DON'T SKIP OUT ON ME

A Novel

WILLY VLAUTIN

HARPER ● PERENNIAL

NEW YORK ● LONDON ● TORONTO ● SYDNEY ● NEW DELHI ● AUCKLAND

HARPER ● PERENNIAL

A hardcover edition of this book was published in 2018 by HarperCollins Publishers.

HarperCollins books may be purchased for educational, business, or sales promotional use. For information, please email the Special Markets Department at SPsales@harpercollins.com.

FIRST HARPER PERENNIAL PAPERBACK EDITION PUBLISHED 2019.

Library of Congress Cataloging-in-Publication Data has been applied for.

ISBN 978-0-06-268447-9 (pbk.)

HB 04.26.2024

For my brother John

DON'T SKIP OUT ON ME

1

Horace Hopper opened his eyes and looked at the clock: five a.m. The first thought that came to him that morning was his mother, whom he hadn't seen in nearly three years. Then he thought about how in a little more than a week's time he'd be alone on a bus heading to Tucson. Awake less than a minute and already there was a pit in his stomach.

He got up and dressed in jeans and a plaid long-sleeve western shirt. He put on his boots and then tried to wake himself. He drank a glass of water and stared at the boxers' photographs he'd taped to the wall of the camping trailer.

The cutouts were from issues of *The Ring* magazine and the fighters were Mexican. The largest image was from the fight between Israel Vázquez and Rafael Márquez. It was the third round of their fourth fight, and Vázquez was hitting Márquez with a brutal left hook. To the right of that photo was Rafael Márquez's brother, the great Juan Manuel Márquez, and to the left of him the legend, Julio César Chávez, wearing a sombrero. Below them was a picture of Horace's favorite boxer, Érik Morales. To the left of Morales was Juan Díaz, and on that one Horace had written with a black marker: "The Scholar." Beside The Scholar was Antonio Margarito. A black marker had crossed out his face. "The Cheater."

He grabbed a worn and frayed notebook from a shelf next to the bed and opened it. The first page read "Log of Bad Dreams," handwritten with a blue pen. He flipped through a half dozen filled pages until he came to "Getting Left in Tonopah." Underneath it were thirty-two marks. He added another, making it thirty-three. He then thumbed to the back pages of the notebook, and near the bottom of a nearly full page he put down the date and wrote the same thing he had written the day before and the day before that, "I will be somebody."

He set a kettle on the propane stove, made instant coffee, scrambled four eggs, and then took them outside to eat at a picnic table in the blue of morning. The 1983 white and orange Prowler trailer was set on a hill overlooking the two-thousand-acre Little Reese Ranch, a hundred yards behind the main buildings. A tin-roofed awning hung out the front of the trailer. Under it was a bicycle, the picnic table, a barbecue, and a lawn chair. Parked beside it was a broken-down four-door Saturn with a flat tire. He'd moved there from the main house when he graduated high school. It was Mr. Reese's idea, thinking maybe Horace wanted his own space, where he could stay up as late as he wanted, play his music as loud as he wanted, and bring over whomever he wanted. A bachelor pad.

Below him, at the bottom of the hill, Horace could see no lights on in the main house, and past it no lights in the lambing shed, and only a faint sign of light coming from the main barn. He finished his breakfast, washed the dishes, made two meals of bologna and cheese slices stacked on top of each other, and filled two water bottles. He put his lunch and an extra shirt and pair of socks, along with his CD player, Pantera's *The Great Southern Trendkill,* Crowbar's *Sever the Wicked Hand,* and Slayer's *Show No Mercy,* in his backpack. He took his coat and sleeping bag and headed down the hill.

Horace was twenty-one years old, stood five feet, seven inches tall, and weighed 125 pounds. He was half white and half Paiute with long black hair that came down past his shoulders. His eyes were dark brown, he had a long, thin nose, and even at his age he only seldom had to shave. Under his shirt, on his left bicep, was a tattoo. In red ink it read "Slayer," and below that in black ink "Hell Awaits," then a black horned skull with two red eyes.

As he walked in the dawn light he looked beyond the ranch and hayfields toward the barren desert floor of Ralston Valley— sagebrush, small patches of prairie grass, the occasional bird or rabbit, and a scattering of lonely pinyon pines. The Little Reese Ranch was ten miles from its nearest neighbor, thirty miles from a paved road, and sixty miles from the closest town, Tonopah.

Inside the barn Horace saw the old man leaning against the workbench writing on a yellow pad. Beside him was a metal cane and curled in a ball at his feet was a retired black and white border collie, Little Lana.

"Good morning, Mr. Reese," Horace said as he came in.

"Morning," the old man replied, his eyes staying on the yellow pad. "The supplies are waiting on the porch and I got you a cup of coffee. It's sitting on the drill press."

Horace walked over to it.

"You about ready?"

"I think so," said Horace.

"Who did you decide to take?"

"Boss and Honey."

Mr. Reese quit writing and looked over to Horace. "You know I've been thinking about Boss. You've done a lot of good work on him. I never thought he would make it."

"He always wanted to be a good horse," Horace said. "He just wasn't sure how."

"I didn't see it."

"You would have, I was just the one working with him."

Mr. Reese nodded and went back to writing. He was seventy-two years old, slender, nearly six feet tall, with short, thin gray hair. He wore faded jeans, a light-blue western work shirt, and weathered cowboy boots. He picked up an English-to-Spanish dictionary and skimmed through the pages until he found the word he wanted and wrote it down on the yellow pad.

Horace drank his coffee and then got two rope halters from the tack room and went to the corral. He haltered Boss first and then Honey, led them both out, and tied them to a rail in front of the barn. He brushed them and saddled Boss, put panniers on Honey, and then carried down the supplies from the house and put them in the truck. After that he waited as Mr. Reese continued working on his letter. When he'd finished, the old man took the letter, a phone card, and three photocopied sections of map, folded them, and sealed them inside a white envelope. He addressed it "Pedro" and handed it to Horace.

"I know I've already gone over this, but do you mind if we do it one more time?"

"I don't mind," said Horace.

The old man cleared his throat. "So we both know Pedro understands English. He acts like he doesn't when it suits him, but he does. This letter is in Spanish 'cause I want everything to be clear. I don't want any confusion. The main things are to see how Pedro is holding up and to see how Víctor is working out. You were gone working for Harrington when Víctor came here and you've only done the one drop since then. The truth is we both don't know much about him. And remember his Spanish is rudimentary and he doesn't know any English. The only language he knows for certain is Peruvian. It's called Quechua. It makes no sense to me when he speaks it. I ordered a Quechua dictionary but it hasn't come yet. So get Pedro to translate. He knows the language. Ask Víctor how he likes it out here, how he likes being a herder. Ask him if he'd be comfortable with his own flock, and then separately ask Pedro if he thinks Víctor's coming along good enough to do it. I'm supposed to talk to Conklin again next week. Knowing how Víctor is doing will help me decide if I want to expand. If I do the deal and buy Conklin's twelve hundred, I'll need another full-time herder."

"All right," said Horace.

"Inside the envelope is a prepaid calling card with fifty dollars on it. Make sure Pedro's still charging the cell phone. Last time I saw him he said he was having trouble with the solar charger, but it worked fine for me when I tried it. He's been out four months now. It was this time last year when he began having problems. It should be better 'cause Víctor is his relative and has been with him. But even so, check if he's shaving, how the camp looks, and how the dogs are."

"It was pretty rough to see him like that last time," said Horace.

The old man nodded. "I've been worrying about him every day, but he said he was ready to go back to work. He said he got help, so we'll see."

Horace nodded. "Is your back any better this morning?"

The old man shrugged. "Don't worry about me. Just make sure everything's all right up there and be careful. The report says it's gonna hit near a hundred so remember to stay hydrated and stop at the creek for the horses."

"I know," Horace said and smiled.

Mr. Reese gave off a short laugh. "I'm sorry. I guess the older I get the more I have to say everything twice."

Boss and Honey swayed in the stock trailer along the gravel road and the sun began its rise over the Monitor Range. For as long as Horace could see there was nothing around him but sagebrush and hills and sky. He put in a Copenhagen, searched for radio stations, and drove thirty miles before turning east on an unmarked dirt road toward the foothills. The road worsened and he stopped, locked in the hubs, and put the old truck into four-wheel drive. He eased over washouts and around rocks until he reached the derelict mine site, where he parked at the foot of a narrow canyon. Across the road were a series of single-jack mines and a tipped-over camping trailer. Farther up was the main mine site, where the rubble of old buildings sat next to a hole filled with rusted-out mine equipment and a tire-less horse trailer.

From the truck's glove box, he took a laminated sign—THIS TRUCK BELONGS TO THE REESE RANCH. PLEASE DON'T VANDALIZE! WE'RE A MOM-AND-POP OUTFIT—and put it under the windshield wiper. He locked the truck, put on a wide-brimmed cowboy hat, opened the dusty stock trailer, and unloaded the horses.

He tightened both cinches, loaded the supplies on Honey, got on Boss, and started off. The mining road narrowed to a trail and the canyon's rise began. Pinyon pine and birch trees appeared with more regularity and the small trickle from the creek that ran along the trail grew to a constant flow. He kept the reins and the pony lead in his left hand, and with his right held a hand exerciser. He squeezed it a hundred times and then switched it to his left hand. He went back and forth and back and forth as he rode. He tried not to think that this would be the last time he'd make the trip, but he couldn't help it, and his heart sank.

"I won't forget you guys," he said to the horses. "I'll miss you every day, but I'll be back. I'll be different when I'm back but I'll be here and I'll make sure you're taken care of. Don't worry too much, okay?"

By midday he had climbed to 7,500 feet. Boss made his way slow and sure-footed along the rocky trail and Honey followed along sluggishly until they left the canyon and came to a plateau, where a large bowl-shaped meadow appeared. The mountains around them rose past 12,000 feet. In the distance Horace could make out the flock, the eleven hundred sheep, and could hear the faint sounds of bleats and the barking of dogs. He took the horses to the creek, let them drink, and continued on.

He saw first Tiny, a brown and white border collie. He whistled for her and got down from Boss. The nub of Tiny's tail wagged excitedly as she came to him. He checked her paws for cuts. With a pocketknife he took two mats of hair off her rump, and then ran his hands through her fur, feeling for ticks, but found none. He put a new flea collar on her and together they walked the horses toward a blue tarp in a grove of aspens at the edge of the meadow.

Mr. Reese's donkey, Myrtle, stood on meadow grass, highlined in between two trees, and the herder, Pedro, lay on his back, asleep on his pad near a spent fire. The grass around him was beat down and above him the aspens quaked in the breeze. Next to his bed were a plastic gallon jug of water and a pair of leather boots. The cooking pans were clean and sitting on a green Coleman stove and a rifle leaned against a tree. Two shirts and three pairs of socks hung on a makeshift clothesline, and farther back, nearly out of sight, was the carcass of a lamb in a dressing bag hanging from a sturdy branch.

"Get him up, Tiny," Horace said gently to the dog. "Go get Pedro." The dog walked to the sleeping man and licked his face. Pedro yelled and sat up, startled.

"Hola, Pedro," said Horace and laughed. Tiny ran back to him and hid behind his legs.

Pedro was clean shaven and smiled a mouth of silver and missing teeth. He was a short, dark-skinned man with a potbelly and thinning brown hair. His pants fell as he stood. He wore no underwear. He pulled his trousers up, buttoned them, and cinched his belt. He put on his socks and boots.

"Mr. Reese's back is still out so you got me again. How have things been?"

Pedro shrugged his shoulders.

"Where's Víctor?"

"Víctor es gone." Pedro sighed and shook his head.

"Gone?" asked Horace.

"Sí."

"Gone where?"

Pedro again shrugged and pointed to the mountains.

"Is he gone just right now or is he gone for good?"

"Loco," Pedro said.

"¿Loco? What do you mean?"

Pedro shrugged his shoulders. "Víctor take rifle and point at me. Say he kill me if I don't get him out of *las montañas.*" He looked at the ground and kicked at the dirt with his boot.

"What happened after that?"

"I got the rifle away," Pedro said and smiled. "The next *mañana Víctor no aquí.*"

"How long ago?"

Pedro put up his hand and showed two fingers.

"¿Dos días?" said Horace.

Pedro nodded.

Wally, an eight-year-old black and white border collie, came into camp. Horace called for him and checked his paws and looked him over for ticks. He cut four mats of hair off him and put on a new flea collar.

"Where's Little Roy?"

Pedro shook his head. *"Con Víctor."*

"Little Roy's with Víctor?"

Pedro nodded.

"¿Donde es Víctor?"

Pedro again pointed to the mountains behind them. "I tell him no city here, but he go to find city. He no like *las ovejas*. Víctor *es deprimido*."

"How are Jip and Whitey?"

"Bueno . . . Con las ovejas."

Horace looked out into the meadow until he saw the two Anatolians hidden in the middle of the flock. He looked back at Pedro and then past him to the carcass behind camp. "What about the lamb?"

Pedro looked at it and then looked at Horace. "Víctor kill it two days ago. We fight. I say no."

"Víctor killed it?"

"Sí," Pedro said.

Horace took the envelope from his backpack and handed it to Pedro. "These are the instructions from Mr. Reese and a new phone card. Let's unload Honey and then you read the letter, okay?"

Pedro nodded and they took the supplies off the mare. Horace unsaddled Boss and led the two horses to the meadow to eat. He held their halter leads, ate his own lunch, and watched the flock as they huddled together eating the high meadow grass. He then high-lined Honey, resaddled Boss, and went to Pedro, who sat on his sleeping bag looking over the letter.

"Where did you last see Víctor?"

Pedro set the letter down and stood. They walked out of the trees to the meadow. He pointed toward the edge of the high valley.

Horace looked up along it. The valley split into two smaller valleys a half mile up, and those each ran a mile more before disappearing into the side of a mountain. "Which side?"

"*No sé.*"

"You don't know which side of the valley he's on?"

Pedro shook his head.

It was late afternoon when Horace rode out. The valley in front of him was covered in sage and bitterbrush, mountain mahogany, and buckwheat. He looked for signs of Víctor but saw none. Where the valley split into two he paused. The right side was rocky and barren with only patches of meadow grass and sage. To the left was the creek, a meadow, three separate groves of aspens, and an easier slope. He took it and rode up another mile before it ended. From there he found a small switchback trail up the side of the mountain. He rode for two more hours and the trail was rocky and narrow. As dusk fell he summited the ridge. He was at over ten thousand feet and had a view of the entire valley.

He tied Boss to a pinyon pine, unsaddled and hobbled him. He carried his backpack and sleeping bag to the open ridge, cleared a space of rocks, and lay out a small tarp on the dirt. He put his sleeping bag on top of it, took off his boots, and sat down. From his backpack he took his food, his CD player, and his binoculars. He ate the last of the bologna and cheese, played Pantera's *The Great Southern Trendkill*, grabbed the binoculars, and looked out.

He saw Pedro's fire first and then searched up and down the

main valley and then the two smaller valleys for another fire but saw none. He took off his jeans, got in his sleeping bag, and again started the CD. He lay on his back and looked at the stars and the passing satellites above him. When the CD finished he again looked out with his binoculars. This time he found a second fire on the far side of the main valley, just before the split. He took note of the location, put the binoculars down, and went to sleep.

2

Mr. Reese watched until Horace's truck and trailer disappeared from sight, and then he went to work on getting the Ford 600 truck started. He limped and leaned on his cane as he went back and forth from the shop to the truck and tinkered on it until black smoke billowed from the exhaust pipes and even Mrs. Reese came from the house and watched as he got it, finally, to idle. He hooked a flatbed trailer to it, got his sack lunch, coffee, and a canteen of water, and left.

He drove along the main gravel road with Little Lana's head resting on his lap, and headed north for thirty miles. He drank coffee and listened to a struggling country station out of Tonopah as a small herd of antelope walked through the sagebrush to the left of him, and farther up in the foothills of the Monitors two wild horses bathed in the morning sun. The radio station disappeared and he turned the radio off. He came to a rough spur road and that brought him, after three miles, to the Morton ranch.

As he parked in front of a red barn he saw Lonnie Dixon, a twenty-six-year-old ranch hand, taking boxes from the main house and loading them into a beat-up and dented stock trailer. Mr. Reese and the dog stepped down from the cab and made their way slowly toward Lonnie.

"Good morning," Mr. Reese called out as he approached.

"Morning." Lonnie smiled. He was thin with brown hair and dark blue eyes. He had crow's-feet and weathered skin that made him look older than he was. He wore a thin gray T-shirt, jeans, and work boots.

"How's it been going?" the old man asked as they shook hands.

"I gotta say it seems like I've been loading boxes out of this place half my life."

Mr. Reese grinned and leaned on his cane. "As far as I know the Mortons never got rid of anything."

"They're serious pack rats all right."

"And I bet when Eddie's folks died he didn't get rid of any of their stuff either."

"You're right," said Lonnie. "He just put it in boxes in the basement. Even their clothes. That shit's been sitting down there for twenty years. He's even got some of his ex-wife's stuff."

"Is he around?"

Lonnie shook his head. "Eddie ain't been here hardly at all since he signed the papers selling this place."

"It's gotta be hard on him."

"He's sure been falling apart over it. Says it's difficult just seeing the place anymore. Says he feels too guilty, but he also doesn't see the point of dying out here alone."

"His folks, if they were alive, would understand," Mr. Reese said. "He's been out here for a lot of years trying to make a go of it. There's not a lot of point to it if you don't have a family to help, to be a part of it. There's sure no money in it."

"Everyone says that since he got divorced he's been having a hard time. But he's been drunk every night since I've worked here and I been here three years. He was divorced ten years before that."

Mr. Reese laughed. "Did he sell the cattle?"

"Most. The rest are in a holding pen in town. I know they want them out, but Eddie won't deal with it. I think for a while he thought he might try it somewhere else. So he didn't sell fifty cows, but now who knows what he's gonna do."

Mr. Reese looked down as Little Lana leaned into his cane. "And how about our plan to get Horace to Arizona?"

Lonnie shook his head and kicked the gravel road with his boot. He sat down on the wheel well of the stock trailer. "I sure tried, Mr. Reese, but Horace said he wanted to take a bus to Tucson. I told him I'd pay for gas and get him there for free but he said he wanted to leave Tonopah by himself. That there were certain times when you had to do things alone. But I'm still taking Eddie's horses down to his uncle's place in Globe. I'm leaving in a couple nights if he changes his mind. I've always liked Horace. We did all those jobs for Mr. Harrington and we had a lot of laughs. And he helped me get my horse, Elroy. So I don't think it's me. At least I hope not."

"It's not you," Mr. Reese said. "He just wants to prove himself, that's all. He was dead set on getting his grandmother's old car running and going that way. But the engine's shot so he said he'd just take the bus. I offered to buy him a car, but he said no. I offered to drive him a half dozen times, too, but he didn't want that either. So when I heard you were heading down to that area I thought maybe he'd go with you. You're his friend, not an old man. I was hoping you could make sure he got settled. He was just a little kid when he came out to Tonopah. So he's never really lived in a city before. At least as an adult. I just worry about him."

"He told me he's going there to be a professional boxer. Is that true?"

"That's what he wants."

"Seems like a rough way to go."

Mr. Reese nodded.

"I'll call him one more time and ask."

"I'd sure appreciate it," said Mr. Reese.

"I hope he does all right down there."

"Me, too."

Lonnie stood back up. "Well, the tractor and all the stuff Eddie set aside for you is in the barn if you want to head down there."

Mr. Reese nodded and the two began walking. Little Lana moved ahead of them and crawled under the Ford to escape the sun.

On a workshop bench sat three cardboard boxes, a plastic milk crate with an old KitchenAid mixer, and a wooden box with a waffle maker, a blender, and a griddle.

"As far as I know it was this kitchen stuff, the broken generator, the tractor, and a few boxes of parts."

"I think that's it," Mr. Reese said and opened one of the cardboard boxes to find sets of colored ceramic bowls. "My wife always admired Eddie's mom's bowls, and the mixer. It's nice of Eddie to remember that. It'll mean a lot to my wife."

"I heard Eddie's mom was a great baker."

Mr. Reese nodded. "When she was alive she made every wedding cake within sixty miles of here."

"Man, I've never baked anything that wasn't out of a box."

"I haven't even done that." Mr. Reese smiled.

"What are you going to do with the old tractor anyway?"

"Well, about thirty years ago Eddie's dad and I bought the same model tractor. We went in on the implements to save money. Eddie's dad and I were good friends since we were kids. Over the years we did a lot of stuff like that. . . . But then he passed away and not much after that their Ferguson's transmission gave out so Eddie bought the Kubota and different implements. I thought I was going to get a new tractor myself, but my main well started giving me fits a couple months back so we have to drill a new one. Now I'm just hoping to part this one out to get mine back in shape. Eddie was nice enough to give it to me."

"Sounds like a lot of work."

"It probably will be."

"Well, good luck," Lonnie said and picked up a box, and Mr. Reese set his cane against the barn wall and picked up another. They made four trips carrying boxes and crates and various tractor parts. Together they lifted the generator into the bed of the truck, and afterward Lonnie hooked a chain from the Kubota to the Ferguson and they towed it from the barn. Mr. Reese used the trailer's winch and pulled the broken-down tractor up onto the flatbed.

It was midday and nearly a hundred degrees when they finished. Lonnie brought two glasses of ice water from the house and they sat on the porch.

"So what are you going to do now?" asked Mr. Reese.

"I ain't sure," said Lonnie. "If Eddie pays me my wages I think I'll take a bit of vacation. Maybe drive around for a while."

"Will he pay you?"

"Sometimes I don't think he will, but usually he pulls through."

"And what's he gonna do?"

"Once the sale goes through he says he's gonna buy a trailer down in Baja, but who knows."

"And who bought this place?"

"That's what's strange. It had been for sale for years and then suddenly out of the blue a rich lawyer from Las Vegas and his wife saw it and made an offer all in one afternoon. I guess she likes horses."

"Maybe they'll hire you."

"Maybe."

Mr. Reese finished the water and nodded. He set the glass on a wooden table and as he did so he could feel his back begin to seize. "I guess I better get moving," he said. "After your vacation if you come back to this area and are looking for work please let me know. With Horace gone I sure could use the help once in a while."

"I appreciate you saying that," said Lonnie, and they shook hands.

Mr. Reese walked down the porch and moved slow and pained across the gravel. Little Lana appeared from the shade of the truck as he opened the driver's side door, and jumped in. They were nearly to the main road when the spasms began in full and he stopped the truck. He cried out in pain and fell along the bench seat. Little Lana whined and licked his hand as the sun beat down in the afternoon heat. The old man reached into his shirt pocket for his vial of pills. He swallowed a Valium, closed his eyes as sweat dripped into them, and waited.

3

An hour past dawn Horace came to the grove of aspens, tied Boss to a tree, and found Víctor snoring in a red sleeping bag next to a small stone fire pit. The pit was swarming with flies. Half-raw and charred meat lay on the rocks. A backpack was next to Víctor's head, and Little Roy, a black and white border collie, lay curled in a ball by his feet. Ten yards behind camp was a crudely butchered lamb hanging from an aspen branch, its entrails in a bloody pile below it. The lamb wasn't skinned or covered in a field bag. The white of its wool was thick with blood.

Horace whistled for the dog, who got up quickly and came to him. He checked him for cuts and ticks, removed five hair mats, and put a new flea collar around his neck. He told Little Roy to sit and then walked over to Víctor. The man's arms were outside the sleeping bag and his hands were covered in dried blood and dirt. Two knives sat on a rock beside him. Horace picked them up and walked to the edge of camp, then dropped them on the ground and kicked dirt over them. He went back to Víctor and shook him with his boot.

The moment Víctor opened his eyes he screamed in fear.

"It's okay. It's me, Horace," he said gently and smiled. "Do you remember who I am?"

Víctor looked at him from the sleeping bag but kept still and silent. He was a small, dark-skinned man, in his mid-twenties, with a swollen right eye and blood crusted around the nostrils of his swollen nose. He had been beaten up. There were blood-stains on the parts of his shirt that were visible. His hair was black and had dirt, grass, and sagebrush in it.

Horace went to his backpack and took a Spanish dictionary from it. "Mr. Reese thought you might understand some Spanish." He looked through the book and said, *"¿No gustar aquí? ¿No gustar en la montaña?"*

Víctor shrugged.

"¿Malo aquí? ¿Pedro malo hombre?"

Víctor nodded slowly.

"¿Pedro es muy malo?"

"Sí," Víctor said and sat up. *"Sí."*

Horace went through the dictionary again. *"¿No trabaja en la montaña?"*

He nodded. *"Víctor no aqui."* He pointed to himself. *"Víctor— Los Angeles."*

"Los Angeles?"

"Los Angeles. ¡Sí!" In a rush of excitement, Víctor unzipped the sleeping bag and stood up fully clothed. His boots and pants were also stained with dried blood. He gathered his sleeping bag and backpack and held them in a loose bundle in his arms.

Horace stared at him and not knowing what else to do, nod-ded. He cut down the lamb and dragged it behind some brush and then checked for embers left hidden in the fire pit. When he found none, they left. Little Roy walked ahead of them and Horace rode Boss while Víctor trailed behind on foot.

The sun was getting high by the time they came to Pedro, who sat by a small fire. On a grill he cooked lamb chops. On the stove was a pan of potatoes and onions, and next to it a pan of pinto beans. Víctor set down his things and stayed at the edge of camp away from Pedro, and Horace unsaddled Boss and high-lined him next to Honey and the donkey. When he'd finished, he sat down across from Pedro.

"I figured you'd cook something good," said Horace.

Pedro smiled.

"But I'm still going to have to tell Mr. Reese about the lamb."

"Víctor. Víctor killed *el cordero*."

"I know, that's what you said. He killed another one up at his camp, too."

Pedro shook his head.

"What should we do with him?"

Pedro shrugged his shoulders.

"Do you want me to take Víctor with me when I go?"

Pedro nodded. He kept his eyes on the food, turning the lamb chops over and putting salt and pepper on them. "Víctor not sheepman," he said. "*Víctor es muy débil*. He my cousin, but I don't know him."

Horace looked to the edge of camp where Víctor leaned against an aspen tree staring at them. His face was covered in dirt. He looked worried. "You'll have to tell him what's happening. He doesn't understand me."

Pedro called for Víctor, who while walking into camp, stumbled over a rock and nearly fell. Pedro shook his head and spoke to him sternly in Quechua. Víctor paced back and forth as he listened and then he rattled off a long reply, his arms waving dramatically and spit coming from his lips.

"*¡No más!*" Pedro yelled finally and again shook his head. He took three paper plates from a canvas bag and dished out the food. Horace took a knife and fork from his pack and began eating next to the fire. Pedro handed a plate to Víctor, who moved back to the edge of camp away from them, and ate with his hands.

* * *

It was past noon when Horace went to the sheep and found the two Anatolians, Jip and Whitey. He checked their paws and put new flea collars on them both. When he got back to camp he and Pedro sat across from each other while Víctor slept on his sleeping bag near the creek thirty yards from them.

"When you write your note to Mr. Reese, tell him about the two Víctor killed. Also tell him what happened with Víctor, why he wants to leave and all that. And tell him where we should send Víctor once we get him into town. Remember we don't understand anything he says and he doesn't understand us."

Pedro got up and took a notebook and pen from his pack.

"Are you gonna be all right up here on your own?"

Pedro nodded as he sat back down across from Horace.

"And your phone works?"

Pedro pointed to the top of the closest ridge. "Up there."

"And you're sure you're okay?"

Pedro again nodded and then began working on the letter.

There were no clouds in the sky and the day was at its hottest as they headed down the mountain. At times Víctor lagged behind or stopped, but eventually he always caught up to Horace and the horses. And after they reached the halfway mark Horace got down and walked as well. Hours passed in silence and they stopped only twice to let Boss and Honey drink from the meager creek. It was starting to get dark when they came to the truck and the stock trailer. Horace loaded the horses while Víctor, exhausted, got into the cab of the pickup and closed his eyes.

At the ranch Víctor took a shower and Horace set out a pair of his own jeans, a T-shirt, underwear, and a pair of socks for him. After that he walked to the main house with Víctor's dirty clothes. He put them in the washer and then went to the kitchen to see Mrs. Reese cooking dinner. The old woman was short and plump, dressed in gray varicose vein compression socks, slippers, and a faded flower-print dress. She had long gray hair she kept in a bun and blue eyes hidden behind thick glasses. At the kitchen table, Horace took the chair across from Mr. Reese and watched as the old man went over Pedro's letter with a Spanish dictionary.

"If I'm translating correctly Pedro says it started out fine but that Víctor got strange after a couple weeks. I guess he doesn't know Víctor as much as he said he did. He gave us the impression he was very close to him. But it turns out he's just a distant cousin who's always had problems. Pedro says that around the third week Víctor began talking to himself. And then soon after, he quit working and quit getting out of his sleeping bag. And then one night he pulled a gun on Pedro, they got into a fight, and the next morning he was gone. I guess after that is when you found him. Pedro says most of their family live outside the city of Cuzco in Peru. But Víctor doesn't want to go back there. He wants to go to Los Angeles. He says he has a friend there who will help him get a job and a place to live. Pedro says to give Víctor three hundred dollars of his own pay and to use his money as well to buy him a bus ticket to Los Angeles. He also wants me to take one of the lambs out of his pay. But he swears, he promises, the two killed were done by Víctor." Mr. Reese took off his glasses and rubbed his eyes. "That's about all of it. It's a mess all right. How did Pedro seem?"

"Okay, I think," said Horace. "His camp was clean and he seemed to be taking care of himself. Myrtle and the dogs looked good. But it's always hard to tell with him."

Mr. Reese nodded.

"What do you think's going to happen to Víctor?"

"I really don't know," Mr. Reese said and sighed. "I'd guess most likely, after some hard times, he'll end up back in Peru if he's lucky. I can't see him making it in Los Angeles without

speaking Spanish, but then I don't know that much about Los
Angeles. Maybe his friend will take care of him. Maybe they
have a good Peruvian community there. I just don't know. We'll
have to hope for the best." The old man got up from his chair,
slow and stiff, and went to the refrigerator. "After all that I think
I need a beer."

"Is your back real bad today?" asked Horace.

"Not so bad," the old man said and poured the beer into a
glass and sat back down.

"Horace, are you too tired to eat?" Mrs. Reese asked as she
chopped carrots.

"I'm starving," Horace said.

The old man took a drink of beer and looked at the boy.
"Would it be all right to talk about something unrelated to Pedro and Víctor?"

"Sure, Mr. Reese."

"I wanted to ask you a few questions about the upcoming
Golden Gloves tournament."

"Okay."

"I know we've gone over this before, but they really said for
certain that you could fight out of Arizona even though you live
in Nevada?"

Horace nodded. "Six months ago when I took those days off
I got my driver's license changed to an Arizona driver's license.
My aunt in Tucson said I could use her address. So in the eyes of
the law I am an Arizona citizen. And I called the Golden Gloves
office and told them, filled out the paperwork, and paid the fee.
I double-checked it all."

"Can't you just box in Las Vegas and live here?" asked Mrs.
Reese.

Horace shook his head. His voice grew quiet and he began
tapping his foot on the faded linoleum floor. "I'm never fighting
in Nevada again. Not ever."

"It wasn't that bad what happened in Vegas," Mr. Reese said. "You're too hard on yourself."

Horace stared at the floor.

"And you're really going to stay in Tucson after that?" she asked.

"You know he is," Mr. Reese said gently.

"But you are, Horace?"

"I'm sorry, Mrs. Reese," he whispered and looked at her.

"And you're for sure staying at your mom's sister's place?"

"She has a back house that I'm renting. I've already arranged it."

"And you've talked to your mom about all this?" Mr. Reese asked.

"Just a little. She's always wanted me to leave Tonopah. She helped arrange it. She said her sister owed her a favor."

"And it's a nice place?" Mrs. Reese asked.

"I think it is, but I haven't been inside it."

"And you're really going to live there?" Mrs. Reese asked.

"A person has to find his own way," Mr. Reese said. "Especially at his age. You know that. We're both just going to miss you, Horace. That's what we're trying to say. We both love you and don't know what we're going to do without you." He paused and looked at his wife. Tears welled in his eyes and his voice wavered. He smiled. "Anyway, I guess you better go get Víctor before I start crying. Let's hope he can at least eat without causing too many problems."

The next morning at dawn Horace went over to where Víctor slept on a makeshift bed on the couch. Horace pushed on his leg until Víctor opened his eyes.

"Uno hora, Los Angeles," he said and stepped outside in his workout clothes. He ran down toward the desert floor and the

county road. Two miles there and two miles back. Afterward he did push-ups and sit-ups under the awning. When he opened the door to the trailer he saw Víctor sitting on the couch, dressed and waiting. Horace showered, put on clothes, and together they walked to the main house.

Mrs. Reese had the table set and they ate a breakfast of bacon, eggs, and potatoes. Afterward she handed each man a sack lunch, and Mr. Reese gave Víctor three hundred dollars from Pedro, the five weeks' pay he was owed, and an extra hundred-dollar bonus.

"Horace will buy the bus ticket for you when you get to Tonopah, okay? Pedro's paying for it out of his wages."

Víctor looked blankly at the old man and said nothing.

"Can we at least call someone for you?" Mr. Reese asked in both Spanish and English, but Víctor just shrugged his shoulders. Mrs. Reese even brought the phone to Víctor, but Víctor only set it back on the kitchen table.

Horace drove the forty-five miles on gravel road while listening to Megadeth's *Countdown to Extinction* on headphones. The sun rose over the Monitors and fell onto Ralston Valley. A truck pulling an empty stock trailer was the only traffic they passed, and Víctor dozed in the passenger seat. Eight miles from Tonopah they hit pavement and Horace got the old truck up to fifty and drove to Deyoe's Mini-Mart, where he parked and shut off the engine. He tapped Víctor on the shoulder and woke him.

"We're here," he said, and they got out of the truck and walked inside. Horace bought Víctor a bus ticket to Las Vegas and a gallon jug of water, and together they sat outside on a metal bench and waited.

"The bus you're going to catch, it's not a Greyhound," Horace tried to explain. "It's just a small-time line that goes to Las

Vegas and back. So when you get there you'll have to find the Greyhound station. The easiest way to do that will probably be to take a cab. Once you're there you can get a ticket to Los Angeles. Understand?"

Víctor just looked at him, his hurt eye still half-shut and his nose swollen. *"Los Angeles,"* he said and tapped his chest with his thumb.

Horace shook his head and took a note from his shirt pocket that he'd written the night before.

MY NAME IS VÍCTOR

1. *I need to get to the Greyhound bus station in Las Vegas.*
2. *I need one ticket to Los Angeles on the Greyhound bus.*

He handed the paper to Víctor. "Show this to the bus driver to get to Los Angeles." Víctor looked at the note and put it in the backpack he carried. Horace told him no and took the paper back out. "You got to hold on to it." He acted like he was driving. "Give to the bus driver, okay? Give it to the bus driver."

Víctor again took the paper and this time held it in his hand, and Horace decided to stay with him until the bus came. For nearly an hour they sat in silence, side by side on the metal bench, and Víctor ate his lunch so Horace gave him his own sack as well. When the bus finally appeared coming up the hill, Horace tapped Víctor on the shoulder and pointed to it.

"Recordar el autobús . . . Goes to Las Vegas, not Los Angeles." He tried to think of more Spanish words, but what little he knew disappeared from his grasp. The bus parked in front of the mini-mart and a small pudgy driver stepped out. Horace spoke to him briefly, gave him twenty dollars, and asked if he could help get Víctor to the Greyhound station. The driver said he'd try, and then Horace shook Víctor's hand, gave him fifty dollars of his own money, and said goodbye.

4

I hate the dentist," Horace said the next day as they sat in Mr. Reese's truck in front of a small dentist's office in Tonopah. It was early morning and Little Lana sat curled in a ball between them as the radio played.

"Everyone hates the dentist," the old man said, "but having bad teeth is worse. Remember that old guy that used to hang out at Tonopah Tire when you worked there?"

Horace laughed. "Ricky. I remember him."

"Most likely he had good teeth at one point, but when you knew him he had nothing left but little rotten nubs."

"He had the worst breath of all time, too."

"See," Mr. Reese said. "That's why you go to the dentist. And look at it this way, you won't have to worry about them when you get to Tucson. You'll be all set. Anyway, you better get in there or you'll be late, and I have a few errands to run while you're getting stabbed and drilled on."

"I can't believe I have two cavities," Horace sighed. "I brush my teeth twice a day and I never eat sugar."

"Soda has a lot of sugar in it."

"But I'm quitting that," Horace said and opened the passenger side door and got out. "I bet you're going to get a real breakfast now, aren't you?"

"Breakfast?" the old man said and grinned. "I hadn't thought of breakfast but now that you mention it, maybe I will. Of course I'd invite you but your face will be numb and swollen and all beat up. I bet it'll hurt too bad even for pancakes."

"Thanks a lot," Horace said, shut the door, and waved him off.

Mr. Reese's first stop was the post office and then to the pharmacy for his and his wife's prescriptions. After that he still had forty minutes left and the thought of waffles and bacon called to him. They had eaten breakfast at dawn, oatmeal with raisins and skim milk, but even after all the years of eating it he'd never grown to like it. It seemed a chore more than anything. He drove to the Stage Stop Cafe and decided to eat whatever he wanted. A man had to have some secrets, he thought, as he walked with his cane across the pavement and went inside.

But as he waited to be seated, Jerry Blano, a seventy-three-year-old retired insurance salesman, came from a hidden corner of the restaurant. Mr. Reese looked at the date on his watch and sighed. It was the first Monday of the month, it was the meeting of the Old Ranch Hands, a makeshift men's social club of retired ranchers and citizens of the area. It was their monthly breakfast meeting, and he'd unknowingly walked into the middle of it.

"Well I'll be, if it isn't Eldon Reese," Jerry Blano said, grinning.

Mr. Reese forced a smile and the two shook hands.

"I got old-man bladder, but let me bring you back to the table before I make my stop."

Mr. Reese nodded and not knowing why exactly, followed Blano past the corner where seven old men sat around a table with a cleaned plate in front of each of them. They gave Mr.

Reese a group hello and Blano took a chair from a nearby table, put it next to R. J. Holmgren and Bob Ringwald, and left.

Two stainless-steel pitchers of coffee sat on the table, and R.J. filled him a cup. Across the table Saul Dennison said, "So you still running your operation, Reese?"

"I'm trying," he replied.

"How's business?"

He smiled. "I'm still afloat."

"They don't make it easy nowadays, that's for sure."

Mr. Reese nodded.

At the end of the table Corbett Dalton said, "How you dealing with those sons of bitches at the BLM?"

"The same as I always have," Mr. Reese said. "It's a hard job to keep any side happy right now."

Corbett was a fat, squat man who had been a bad doctor in Sacramento and then Reno and then Elko and finally Tonopah. Mrs. Reese said he was like a bad priest. Due to incompetence and malpractice he was getting shipped to smaller and less desirable places until he landed at the end, Tonopah.

"You been keeping up on the Bundy fiasco?" asked R.J.

Mr. Reese shook his head and looked for a waitress, but the two women waiting tables stayed clear of the old men.

R.J. said, "They should put the entire federal government in a Sani-Hut and have NASA send them up to space."

Bob Ringwald, a retired highway paver, laughed. "Take that so-called president with them, too."

"And Harry Reid," said Corbett.

They all laughed except the two men in the corner, Hudson Dreary and Vince Pollen. They were talking University of Nevada, Reno football. Jerry Blano came back to the table and began going on about driving to Reno for a doctor's appointment. That led to a long rant about the city's growth and crime, and that led to a talk about Las Vegas and golfing fees and then to a series of tirades among Blano and Corbett and Saul about Obamacare.

Mr. Reese drank the lukewarm coffee and wondered if he could move to the counter and order his waffles and bacon there. Would they leave him alone then or would it cause more of a disruption? Would he then become the focus of the table when all he wanted was to eat waffles? He again looked out, but both waitresses had disappeared from view.

"Reese, what's your personal experience with the BLM?" asked Corbett.

Mr. Reese turned back around. "It's a hard job managing the public's land. In my experience no one's that happy on any side, but they've got good people there. Most of them, in their own way, care about the land."

Corbett shook his head at the answer and turned to R.J. and whispered.

Everyone started talking around him. Mr. Reese figured he could wait a few minutes and then move to the counter to eat. Anyway he had to pick up Horace. He was running out of time. He looked out across the table. None of these men worked anymore and only two of them had been ranchers, Hudson and Vince. Both of them had sons who had taken over for them. Mr. Reese's younger daughter, Lynn, went out with Hudson's youngest son for a year and a half in high school but then the boy was killed when his horse slipped down a gully. If the horse hadn't slipped, maybe the boy would still be alive and maybe his daughter would have married the boy. Maybe if the boy would have knocked up his daughter in high school she would have stayed. He was handsome enough to fool her for a little while. If she'd been reckless and he hadn't been killed, Hudson's son would have, by now, taken over the Little Reese ranch. He wasn't the smartest kid, but he would have been an all right son-in-law.

Mr. Reese couldn't remember the boy's name. Terry, maybe? How many times did he think about Terry running the ranch? A dozen times, ten dozen? His daughter was smarter than Terry or himself, and after a year or two of him being in charge she would have ended up running things. She'd fix it right. Maybe they'd get a divorce and she would take up with Vince Pollen's littlest son. That boy knew how to run a ranch. Luke Pollen was a born livestock man. He wasn't much to look at, but once she had her fill with Terry, if Terry hadn't died, Luke would have seemed like a good catch in the ranching world. He worked from sunup to sundown. With her smarts and Luke's work ethic, that would be something. If she was three years younger and had been in Luke's class maybe that would have happened. Maybe somehow and for some reason she would have liked him.

"Excuse me, fellas, I gotta hit the can," Mr. Reese said and stood up. He nodded to Vince and Hudson and made his way across the restaurant. He found one of the waitresses behind the counter and told her he drank a cup of coffee, left three dollars, and headed out the door.

5

Horace came alone into Tonopah three days later. He picked up the ranches' mail, stopped at the auto parts and hardware stores for Mr. Reese, and then parked in front of a small yellow house with brown trim. A dented green Buick Regal and a 1960s camping trailer filled the carport, and a chain-link fence surrounded the yard. As he went through the gate a scraggly Pomeranian shot out from a doggy door on the side of the house and frantically barked.

"It's just me, Pom Pom," Horace announced. The front door then opened and an elderly lady appeared. She wore a navy-blue muumuu with orange and red tropical flowers on it. Her long gray hair was pulled back and held together with a ballpoint pen.

"Shush your ass, Pom Pom," she yelled in a graveled smoker's voice. "Horace, just kick her if she tries anything funny."

"Okay, Mrs. Poulet," he replied and walked up to the house as the dog continued to bark and run circles around his feet.

The old woman led him through a cluttered hall to the living room, where she sat in an easy chair. On a wooden table in front of her were two sewing machines. Fabric lay in piles on metal shelves against the back wall and on the floor around her.

She picked up a thin cardboard dress box, opened it, and lifted out red boxing trunks. The legs were trimmed in gold, as was the waistband, which was three inches wide and had "Hector" embroidered in red cursive letters at the front. Halfway down the front of each leg, stitched in gold thread, was a Thompson machine gun. She flipped them over. On the back of the waistband, in the same red cursive lettering, it read "Hidalgo" with a small embroidered Thompson machine gun on each side of the name.

She handed the trunks to Horace, and softly he ran his fingers over the cursive letters of the name. "I can't believe they came out so nice," he whispered to her. "It looks even better than I thought it would."

"I found a book on machine guns. There's a lot of different kinds but I thought the Thompson worked the best. It's the most dramatic. Why did you want a machine gun on there anyway?"

"Do you remember Arnaldo?" asked Horace.

She sighed and shook her head grimly. "Your poor grandmother, I don't know why she would date him. He was such an awful man."

Horace nodded. "When he trained me he said my combinations had to be like machine-gun fire. 'Faster, Horace, faster like a machine gun. Like a machine gun!' That's what gave me the idea." He again looked at the trunks and ran his fingers over the embroidery. "I just can't get over how nice it looks."

"I'm glad you like them," said Mrs. Poulet.

Horace put them back in the box and took a hundred-dollar bill from his wallet and handed it to her. "I have to go now," he said and stood up. "But when I become a champion I'll hire you to make all my trunks and robes. It's gonna take me a while but I'll get there and I'll hire you to make me custom embroidered shirts and coats, too. It'll be a lot of work but I'll pay you better than you've ever been paid. I'll make sure of it."

* * *

It was noon when he headed back to the ranch. He drank off a Coke and chewed Copenhagen and drove through the desolate valley trying to stay awake in the midday heat. The afternoon was spent helping Mr. Reese dismantle Morton's tractor. Mostly the old man sat in a chair resting his back, telling Horace what to do. At six-thirty they ate dinner on the porch and listened to a San Diego Padres game on the radio. When the meal was finished Mr. Reese opened a can of beer and Mrs. Reese headed to the kitchen with a stack of plates. There was a slight breeze as the sun moved behind the mountains. The sky was cloudless and darkening blue and the two men sat across from each other at the picnic table.

"I hate to do this but I have to ask you something," Mr. Reese said. "You're heading out the day after tomorrow, right?"

Horace nodded. "The bus leaves at seven a.m."

Mr. Reese drank from the can of beer. "Well, I'll just say it. As you know I still can't get on a horse and I have to get the supplies to Pedro. I thought I had Rico's kid, Lenny, coming to help for the next month. He promised he could do this week's drop, but today his mother called and now he won't be able to start until next week. I don't know why they didn't tell me earlier, but they didn't. I hate to ask this, but I was hoping I might be able to convince you to stay on an extra couple days and do one more run. We'd get you packed tonight and then tomorrow I'd take you. I know could make the drive alone but I was hoping to spend a bit more time with you before you leave. I'd pick you up the day after tomorrow at noon. I think that gives you plenty of time to get back if you leave at dawn. Then you could take the bus out the next morning. I hate to mess up your plans, but I'm afraid I don't know what else to do."

Horace looked down at the picnic table. "It's okay, Mr. Reese," he said. "I knew I'd probably have to do this week's drop. I guess I just forgot to tell you that I knew." He stood up but he didn't look at the old man. "Well, I guess I better get my things together and start packing. And I have to get the trailer cleaned out."

"Don't worry too much about cleaning the trailer. It's your home. You keep it the way you want it."

"You never know when someone else might need it. I want to make sure I leave it the way I found it."

"You don't have to. That trailer is yours."

Horace half nodded.

"I'm sorry," Mr. Reese said.

"No need to be sorry," Horace replied and walked down the steps of the house and headed toward the trailer.

He slept until three a.m. When he woke he got up and filled his duffel with all he was going to take to Tucson, put what remained in cardboard boxes, and spent the rest of the night cleaning the trailer. He washed out the cupboards, the refrigerator, the bathroom, and the kitchen. When dawn came he showered, put on clean clothes, and moved the belongings he wasn't going to take to an unused tack locker in Mr. Reese's barn. He set his sleeping bag and backpack in the bed of Mr. Reese's pickup and went inside for breakfast.

By sunrise they were on the road. Mr. Reese drove, Horace chewed Copenhagen and worked his hand exerciser, and the bay gelding, Lex, and the old mare, Honey, swayed back and forth in the stock trailer.

"I know it's early to talk, but I was hoping we might," Mr. Reese said. He held a cup of coffee in his left hand and steered with his right.

"What is it?" said Horace.

"I'll need you to be honest with me."

"I'll be honest."

"Even if it hurts my feelings?"

"Well . . . I'll try, Mr. Reese." Horace spit into an old McDonald's cup and the truck shook as the road worsened. The old man slowed to twenty-five, finished his coffee, and set the mug between them on the bench seat.

"If I'm optimistic about my back I have maybe four years left where I can work. As you know after I hurt it the first time, we hired Albert and his wife to help out. You were still in school. He and his wife had talked about buying the ranch someday, but then his wife left him and that idea fell apart. . . . The reason I'm bringing this up is sooner or later I'm going to have to sell the place. We'll have to move into town or in with one of our daughters. I know we've talked about this before, but I wanted to again before you left. You seem a natural for this sorta work and you're good at it. I know you're young and you don't have a woman or a family and it's a lonely life. That's something only you know if you can take. What I'm saying is after your boxing career why don't you come back? We'll set out a plan for you to take over the ranch. For you to own the ranch yourself. I'd hate to see all the hard work we've put in these years disappear like it has with the Casey place and the Hass place. We've seen both those go from working ranches to nothing. Now Morton's is sold, too. And who really knows what will happen to it. Working a ranch is hard, especially if you're single. There's not a lot of money in it either. I know you've been skittish with us and it's hard for you to accept gifts. I also know it's been hard for you to relax around us. To trust us. But we trust you. What I'm trying to say is that Mrs. Reese and I think of you as our son and we want you to have the ranch when you're ready for it."

Horace looked at the old man but he couldn't speak. Tears welled in his eyes. He looked out the window at the hills of sage and the distant mountains behind them. They drove for miles before he said anything. "I don't think anyone has ever thought I could run a ranch," he said finally. "But that you and Mrs. Reese think I could, well that's the nicest thing I've ever heard. I won't forget that you said it. I really won't. You and Mrs. Reese saved me. I know that."

"Well, you saved us, too," Mr. Reese said. "And you helped Mrs. Reese. She wasn't herself after our daughters left. You know how she was, how she gets. You helped her."

Horace again looked over at him. "There's been a lot of years I dreamed that I was your son. A lot of years. But, Mr. Reese, I'm going to be a world champion boxer someday and I don't know how long that's going to take. And to do that I have to move to the city. I have to change the way I live and where I live. I wish I could do both at the same time, but I've thought a lot about it and there's no way I can."

"But boxing's such a hard life, Horace."

"It's not going to be that bad."

"But fights are hard to get. You're the one who told me that. That the other way of fighting is more popular now."

"MMA is more popular, but people still like boxing. They really do. So I'm not too worried," he said, but his voice grew uncertain. "I'll get the fights, Mr. Reese, and I'll be okay. You'll see. It just takes work. You're the one who told me that. You're the one who said if you just keep working hard, things tend to break your way."

"That's true, I have said that . . ." Mr. Reese's voice trailed off. He rubbed his face with his free hand and cleared his throat. "Can I ask you another question?"

"Sure."

"Why do you have to change who you are? Why do you have to become a Mexican boxer?"

"I should have never told you that," said Horace.

Mr. Reese looked over at him. "I'm glad you did. I'm glad you told me. It's good to be honest. And I'm honored you'd share that with me. But I just have to ask, why?"

"Because Mexican boxers are the toughest," said Horace. "Everyone knows that. They go toe to toe. They're true warriors who never quit, who never back down, who are never scared. Érik Morales was never afraid of anybody. Not anybody."

"I bet he was."

"He never was. I know he wasn't."

"But you're not Mexican," Mr. Reese said.

Horace didn't answer. He rolled down the passenger side window as the sun began to come over the Monitor Range. He let his arm hang out, and the morning air was cool and smelled of sage and dust.

"Did I upset you, Horace?"

"No," he said, but it wasn't true. He wanted to jump out of the truck. He wanted to be a million miles away from that old truck. "The thing is, Mr. Reese, there's no tough Indian boxers."

"But that's where you're wrong," the old man said, suddenly excited. He slumped down in the truck's seat and steered with his legs. He took the wallet from his back pocket and pulled out a piece of paper with Mrs. Reese's handwriting on it. In bold letters at the top of one side it said "Indian" and on the other side it said "Irish." "Mrs. Reese and I went to the library and looked on the computer. We found out some things. There was a boxer in the seventies named Danny 'Little Red' Lopez. He was part Ute and part Mexican and part Irish. You're part Irish, your grandfather, Doreen's husband, was from there, and you're part Paiute. That's different, sure, and he has some Mex in him but not as much as you'd think. And then there's Marvin Camel. He was a Flathead, and it says here he was a champion, too. Now Flatheads are out of Montana. He isn't from Nevada but he's close. Not that far away when you really think about it. And last is a guy name Joe 'The Boss' Hipp. It said he was the first Native American heavyweight world champion."

"I don't want to be like Marvin Camel or Joe Hipp. I know who they are." Horace fell silent for a moment and then looked at the old man. "Mr. Reese, I don't want to be an Indian. No good fighters are Paiutes. Paiutes aren't good for anything."

"That's not true," the old man said, "and you know it's not. That's your grandmother talking. It's a bad thing to say. Anyway, like I said you're part Irish too, and there's a lot of great Irish boxers. I have a list of those on the other side."

"Don't bother, Mr. Reese," Horace said and shook his head. "No one thinks I'm white 'cause I don't look white. I don't look Irish, so I'm not Irish. But I look like a Mexican. Everybody who doesn't know me thinks I look Mexican. They really do." He again looked out the window and his feet tapped down on the floor of the truck faster and faster. He began to pick at his fingernails. His voice faltered. "I appreciate all you're saying, Mr. Reese, but I'm going to be a champion. I am. It's like the B.O.A.T. book said. To be a champion you have to create your own future, you have to make it yourself. You have to build your boat little by little and brick by brick until it's unbreakable and unbeatable. And that boat will take you to the next level, to the level of champions, and that's what I'm going to do."

"But what if it doesn't happen? What if you don't become a champion? What will you do then?"

"A winner doesn't think like that, Mr. Reese." And for the first time in Horace's life he was mad at the old man. His voice shook. "Don't you get it? A winner only thinks about winning. A champion only thinks about being a champion."

The old man slowed the truck to a crawl and again looked at the boy. "I didn't mean to upset you, Horace. I'm sorry, I am. I just feel I have to ask these questions 'cause you're my friend and that's what friends do, they watch out for each other. What if you get hurt in some permanent way?"

"I won't get hurt," Horace said. "Anyway, I can't worry about things I can't control. A champion doesn't think that way. A champion only thinks of the things he can control and he does the work on those so he can get to the next level. And when he gets to the next level he just thinks of the level after that. He just keeps building the boat."

Mr. Reese again rubbed his face and tried to think. He cleared his throat. "I hate to bring this up," he said, "and I hope you'll forgive me someday for what I'm about to say, but I feel I have to. I have to because boxing's so dangerous. Remember, Horace, I took you to your fight in Las Vegas. I've seen you box. I've seen what happens when you get pressured or cornered. I've seen how you panic."

"Don't bring up Las Vegas!" Horace shouted, and tears fell suddenly from his eyes. His feet tapped harder against the floor and he fidgeted uncontrollably. A mile passed in silence and then his voice became nothing but a broken whisper. "Please don't bring up Las Vegas. Please don't ever bring it up again. I'm begging you. I'm seriously begging you, Mr. Reese. It was just one fight. And I told you I never wanted to talk about it again and you promised me you wouldn't. You promised me you'd never mention it, not ever."

"I did promise, that's true," the old man said, "and I'm sorry I broke that promise. This conversation hasn't gone the way I was hoping it would go. I didn't mean to upset you so much. I'm not the most eloquent, but I mean well. I just want to help you. I'm running out of time and I believe I have an answer to some of your problems and some of mine, too."

Horace wiped the tears from his eyes. "I know what you're talking about, Mr. Reese. I do. I appreciate it. And don't worry, when I come back I'll buy the ranch for a lot of money. One of my main goals is to make sure you and Mrs. Reese can live the easy life. You deserve that and I'll make sure it happens. I'll take care of you both and I'll take care of the ranch. All the horses and dogs, too. Everybody. I really will, you'll see. You've been the best parents I've ever had. I know that and I know my own mom and dad don't care. So it's my solemn promise that I'll help you. And I don't break promises, Mr. Reese. I'd rather die than break one. But for right now I'd rather if we just quit talking."

The old man nodded. "You're right," he said. "I've talked enough and I'll stop. I just hope someday you'll forgive me."

Horace looked at the glove compartment in front of him. "There's nothing to forgive, Mr. Reese. You're just trying to look out for me, I know that. You and Mrs. Reese are my best friends and you're the only ones who've really cared about me. I know all that. But you shouldn't worry so much. I have a good plan. I'll be okay and I'll make sure you're okay, too. Because that's what champions do. They take care of the things they should take care of."

Horace stopped Lex and Honey at the first turn into the canyon. Mr. Reese was finally out of view and he could hear the old man starting the truck and leaving. He took his backpack off, found his CD player, looked through the small stack of discs, and picked Metallica's *Ride the Lightning*. He put on his headphones and turned up the music so loud that Lex's ears swung back and both horses looked nervously about. Horace ran a hand over Lex and moved them on. The morning was quiet and still but for the faint sound of the music and the horses' shoes clanking against the rock and gravel. They headed up through the canyon and into the Monitor Range.

* * *

It was afternoon when they arrived at the same high mountain valley from which Horace had brought Víctor down. At the meadow's edge he stopped and took a pair of binoculars from his pack. He saw the sheep and heard the faint barking of the dogs and finally made out a blue tarp in a different location on the far side of the valley. He put the binoculars away and headed for it.

He called out to Pedro as he came into camp but only the dogs came to greet him. He got down from Lex and high-lined the horses next to the donkey, Myrtle. He unsaddled Lex and unloaded the supplies from Honey's panniers. In camp he called out Pedro's name a half dozen times, but Pedro was facedown on his old canvas sleeping bag, snoring. Horace set his backpack and sleeping bag under the shade of the aspens and walked back to Myrtle, who stood half asleep in the sun. He picked her feet and looked her over for any cuts or signs of lameness and then walked out to the meadow and whistled for the dogs. Each one he checked for ticks, cuts, and mats, and then let them go.

When he came back Pedro was making coffee on the Coleman stove.

"We took Víctor to the bus," said Horace. "He's gone now."

Pedro nodded but said nothing.

"Mr. Reese is hiring a kid named Lenny. He'll be up next week with your supplies 'cause Mr. Reese's back is still hurting. Anyway, I'm going to go look around and I'm gonna take Little Roy with me."

Pedro again nodded but remained silent. Horace took his CD player, the binoculars, his water bottle, and a Spanish-to-English dictionary, and called for the dog. Together they climbed for an hour until they came to a small ridge overlooking the meadow. There was no sight or trace of humanity for as far as he could see but for the blue tarp, now just a dot at the edge of the meadow grass. He sat on a rock, and Little Roy curled in a ball at his feet. Horace opened the dictionary and randomly went through Spanish words.

Carrot: *la zanahoria*
Tree: *el árbol*
Cow: *la vaca*
Tire: *el neumático*
Sleep: *dormir*
Head: *la cabeza*

But no matter how hard he tried the words wouldn't stick. For a year he had listened to Spanish lessons on CDs, read books on learning Spanish, and left sticky notes on his things in the trailer: *el plato, el bol, el baño, la mesa, la puerta, el fregadero, el colchón, la ventana.* He took the Macy's advertising section from the Sunday *Las Vegas Sun* newspaper and wrote next to a woman modeling underwear *el sostén, las bragas, la pierna, el brazo.* The words would stay with him for an hour, sometimes a day or even two, but if he took the note away from, say, *el plátano,* it would soon become "the word that started with a *p*" and then there would be nothing left but the banana.

A high mountain breeze blew constant and cool and the sky was empty but for a few lone clouds barely visible in the distance. Horace closed the dictionary and lay on the dirt and rocks next to Little Roy. Why had Mr. Reese had to see him in Las Vegas? And why had Las Vegas happened at all? He'd won three Golden Gloves fights before that, hadn't he? And why did he have to remember the loss so clearly, and why did he have to remember it every single day of his life?

It had happened at the Nevada Golden Gloves Championships and it was his first bout of the tournament. His opponent was a black kid named Cordarrel Watkins. Watkins was fast and hit hard and had won the state championship the year before, but Horace had seen him fight three different times and knew he had a weak chin and a bad temper, and, worst of all, was careless.

He and Mr. Reese had made the trip to Las Vegas the day before and got a hotel room. Mr. Reese arranged for a trainer from Carson City named Eru Rios to be Horace's cornerman. They ate an early dinner in a casino restaurant—New York steak and broccoli for Horace—and then walked the Las Vegas Strip. They saw a high-wire act and a dog show at Circus Circus and watched a fake pirate ship battle in a fake ocean in front of Treasure Island. They were in bed with the lights out by nine-thirty and Horace slept well and woke refreshed.

The bout was scheduled for three p.m. at Barry's Boxing Center. He and Mr. Reese ate breakfast and took another walk through the casinos before coming back to the hotel to rest. Horace ate again at eleven—a hamburger patty with mustard and ketchup and a side salad—and then they left for the match.

When he entered the ring at Barry's it was exactly three p.m. There were fewer than fifty people watching. Cordarrel Watkins stood nearly six feet tall and was rail thin at 120 pounds. He lived with his aunt and her four children in a run-down two-bedroom apartment in South Las Vegas. All five of them were there along with his boss from Jiffy Lube, a chubby white man in orange sweats. They all sat ringside screaming "Cordarrel!" as the bell rang.

Watkins's long arms were reluctant to throw a punch for the first minute. Horace, a bundle of raw nerves, danced around the ring and connected four jabs and an uppercut. The uppercut stunned Watkins. At the two-minute mark Horace saw another opening and threw a hard right that landed on Watkins's nose and Watkins stumbled back, his nose suddenly bloody. But more than anything, the punch had awoken Watkins. It caused him to lose his temper. He began throwing wild combinations and they came in barrages so fast that Horace fell back against the ropes and was unable to move. He froze. It wasn't that there was power to Watkins's blows, it was just that Horace panicked. He became suffocated by punches that didn't even hurt. He knew he had to get away from Watkins and he knew he had to get away from the ropes but he could do neither. He was stuck. He saw the gloves coming, he heard the sound of them landing, but he could do nothing to stop them. It was as if he'd somehow become paralyzed. Watkins continued punching at will until he tired and moved back to the center of the ring to rest and the round ended.

Eru Rios gave Horace a drink of water and said, "You have to hit him before he hits you. You're not good under pressure. You know you can hit him, but you have to throw punches to do so."

Horace came out for the second round and threw a jab and followed with a hard right that hit Watkins in the kidney and the kid stumbled back, hurt, but once again he became enraged. He said things through his mouth guard and began stalking. Even so Horace got him with a hard right to the face. But again Watkins forced Horace into the ropes and let off a seemingly never-ending series of combinations. Horace froze terribly and the panic grew and grew until he forgot to breathe. And then it happened. It felt as though he was falling and spinning at the same time. Suddenly, out of nowhere, he collapsed. He fell to the ground unconscious. He was laid flat in the second round of his first preliminary fight. He was laid flat while wearing full headgear at a Golden Gloves qualifying tournament in a state that barely had enough boxers to even hold a tournament.

The officials were anxious to get him off the mat, but Horace couldn't move. The overhead fluorescent lights blinded him and a wave of despair consumed him. He could hear people talking.

He could hear, in the distance, the voice of a worried Mr. Reese saying, "Is he okay? Is Horace gonna be all right?"

An announcer came on the PA and spoke of the upcoming raffle and said that the food stand was now selling dollar hot dogs and dollar popcorn. He then cleared his throat and called the next fighters while two men helped Horace to his feet and a doctor came to the edge of the ring where Horace leaned against the ropes. The doctor asked him a few questions, shone a small flashlight in his eyes, and nodded to the referee. "He's fine."

Eru took the headgear and gloves off, and Horace was helped down the steps while a handful of people clapped. They brought him to the locker room and sat him on a long bench. Eru wished Horace good luck, patted him on the shoulder, and left. Mr. Reese sat down next to him in silence and watched as the boy took the wraps from his hands and unlaced his boxing shoes. Around them were boxers of all ages. Kids were laughing and screaming, other fighters were shadowboxing in front of the sink mirrors. Horace kept his head down as he changed back into his street clothes. When he finished he looked at Mr. Reese. "I guess I'm ready to go now," he whispered.

"You don't want to stay and see the rest of the matches?"

"Not really," he replied. He couldn't look at the old man's face. He just stared at the damp concrete of the locker room floor. "I guess I'd rather just go home."

Mr. Reese put his hand on the boy's shoulder. "You gave it your best, Horace. That's all a person in this world can do. You worked as hard as you could. You came prepared. Every morning you went on your runs and then went to the barn and hit the bags. You worked as hard as a boy could. You should be proud of that. I know I am."

Horace looked past the gray, rusted lockers to the emergency exit. "Do you mind if we go out the back way?"

"There's no reason for that," Mr. Reese said and stood. "There's no reason for you to be ashamed. You tried your best."

But Horace put his gym bag over his shoulder and walked toward the red sign of the back exit.

It was dusk when Horace came back to camp with Little Roy. Pedro had built a fire and was sitting on the ground in front of the Coleman stove stirring something in a pan. Horace sat across from him and ate the insides of two of Mrs. Reese's sandwiches and threw the bread onto the fire. Pedro took a saucepan from the stove, poured stew into a cup, and handed it to Horace. They didn't speak while they ate, and then Horace rolled out his pad and sleeping bag. He sat on them and watched the fire. Pedro got in his bed and was soon snoring. Tiny and Wally slept next to him and Little Roy stayed with Horace. He fed the fire one last time and got into his bag.

Before sunrise he woke and stared up at the fading black sky thinking about his future. To be a champion he knew he would have to sacrifice more. He'd have to quit listening to white people's music and he'd have to quit eating fried food and drinking Cokes. Most of all he'd have to get to the bottom of why he continued to panic under pressure.

He got out of the sleeping bag in his underwear and stood in the cold morning. He put on his clothes and boots and started a fire. Once it had gathered coals he walked away from camp and did push-ups and sit-ups. He drank water, ate the insides of another of Mrs. Reese's sandwiches, and took the CDs out from his backpack.

PANTERA: *The Great Southern Trendkill*
CROWBAR: *Sever the Wicked Hand*

SLAYER: *Reign in Blood*
CANNIBAL CORPSE: *Tomb of the Mutilated*
METALLICA: *Ride the Lightning*

He removed the paper booklets from the plastic cases and set them on the fire. He found a small shovel leaning against a tree at the edge of camp, and walked to where the meadow ended and the sagebrush began. He dug a pit and threw the CDs and cases into it. He covered them with dirt and went back to camp.

6

Mr. Reese awoke in the dark to the sound of his wife crying.

"Are you all right?" he whispered.

"No," she said.

"What's wrong?"

"I'm worrying about Horace." Her back was to him. "I didn't mean to wake you."

"It's okay," he said.

"Why does he have to go?"

"He needs to be his own man, you know that."

"When he gets back we only have one last night with him."

"I know," he said.

"Why does he need to be a boxer?"

"I'm just not sure," he whispered. "I've thought about it over and over and I'm just not sure. But remember, he's young, and a lot of young men want to prove themselves."

"Will he get hurt?"

"I don't know."

"Will he come back?" She rolled over and looked at her husband in the dark.

"He will."

"Do you really think so or are you just being nice?"

"He'll come back."

"You promise he'll come back?"

"I'd bet my life on it," he said.

They were silent after that and he put his hand on her hip and rubbed it until he could tell she was asleep. He lay motionless trying not to think, but all that did was make him think more. He remembered the day he parked his truck in front of Horace's grandmother Doreen's little white house and walked up the gravel drive and knocked on her door. She answered dressed in a faded pink robe and stained white slippers. She was white, sixty-seven years old, and frail, and pulled behind her an oxygen tank in a makeshift cart. A plastic tube ran from it to both nostrils.

"I appreciate you coming," she said, her voice hoarse and full of phlegm. She led him inside to the living room. There was an old flowered couch and next to it an armchair where she pointed him to sit. She collapsed on the sofa, turned off the oxygen, and pulled the tubes from her nose. Beside her, on an end table, was a pack of Marlboro Reds. She took one and lit it.

"I'm not supposed to but what difference does it make now? And anyway, this conversation is going to be upsetting enough."

Mr. Reese took off his cowboy hat. "So it's pretty certain with your health?"

She nodded. "I just don't want Horace to find me, and if he stays, sooner or later he will."

"Like I said on the phone, Louise and I would love to have him. This last summer he spent with us was one of the best summers we've had since our daughters left. He's a good boy, and funny, and such a hard worker."

"It's surprising he's a hard worker," Doreen said. "I know his father is, too. It's not ordinary, I don't think, with Indians. Especially around here, but I'm glad he is. Maybe he can be some kind of help to you."

Mr. Reese half nodded. "The plan we've come up with, if it's all right with you and Horace's mom, is that he'll stay with the Pearsons Monday, Tuesday, and Wednesday nights after school. Thursday after classes I'll pick him up and he'll spend Friday, Saturday, and Sunday at the ranch. I'll drive him in early Monday morning before school. It's not the best setup, but it worked for our daughters pretty well. The Pearsons have housed a half dozen ranch kids over the years and I think all enjoyed it more than found it a burden."

Doreen smoked her cigarette and listened. She wore glasses with silver wire frames, and her hands trembled as Mr. Reese continued.

"And I talked with the school and they're fine with him not coming on Fridays if he does the extra work. I do worry that it'll be a problem with his grades, but the Pearsons are slowing down and they're not sure they can handle a fourteen-year-old boy more than three nights. If we find that him staying with the Pearsons isn't working for them or Horace, then we'll figure out a different plan. But he likes them and of course they love him. And then when he's old enough we'll get him a car and he can drive in each morning. We'll have him full time after that."

"He can have my car," Doreen said and coughed. Her eyes watered from it and she used a Kleenex to wipe her mouth. "Horace's dad sends me a check every month. I'll give the Pearsons some of that money."

"They'd appreciate it."

"I'll give you the rest," she said.

"You don't have to," Mr. Reese replied. "We're not doing it for the money. Maybe we could put that in a college fund."

Doreen nodded, knocked the ash off her cigarette, and drank from a can of ginger ale.

"And you're sure Horace's mom's okay with this arrangement?"

"My daughter thinks it's best for him to stay in the same

school. Horace spoke with her about it on the phone and he told her he'd rather stay here than go back to Las Vegas."

Mr. Reese nodded. "I also spoke with a lawyer and we'll need to sign some papers for guardianship."

She again nodded and then closed her eyes. When she opened them she looked at Mr. Reese. "Send me the bill for that. I'll forward it to Horace's father."

"And he's okay with this?"

She just nodded and pointed to the kitchen. "All Horace's food is in the freezer. I don't care for the dinners he likes and I won't eat them. They'll just go to waste if you don't take them."

She put her hand in her robe pocket and pulled out a folded scrap of paper and handed it to him.

"Written on there are the names of his doctors. He had an ear infection not too long ago. It gave him a horrible headache for a week but it seems to have cleared up. Will you keep an eye on it?"

"Of course," Mr. Reese said. "Are there any other medical things I should know about?"

She shook her head. "I did the best I could with him, but who knows? Maybe he'll end up a town drunk like Ricky Lonsdale or Big Tim. You never can tell with Indians, they all seem to end up drunks one way or another. But I've tried my best to keep him away from them."

Mr. Reese looked around the room. "Well, hopefully we'll be an asset to the boy. That's what we'll try to be," he said.

Doreen nodded, put out the cigarette, and turned the oxygen tank back on.

Mr. Reese stood up. "One last thing. Horace told me he'd left his shaving kit in the bathroom and a cardboard box full of things in his bedroom. He's pretty certain he has everything else."

"His room is off the kitchen," she said. Her voice had grown weaker in the short time he'd been there. Tears welled in her eyes. "Tell him to visit me. Tell him it'll be lonely without him and that I love him."

Mr. Reese nodded and walked through the kitchen to a small door. He opened it to find a pantry barely large enough for a twin bed. The ceiling was five feet at its lowest and six feet at its highest. He picked up a lone box off the plywood floor, carried it to the front door, and set it down. In the bathroom he found no shaving kit.

"I can't seem to find his Dopp kit," he said to Doreen as he came back to the main room.

The TV was now on. She took her eyes off it. "I don't let him use the bathroom in the house. The one he uses is in the shop. That's where he does his hygiene."

Mr. Reese nodded and walked out the back door to a metal pole barn. Inside, in the corner, was a toilet, a shop sink, and two shower curtains that hung by a badly built wood-and-wire frame. A garden hose was hooked from the shop sink and ran from it to the makeshift shower. He saw the canvas shaving kit, grabbed it, and left.

When Mr. Reese woke next it was five a.m. He nudged his wife three times before she woke.

"Is it time?" she said, half asleep.

"It is," he said.

She lay still for a minute and then sat up. She rubbed her face, set her feet on the floor, and turned on the bedside lamp. Their bedroom was on the main floor in a room that had once been their younger daughter's. Mrs. Reese put on her robe and slippers and went to her husband's side of the bed.

"You ready?" she asked.

He nodded.

She pulled back the sheet and thin blanket. The old man lay in boxer shorts and a white T-shirt. She took both his ankles in her hands and moved his feet off the bed. He groaned from the pain as he set his feet on the floor.

"Is it bad this morning?" she asked.

"Not too bad," he managed to say. "Once I get moving I'll be all right."

He put out his arms. She took his hands in hers and helped him up.

"Got it?"

"Yep," he said, and she left for the bathroom. He walked stiffly to the main room, where Little Lana lay on a blanket near the woodstove.

"How you doing this morning?" he asked her.

The old border collie wagged the nub of her tail and got up. She walked to Mr. Reese, licked his calf, and then watched as he walked back and forth from the kitchen to the living room. Mrs. Reese came from the bathroom with a jar of heat lotion, and Mr. Reese took off his T-shirt and she rubbed it into his back. She then started coffee, put a pot of oatmeal on the stove, and helped him dress.

They ate breakfast while listening to the radio and they didn't speak. Mr. Reese got to his feet and again walked from the kitchen to the living room back and forth.

"Do you mind if we go over it one more time before they get here?" he asked.

Mrs. Reese nodded and went to their bedroom. She came out with a yellow notepad. "We have $38,765 in the tractor account."

Mr. Reese nodded. "And you're sure this is a good idea?"

Mrs. Reese looked at him. "We've always grown our own hay. Always. Wells run dry, lines break, but there's water here. Trujillo thinks so and he's the best we know. A new well is an investment. We'll have to go deeper but we've always known that. And you can rebuild our tractor now that you have Morton's for parts. I know you can because you can rebuild anything."

"What if we just sold out?" he said.

"I'm not going to talk about that again. This is our home and I don't want to leave. You know that. You're just nervous 'cause it's a lot of money and you've been wanting a new tractor for years and now we're going to spend it all on a well that may or may not pan out. But I think it's exciting. That well's been giving us a headache for a long time now and soon we'll have good water again. We won't have to worry about buying hay and we won't have the constant headache about that damn well not working."

"You're pretty optimistic that the new one will turn out all right."

"It has to turn out all right so it *will* turn out all right."

"You always did like to gamble," Mr. Reese said.

Mrs. Reese smiled. "But let's not tell the girls."

Mr. Reese laughed. "If we told them we'd be sunk. They'd be here packing our bags and throwing us in the loony bin. No, we won't tell them about the well or any of it. We'll be undercover."

"Good," Mrs. Reese said.

"Now I need help with my boots," he told her and pulled out a kitchen chair and sat down.

Mrs. Reese found the boots and helped put them on. After that she began clearing the table and Mr. Reese and Little Lana left the house and walked across the long gravel drive to the barn, where he threw a flake of hay to each of the four horses while Little Lana watched quietly from the gate. It was then he heard the sound of a vehicle parking in front of the barn. He left the corral to see a large flatbed with TRUJILLO WELL DRILLING stenciled in faded red letters on the driver's side door.

7

The pickup truck was parked outside Deyoe's Mini-Mart as the bus made its way up the hill toward them. It was early morning and Little Lana sat between Horace and Mr. Reese.

"Will you give Lonnie this the next time you see him," Horace said and reached into a duffel bag at his feet. He took out a half roll of Copenhagen and set it on the dash. "I'm not gonna need it anymore."

"You're giving it up, huh?"

"If I'm going to make it all the way I have to change a lot of things and that's one of the things I have to change."

The old man nodded.

"I hate to admit it, Mr. Reese, but I'm pretty nervous to get on that bus."

"It's normal to be nervous," the old man replied. "You're going on an adventure to test yourself. It would make anyone nervous. I'm just glad we got to eat one last breakfast together."

"Me, too," said Horace. "And thank Mrs. Reese for the lunches she packed."

"She sure is going to miss you."

"I'm gonna miss her, too."

The old man cleared his throat as the bus pulled up to the mini-mart and parked. "I just want you to know that I believe in you, Horace. I always have. I hope you know and remember that. We both love you. Best of luck in Arizona, and no matter what you always have a home and a job and a family with us."

"Thank you, Mr. Reese."

"And will you call Mrs. Reese now and then just so she doesn't worry?"

"Of course."

"And remember to work on your defense and your breathing."

"I'll work on them," Horace said and tears welled in his eyes. "It sure is hard saying goodbye to you."

"It's hard for me, too," the old man said and opened the driver's side door and stepped down. Horace got out with his duffel and took a second suitcase from the bed of the truck.

"Well, I guess this is it," Horace said.

Mr. Reese went to his billfold and took a thousand dollars from it. "I know it's not much, but maybe this will help you get on your feet."

"You shouldn't give me more money," Horace said. "You already gave me a bonus."

"The bonus was because you're a good worker. You earned that. The thousand is from Louise and myself. Just keep it for emergencies and for maybe going to see one of your music events. Treat yourself."

Horace took the money and then set down his bags and hugged the old man.

"I'll never forget you, Mr. Reese."

"Please be careful."

"I'll be careful as much as I can, but a champion has to take risks. I won't be able to be careful all the time."

"I know," the old man replied. "I know."

"I'm gonna do great down there so don't worry." Horace smiled, picked up his bags, and left for the bus.

* * *

He arrived in Tucson the afternoon of the next day. He stepped down into the hottest weather he'd ever felt and made his way inside the terminal, where he called a cab. The driver took him down South Sixth Avenue, where stores, buildings, tire shops, and restaurants lined the sidewalks for miles upon miles. They came to Fortieth Street and Horace told the driver to pull over in front of a white adobe house with blue trim. There was a four-foot chain-link fence around the yard. The carport to the left of the house was empty. He paid the driver and got out.

He knocked on the front door but no one answered so he moved to the shade of the carport, sat underneath it, and waited for two hours. It was past six p.m. when a green Toyota Camry pulled up to the fence and his mom's sister, his aunt Briana, a large white woman with red hair dressed in a black business suit, got out and opened the gate. She moved the car into the carport and shut off the engine. She seemed neither happy nor upset when she saw Horace. She asked him briefly about his trip and then took him past the carport to the guesthouse. The yard around it was dirt and concrete with one large mesquite tree giving the only shade. There were no chairs or tables, no barbecue or plants or shrubs of any kind. She unlocked the door, handed him the key, and told him to make a copy. Inside, the windows were shut and the temperature was over 110 degrees.

"Like I told you I haven't had the heart to change anything," she said. "What you might not know is your great-aunt raised me more than Doreen did. So it's hard. It's been hard. I took out her clothes but left everything else the way she liked it. You can rearrange some things if you have to, but I'd rather you didn't get rid of anything. At least not without asking me first." His aunt's face was covered in thick, pale foundation. She wore blue eye shadow and dark red lipstick.

The little house was filled with old lady furniture. On the walls were pictures of flowers. There was a TV and a small AC unit against the back wall and a yellow-tiled kitchen in the opposite corner that had a gas stove, a refrigerator, and a sink. On a yellow kitchen table sat miniature porcelain figurines and next to it was a stainless-steel walker.

From his wallet Horace took out a money order. "My mom said it was five hundred a month plus two hundred a month for utilities. So that's forty-two hundred for six months."

His aunt Briana took the money order and looked at it.

"And don't worry, I won't be here longer than six months," said Horace.

His aunt was sweating in the room's heat. Drops were running down her temples. "Just be careful when using the air conditioner," she said. "It's an old unit and it costs a lot to use. Turn it off when you go out or when you go to sleep. Okay?"

"All right," he said.

"You come and leave through the gate so remember to always shut it. I go to bed by eight so if you could keep it down after eight I'd appreciate it."

He nodded.

"And like I told your mother, I don't want other people around here. No parties or friends and no smoking in the house."

"My mom told me all this. I won't mess anything up."

She looked at him and tried to smile. "I don't mean to sound rude. I'm okay with you here. It has nothing to do with you. It's just strange. I've only met you twice, once as a baby and the other time was when you came down here for the day to get your license. And I haven't seen your mom in years. And then out of the blue she calls and asks if you can use this place as an address and asks if you can move in."

"I know it doesn't sound good," said Horace. "I don't talk to her that often. But she called on my birthday and I told her I was thinking of moving and she mentioned Tucson and you and the house. She's always wanted me to leave Tonopah. So when I said I was thinking of leaving I guess that idea just came to her. I didn't mean to impose. And I'm sorry about your aunt. I know you're doing me a big favor. I'll be careful here, don't worry. And I'll only be here six months."

She began to say something more but stopped. "I'll let you get settled then," she said and left.

The bathroom was small and had yellow tile on the floor. Yellow bath towels hung from a rack and there was a stainless-steel railing around the shower wall. On a metal shelf above the sink sat a small mirror and next to it vials of medication. Even the aunt's old toothpaste and hand lotion were still there. The bedroom had an electric hospital bed that moved up and down by remote control, a dresser, an old TV on a wheeled stand, and a window that looked out to a rock wall. The room smelled of overheated air freshener and dust. Horace opened the window and then saw a fan in the corner, turned it on, and went back out to the main room, turned the AC unit on full, and lay in front of it.

The first night he tried to sleep in the bedroom on the medical bed. But even with the fan and the bedroom window open it was too hot, and the plastic mattress cover made noise every time he moved. And worse was knowing that his great-aunt had died in there, on that bed, and no matter what he did he couldn't stop thinking about that. At six a.m., he got up, did his run, and his push-ups and sit-ups. He showered and made a makeshift bed of a blanket, a sheet, and a pillow on the floor in front of the AC unit, then fell back asleep.

When he opened his eyes next the first thought that came to him was of his mother. He was eight years old and sitting

next to her in the car as she drove. She seemed to cry the entire
way and he didn't understand why she was leaving him with his
grandmother if she was crying so much about it.

"It's only for the summer," she had promised. "Your father
said he could take you but then, as you know, things came up.
But you've always liked Grandma. It'll be fun."

Two large suitcases were in the trunk and his bike and four
cardboard boxes were in the backseat of the small car.

"I want you to remember this is not because of Larry or the
baby. I don't want you to think they're the reason you're spending the summer with Grandma. I'm just so tired all the time,
and going back to work's been harder than I thought. And you
have to admit you were a handful all year. Leaving school, running away at recess, and you didn't try even a little in class. And
I've been at a loss about what to do with you this summer. Both
Larry and I have to work and now we have the baby to juggle
and Larry's worn out by it all, too, and he isn't very pleasant
when he's tired. I suppose nobody is. But we both know how he
gets and that makes things hard on the baby, hard on me, and
hard on you. We all just need a break. It won't be forever, just
the summer, and I don't want you to think it's your fault. It's not.
It's my fault and it's nobody's fault. I think we just need a reset,
a break to clean the table and get fixed up."

Horace looked at her. Tears streamed down her face as she
drove. It was hours like that. Her talking and crying. Saying the
same things over and over again.

The only other thing he remembered was that when they
finally stopped in Tonopah he was allowed to order whatever
he wanted at the Stage Stop Cafe. She never let him get milk
shakes, but that day she ordered him one and let him have
French toast and bacon for lunch.

It was all tears as they unloaded his belongings into a small room off the kitchen of his grandma's house, tears when his mother bought a twin mattress and box springs from the Senior Thrift Shop, and more tears as she hugged and kissed him and left him with a grandmother who drank Coors Light on ice from eleven a.m. until she fell asleep on the couch at nine, who chain-smoked cigarettes, who ate only frozen dinners, and who was scared of Indians, blacks, and Mexicans.

8

It was late morning when Horace got dressed and left. He walked to South Sixth Avenue and struggled under the heat. T & T Market, McElroy's Auto Repair, and Food City shopping mall came into view. He walked on until he saw Grand Central Barber Shop and went inside to find two Mexican barbers watching TV. The younger of the two stood up and asked in Spanish if he needed a haircut.

Horace shrugged his shoulders and said, "Can I get a haircut?"

"Sure," the man said.

Horace took out his wallet and from it a picture of the boxer Érik Morales and one of Canelo Álvarez. "Can you cut my hair like that?" he said, pointing to Morales. "But I want it to stick up like it does on this one," he said, then pointing to Álvarez.

The barber nodded.

"How do they get the hair in front to move forward like that?"

"Hair product," the man said and told him to sit down. He put a black sheet around him, took electric clippers, and began cutting off Horace's hair. The two barbers spoke to each other in Spanish while Horace stared at the TV.

A half an hour later he left with his hair short and coated in styling gel. In his back pocket he carried a plastic bottle of it.

He walked down the street and came to Discount Tires. He went inside, and asked if they were hiring. After that he tried Temo-Tires, Big Dog Offroad Discount Tire, a Mexican clothing store, and finally a mini-mart. But none of them were looking for help.

Two days passed the same way. He woke at dawn, did his workouts, and then slept in front of the AC unit. In the late afternoon, when the heat began to ease, he looked for work. He went from place to place searching. On his fourth day he began to grow worried. He even put in applications at Burger King, McDonald's, and Wienerschnitzel. But then as he walked home he took a side street and came to a small cinder-block building with a hand-painted sign that read MÁXIMO'S USED TIRE SHOP. A middle-aged Mexican man sat outside it on a weather-beaten couch, under an awning, drinking a beer.

"Are you hiring?" asked Horace.

"You know how to change tires?" the man asked.

"I worked at a tire place in high school three days a week after school," said Horace. "I can fix flats, put on new sets, and I can tell when used tires are good or bad."

The Mexican man was short and skinny and wore sandals, dirty blue pants, and a stained Tucson Padres T-shirt. He looked at Horace and coughed. "My nephew's my employee, but he hasn't shown up in two days and I don't know where he is. Can you come tomorrow morning?"

"Sure," Horace said.

"Be here at eight o'clock and we'll see if you know anything. I pay twelve dollars an hour, but if we're slow I'll send you home. I can't guarantee hours. And if you don't know what you're doing I can't use you, all right?"

They shook hands.

"What's your name?" the man asked.

"Hector Hidalgo," said Horace.

"*¿Habla usted español?*"

"No, not really."

"Where are you from?"

"Nevada. I just moved here. What's your name?"

"Benny," the man said.

Horace walked home in great relief that he might have gotten a job. He changed into shorts and running shoes and did his afternoon push-ups and sit-ups in front of the AC unit. When finished, he took a manila envelope from his bag of clothes. Inside were thumbtacks and the pictures of the Mexican boxers. He stuck them on the wall next to a full-length mirror in the main room, then stood in front of it, and worked on his combinations.

That evening he made his way down Sixth Avenue to Food City grocery store. Piñatas hung from the ceiling and the aisles were marked in English and Spanish. He bought tortillas, cheese, beans, and hot sauce. He bought precooked chorizo, instant coffee, a dozen eggs, and a carton of milk. He couldn't think of any other Mexican food besides rice, and he had never been good at cooking rice. He also bought orange juice and oatmeal, and filled the rest of the basket with broccoli, carrots, bananas, and oranges.

The next morning, he woke at five, did his workout, showered, and made a lunch of tortillas layered with canned refried beans and cheese slices. He wrapped them in foil and walked to Máximo's Used Tire Shop to find the man, Benny, sitting on the same couch drinking a cup of coffee, eating a candy bar, and reading a newspaper.

"I didn't think you'd show up," Benny said. He was dressed in black work pants, an oil-stained red T-shirt, and sandals.

"Do you still need a worker?" Horace asked.

Benny nodded and went back to reading his newspaper. "A truck will be here soon, just hold tight."

Horace sat on the edge of the couch and waited until a white semi arrived towing a twenty-eight-foot trailer. A stout Mexican man pulled down a ramp from the back and rolled the tires into a paved storage area that was surrounded by a ten-foot chain-link fence topped with barbed wire. The tires were high-quality brands with little or no tread wear. They seemed nearly new. Benny told Horace where and how to stack them, and they unloaded the truck.

Afterward Benny sat on the couch and went through a small book with phone numbers handwritten inside. He was on the phone for the next two hours, and each time he hung up he gave Horace a note with the size and number of tires and Horace took them from the storage area and staged them outside the shop door. Every hour a car or truck came and they changed out sets. Benny supervised on the first three and then moved back to the couch, drank beer, and watched as Horace worked. They finished at seven o'clock. Benny handed him $120 and told him he was hired.

It wasn't a great job, but Horace had accomplished the first thing he told himself he'd do. He was employed. Next was the trainer.

The Eleventh Street Gym was in a run-down strip mall. It wasn't much to look at, only a faded white storefront. But Horace knew from movies that most gyms weren't much to look at. Even gyms in the city, even famous gyms. The lights inside were on and he could see a ring, two big bags, and three small bags. A handful of kids were running around, and he asked a boy of about ten where Alberto Ruiz was. The boy pointed to a barrel-chested middle-aged Mexican man in the corner, who was yelling in Spanish at a kid working a heavy bag.

Horace waited at a distance until they finished, and then the boy left and Alberto Ruiz sat down in a plastic chair and began looking at his phone.

"Mr. Ruiz?" asked Horace.

Ruiz looked up. He had a boxer's face: a nose with no cartilage, rubbery and flat, eyebrows swollen with scar tissue, and his left cheek looked larger than his right. "Who are you?"

"My name is Hector Hidalgo. I talked to you on the phone. I'm from Nevada."

"Hector?"

"I'm fighting in two weeks at the Arizona Golden Gloves Championships in Mesa."

Ruiz shook his head.

"I called a few times. You were driving once and you had your kids in the car. You were going to get pizza. I'm from Tonopah, Nevada. We talked about the heat."

"The heat?"

"Yeah, about how it's really hot here."

Ruiz again shook his head. "Well, what can I do for you?"

"I was hoping you would train me for my fight in Mesa."

"I'm going to Mesa with a few of my fighters," he said.

Horace nodded. "I know, you said that on the phone. That's why I was hoping you could get me ready, too."

Ruiz looked at him and then reached into his sweatpants pocket, took out a packet of Nicorette gum, and put a piece in his mouth. "We'll sign you up. Do you have the monthly fee? It's a hundred to join and then a hundred a month."

"I have the money," said Horace.

"For an extra hundred I can give you more one-on-one time before the fight."

"So three hundred total?"

Ruiz nodded.

Horace looked around the gym. Signs for Zumba and a boxing workout class hung from the walls. He saw five Mexican boys: one was jumping rope, two were working the heavy bag, and two were in the ring chasing each other around. "Do you train professional boxers, too?"

"I train all kinds of people," he said.

"Well," Horace said and tried to think. "Can I start tomorrow after work?"

"I'll be here until nine. We'll talk then and I'll see what I can do to help."

"Thank you, Mr. Ruiz."

"Just call me Ruiz, okay?"

"Okay."

"And what was your name again?"

"Hector."

Ruiz nodded. "Be in gym clothes and bring your fees tomorrow, okay, Hector?"

When Horace arrived at the tire shop the next morning, Benny was asleep on the couch snoring with a mug of coffee between his legs, and a half-eaten Snickers bar in his hand. Horace sat on a wooden chair beside the couch and waited. The sun rose over the houses and Benny continued to sleep. An hour passed and Horace leaned back in the chair and closed his eyes, and when he opened them Benny was standing above him pushing on his shoulder with a hand that had only a thumb and two fingers.

"Hector," he said. "Wake up. The trailer's here."

Horace stood in a haze and saw a twenty-eight-foot trailer parked at the storage gate. The driver opened the back, hopped up into the half-empty trailer, and began rolling tires down to

Horace, who on the command of Benny stacked them in different areas until the trailer was unloaded. After that Benny sat on the couch and fell asleep again until an obese man on a small motorcycle arrived and began honking his horn.

Benny opened his eyes and smiled. He rubbed his hands together, took fifteen dollars from his wallet, and gave it to the man on the motorcycle, who handed him a plastic bag and drove off. Benny then took two twenty-four-ounce cans of beer and a Styrofoam container from the bag, opened one of the beers, and began eating a barbecued-rib lunch with greens, beans, coleslaw, and corn bread.

Horace took his lunch from the refrigerator and sat in the wooden chair next to the couch and began eating.

"You're not married, huh?" Benny said as he looked at Horace's food.

"No."

"I bet you don't live with your mother either."

"No."

"I didn't think so." He gave off a short laugh. "Your lunch is about as depressing as a lunch could be."

Horace nodded but kept eating. He looked around the property and said, "Who's Máximo?"

"Máximo?"

"The name of this place."

"Ah, that Máximo. He was my uncle. I inherited this place from him. I'd retired from working for the city but all I did in retirement was watch TV. Then my uncle Máximo died so I have a job again."

"Are you from Mexico?"

He shook his head. "I was born in Hudson, Michigan. You know where that is?"

"I know where Michigan is."

"My parents worked at a poultry processing plant there, but I moved in with my aunt and uncle in Tucson and went to high school here."

"Do you like Tucson?"

"What's not to like?"

Horace shrugged his shoulders.

"And you're from Nevada?"

Horace nodded.

"Where?"

"Tonopah."

Benny shrugged his shoulders.

"It's in the middle. A few hours north of Las Vegas."

"What did you do there?"

"Worked on a ranch."

"Like cows and shit?"

"Sheep."

Benny nodded. He closed the Styrofoam container, set it on the ground, took a plastic toothpick from his pocket, and began working on his teeth. "You know how to drive?"

Horace nodded.

"How old are you?"

"Twenty-one."

"And you have a driver's license?"

"Yeah."

"Let me look at it."

Horace took it from his wallet and nervously handed it to the man, but Benny didn't realize the name was different, that it said Horace Hopper. He just glanced at it and gave it back without saying anything. He took sixty dollars from his wallet. "I want you to get me two cases of Tecate tallboys. Tallboys are the big beers. Sixteen-ounce cans. You know where Food City is?"

Horace nodded.

"My son's car is behind the lot. You can drive it. And remember, don't buy warm beer. Get them cold, and if they don't have them cold go somewhere else." He took a key from his chain and handed it over. "And don't get in a wreck or steal it or buy the twelve-ounce cans."

Horace again nodded. He walked behind the small cinder-block building, got into a dented blue Ford Ranger pickup, and drove to the store. When he came back he found that Benny was now sitting under the awning with two Mexican men at a portable card table. They all clapped when they saw Horace carrying the two cases. Benny took three cans and told Horace to set the rest in the refrigerator. Afterward Horace stood at the edge of the garage as the men spoke Spanish and played cards, drank beer, and ate ceviche. One of the old men wearing a Boston Red Sox baseball cap grabbed a paper plate and set a large helping of ceviche on it, drenched it with hot sauce, squeezed lime on it, put a handful of saltines around it, and called out, "Hector."

Horace took the plate, thanked him, and sat down on the couch and looked at the food. He'd never eaten much seafood except for fish and chips at the Stage Stop in Tonopah, and he hadn't liked it. He hadn't even liked the trout Mrs. Reese cooked when they fished Pine Creek. The plate sat in front of him heaped with shrimp, cilantro, cucumber, peppers, tomatoes, onion, avocado, and hot sauce. The old men couldn't stop shoveling it into their mouths.

Horace looked at the food for a long time and then ate it as fast as he could to get it over with. It was spicy and felt awful in his mouth, and there were two times he thought he might throw it up. The men put more on their plates and he didn't understand how they could. His entire mouth burned, and he asked Benny if he could have one of the Cokes in the fridge.

In three swallows he drank the soda and then he sat back down on the couch and watched the men play cards. He tried to pick up on their Spanish, but they spoke so fast that almost none of the words he heard were recognizable. Finally, he got back up and went to Benny and asked him what he should do next, but Benny told him he was done for the day and took sixty dollars from his pocket and handed it to him. Horace put the money in his wallet and, not knowing what else to do, headed back to his aunt's house.

9

Mr. Reese parked his truck in front of A & C Auto Parts and he and Little Lana went inside. The shelves of the store were half empty and the products that were there were covered in dust. There were no other customers. In the back a middle-aged man in gray coveralls sat behind a chest-high counter listening to the radio.

"Morning, Hank," Mr. Reese said.

"Morning, Eldon," he replied. He was a big man who was bald on top and had greased-back brown hair on the sides. At one time he'd been an amateur bodybuilder, but he had let himself go. "I ain't seen you in a while," he said.

"I've had a run of luck with the truck." Mr. Reese knocked his fist on the wooden counter and handed Hank a parts list. "But now I'm gonna rebuild my old Massey and see if I can get a few more years out of it. That's what these parts are for."

Hank looked over the handwritten list. "I'll have to order some of this stuff."

"I figured you would."

Hank got up from the stool and disappeared into the back. He came out minutes later with the parts he had in stock, set them on the counter, and began writing up an invoice. "You still got that kid working for you?"

"You mean Horace?"

"The Indian kid."

"That's Horace. No, he's moved on."

"I thought I should let you know that I've seen him walking around town in black tights with a long chain belt hanging down to his knees and a ripped-up black T-shirt. He had his hair teased out like he was a woman. He looked like a woman."

"It's none of my business how Horace dresses on his own time," said Mr. Reese.

"I'm just telling you what I saw," said Hank. "He walked up and down this street like some kind of fag prostitute. He's done it a half dozen times that I've seen myself."

"Why are you telling me now if it's bothered you for so long?"

"I just thought of it," said Hank.

"He's a boy who's stuck out on a ranch with a couple old people for months at a time. He likes heavy metal music. From what I can tell they all dress like that. Anyway, like I said, what he wants to do in town is his own business. And it isn't against any law that I know of. So either sell me the parts or don't but I'd appreciate you not talking about him anymore."

Hank nodded. "Fine by me. Just tell him to skip my street the next time he's in town."

Mr. Reese shook his head and took the list he'd written off the counter and put it back in his shirt pocket. "Every time I step foot in here you get meaner and the store looks worse. Horace hasn't done anything to you but spend his money here trying to fix that old Saturn of his grandmother's. And he only came here because I told him to because I liked your dad. But I'm tired of it and tired of you. From now on I'm just gonna head up the street."

Hank's face fell and he took off his reading glasses. "I didn't mean nothing, Eldon. I was just talking. You don't have to get all upset. I always talk too much, you know that."

But Mr. Reese and Little Lana had already headed for the door.

It was ninety degrees out as the two walked to the Clubhouse Saloon. Mr. Reese thought of Horace on that same street dressed in his heavy metal outfit, walking around, lonely and different and lost. Other people had mentioned it to him as well and his heart grew heavy thinking about the boy. "Maybe Tucson will be the best place for him," he said softly to Little Lana, and they went inside the empty bar, where a young woman sat behind the counter, looking at her phone.

"Good morning, Mr. Reese."

"Good morning, Janie."

"A can of Coors?"

"That sounds about right," he said and sat on a stool near her.

"Can I give Lana some water?"

"I bet she'd like that quite a bit."

Janie opened a Coors and then filled a bowl with water and walked from behind the bar, set it down for the dog, and petted her.

"How's the baby?" Mr. Reese asked.

"I'm not getting much sleep," Janie said and stood back up. "I can't remember the last time I slept all night. But other than that she's great."

"The first years are tough," Mr. Reese said and took a drink of beer.

"You have two daughters, right?"

He nodded. "Cassie's in Reno and Lynn's in Denver. They're a few years older than your mom. I think they'd just left high school when your mom started."

"I can't imagine my mom in high school."

"She was a great basketball player."

"I can't believe that either," Janie said and laughed.

The old man took another drink of beer. "I got a question for you. Have you ever been to the NAPA Auto Parts?"

She shook her head. "But my boyfriend, Cody, he goes there all the time."

"Cody's the Henderson boy, right?"

"That's him."

"And he likes NAPA?"

"I don't know if he likes them but he's always going in there."

Mr. Reese took another drink of beer. "You know Cody's grandfather was a friend of mine growing up. I guess it would be over thirty years ago that he sold his ranch and moved to Reno. I don't think I've seen him since."

"He just retired from Ponderosa Meat," Janie said. "We went up for his retirement party last month. They've just moved to Arizona."

"Arizona?"

"They got a condo on a golf course somewhere near Scotts-dale."

"A golf course?"

"He's a golf fanatic," she said, and then two men in motor-cycle leathers came into the bar. They sat in the corner, near the door, and as she walked over to help them Mr. Reese finished his beer. He said goodbye to her and then he and Little Lana headed up the street to NAPA Auto Parts.

10

Ruiz was yelling at a Mexican boy shadowboxing in front of a full-length mirror. The boy was a chubby seventeen-year-old who wore cutoff sweats that hung low on his hips, showing red underwear. On his feet were fluorescent orange high-top basketball shoes.

"At least tie your goddamn sneakers," Ruiz yelled and pointed to the boy's untied laces. "What happens when you trip and a guy gets you with an uppercut that blinds you?"

"*Blinds* me?" the kid cried and stopped punching.

"You have to be aware both in and out of the ring. Anything can happen at any time. When you realize that you'll be better prepared for what's coming. You can't walk around like a jackass with your pants falling down and your shoes untied. There's a reason people wear belts and there's a reason people tie their shoes. I've seen you trip five times in the last hour."

Horace watched from the corner of the room as Ruiz ranted. He kept at the boy five minutes more and then called the session. The boy left, and Ruiz sat in a folding chair near the back wall and looked at his phone. Horace approached, his face dripping with sweat. He'd run two miles in jeans and work boots in the evening heat to get there.

"I'm sorry I'm late," he mumbled. "We got more cars in than I was told we'd get."

Ruiz looked at him. "Who are you again?"

"Hector. Hector Hidalgo. I came in yesterday and we talked."

Ruiz rubbed his face with his hands. His fingers were short and stubby and he'd shaven badly with missed spots under his nose and lower lip. "I remember now," he said.

"Is there still time for a session tonight?"

"Do you have gym clothes?"

Horace nodded.

"You have the money?"

Again he nodded. He handed Ruiz three hundred dollars. Ruiz counted it and then pointed to a locker room. "Change in there," he said.

Horace came out minutes later in his gym clothes and Ruiz waved him over.

"So where are you from again?"

"Nevada," said Horace.

"And you say you've boxed before?"

"Yes."

"Well, regardless, the first thing I'll teach you is how to protect yourself. If you don't learn that, you'll end up with a face like mine. But that's the life of a prizefighter."

"You really fought pro?"

"For fifteen years," said Ruiz.

"What was your record?"

"Twenty-five and twenty. Not much of a record. But they stole at least ten from me, I could argue fifteen."

"I want to turn pro," said Horace.

Ruiz smiled. "You're the kid fighting in Mesa? The kid who kept calling me."

Horace nodded.

"It's all coming back to me now," Ruiz said and laughed. "We'll concentrate on that first, okay? Mesa first."

Horace walked home from the gym that evening thinking over the session. Ruiz said he hit harder than anyone he could remember training. "There was a guy I fought in Houston once. A wiry, ugly son of a bitch from Cuba who escaped to Florida on a raft made of truck inner tubes. That's how tough he was. He used a handmade oar and gutted out the entire trip on his own. Pushing through the waves, in the ocean, with sharks and the Coast Guard trying to get him. That kind of life, going through things like that, makes you tough. He hit like a cement truck shot out of a rocket. I survived the fight on my feet, but I was finished after that. I kept going, fought eight more times, but I wasn't the same fighter. He took something away from me that I could never get back. You hit nearly as hard as him. My hands are sore from the mitts and they never get sore from the mitts. But look, Hector, I was able to make you freeze up a half dozen times. Is that normal for you?"

Horace nodded. "Can you fix it?"

Ruiz shrugged. "We can try, but it's hard to fix something inside of you like that. We'll give it a go though. We'll make it better at least."

Horace had left the gym let down and depressed. He had held it as truth that a professional trainer would somehow fix him of his freezing and that it would be remedied quickly. That it would be, after a session or two, solved and out of his way, and then he could get on the road to becoming a champion. But as he walked down the street his guts began to hurt. What if it could never be fixed? What if he was just basically flawed forever?

He arrived home and went inside. He looked at the food he had in the refrigerator but none of it was what he wanted. The truth of it was he didn't like Mexican food and he wasn't used to spicy food. His grandmother's stomach wouldn't allow it and the Reeses didn't like it either. He enjoyed hard-shell tacos well enough, but he didn't like making them himself. He would have to cut up a head of lettuce, slice tomatoes, and grate cheese. He didn't know how to season the meat and the store-bought shells didn't seem as good as the ones in restaurants. It was too much work and he got tired of them after two nights anyway.

As he stood looking into the refrigerator, he thought that maybe, at least for a while, he could eat non-Mexican food at home. That he wouldn't have to act Mexican there, alone. He would make BLTs, cheeseburgers, egg and ham and potato chip scrambles, and always he'd keep spaghetti around. If he was honest with himself his favorite food besides fried chicken, mashed potatoes, and gravy was Italian food: spaghetti, lasagna, pizza, and ravioli.

He showered, ate three bowls of cereal, and then underneath the AC unit lay on his makeshift bed, turned on his CD player, and listened to disc one of *Learning Conversational Spanish*. But as always the words came and went from his mind and he fell asleep and didn't wake or move until the next morning at dawn.

For the following eight days he did the exact same thing: morning workout, changing tires at Máximo's, night sessions with Ruiz, and then home and listening to his language CDs.

The morning of the ninth day, the day of his Golden Gloves fight, he woke to his phone ringing.

"Morning, Horace. Are you up?"

"Is that you, Mr. Reese?" Horace whispered.

"It is."

Horace sat up and rubbed his face with his free hand. "Is there anything wrong? Did anything bad happen?"

"Nothing like that. We just wanted to wish you luck." Mr. Reese pulled off the phone. "I think we woke him," he said to his wife. He cleared his throat and said into the receiver, "We're sorry to call so early. We just remember that even when you had a day off you got up at five so that's what we decided to do. Try you at five. Are you sure you're okay to talk?"

Horace stood up. He went to a small end table near the room's main window and turned on a lamp. "It's a good time to talk, Mr. Reese. But if it's five here that means it's four where you are."

"Mrs. Reese and I have a hard time sleeping, you know that. We were up already talking about you, excited about your fight today. We couldn't wait to hear how things are going in Tucson. Are you getting settled all right?"

"I think so," Horace said. "I got a job anyway."

"You got a job already?" Mr. Reese again pulled off the phone. "He got a job. . . . Well, I knew you'd get hired fast. You're a hard worker. Everyone knows that. They'll be lucky to have you. What kind of work are you doing?"

"I'm working for a tire shop."

"Like Tonopah Tire?"

"Yeah, but it's all used tires. It's not the best job, but it'll be okay for a while."

"And the boss is okay?"

"He seems good enough. He doesn't talk much so I don't know. I'll switch jobs later on, but it's a start. How are things at the ranch?"

"They're going fine," the old man said.

"How is Lenny working out? Does he get to Pedro okay?"

"Lenny didn't take the job."

"He didn't?"

"No. His mother called and said he was suddenly unavailable for the rest of the summer. After all that time of him promising he could. I'm not sure what happened. It seems harder with kids now. They just don't seem like they want to do this type of work."

"What did you do about Pedro?"

"I went myself."

"With a broken back?" Horace said and began pacing the room.

Mr. Reese laughed. "My back's not broken, I just have muscle spasms. Anyway, don't worry about us. I didn't mean to burden you. That's not the reason we called."

"You'd never burden me, Mr. Reese," said Horace. He sat down at the old woman's kitchen table and picked up a ceramic fawn and looked at it. "You learn things when you live in the city. You learn that you're on your own even when you're surrounded by people. I guess I never realized that in Las Vegas."

"You were just a boy when you lived in Las Vegas. Things are different when you're grown up and out on your own in a city. And how do you like Tucson?"

"It's hot here. I didn't think it would be so hot."

"That's true," the old man said. "It is hotter down there than it is here."

"And I haven't gotten used to how many people there are. There's people everywhere."

"That's a hard thing to get used to when you've lived on a ranch for as long as you have."

"Can I ask you a question?"

"Of course."

"Where does all the toilet water in a city go? Does everyone have septic tanks? I got to thinking about it when I was walking down a street and there was a long traffic jam. Behind that street was another street that also had a traffic jam. And behind all that was a freeway overpass with more cars than you could count. There's just so many people. It got me thinking about how everyone takes showers and uses the toilet and does laundry. I don't mean to sound like an idiot, but where does it all go?"

Mr. Reese again cleared his throat. "Every house, store, and building, all their plumbing is connected. They all have pipes leading to bigger pipes and they send all that stuff somewhere out of town and treat it. They try and clean the water the best they can and then the water goes on its way back where it should go, and the remaining stuff, the sludge, is dumped somewhere."

Horace set down the ceramic fawn and picked up a brown ceramic burro. "Where does all the water come from? There's no river or lake anywhere near here."

"Water's a big problem in that part of the world. It's a problem for us, too, as you know, but more so for a place like Tucson with its large population. They pipe some in and then of course they drill for some. They have huge aquifers in that area. They pump a lot of water out of the earth."

"You must think I'm pretty stupid," said Horace.

"No, I don't think that at all," Mr. Reese said. "You're just living in a city now, and people think about those sorts of things when they live in a city. You have to remember you were just a boy when you left Las Vegas. And you haven't been to any other city, have you?"

"No, Mr. Reese. Just Las Vegas and now Tucson."

"These are big changes, big adjustments. So it makes sense you have questions. How's everything else? How's your aunt? How's her place?"

Horace sighed and set down the burro and picked up a ceramic cactus. "She's okay I guess," he said. "But every time I talk to her I can tell she doesn't want to talk to me. And the house is kind of weird. It has nothing but old lady things in it.

When I get enough money, I'll get my own place. It'll take a while, but before too long I won't have to stay here."

"Well, you thought she might be tough," Mr. Reese said. "Your mom and her never got along so it makes sense she might be standoffish. But once she gets to know you, she'll like you."

"I hope so."

"Did you meet the trainer who you were talking with on the phone?"

"I did. His name's Alberto Ruiz and I found him all right. He has his own gym. I think he really was a professional boxer like he said. We've been working together eight days in a row. It's more expensive than I thought but I'm realizing everything is more expensive in a city."

"That's true. Things do cost more in the city. Have you gotten to see any of your music events?"

Horace laughed. "You mean concerts?"

"Yes, concerts."

"I gave up all that. I don't listen to that sorta music anymore." Horace could hear Mrs. Reese talking in the background.

Mr. Reese paused and then came back to the phone. "Louise says I'm leaving out the important questions. Are you eating properly?"

"Tell her I'm trying to, but I'll never eat as good as the food she makes."

"I'll tell her," Mr. Reese said. "Well, Horace, I'll let you go. We love and miss you and think about you every day. We wish you the best of luck in Mesa. We know you're going to do great. You're the hardest-working person we've both ever met. Just remember your defensive skills. Tell your coach about defense. Have him help you with that, and your breathing."

"I will, Mr. Reese. I'll make sure to tell him."

Horace hung up the phone, and the uncertainty of the night before, the loneliness, waned and he began to focus on the day ahead of him. He ate four fried eggs, showered, and then walked two miles to Alberto Ruiz's house. In the cool of dawn, he sat at the edge of the carport and waited an hour until the lights in Ruiz's tract house came on. Two cars arrived separately after that. A nine-year-old boy named Owen was dropped off by a haggard-looking man in a mid-eighties, dented work van. The second boy, Johnny, came in a rusted-out white Nissan with Minnesota plates. The woman driving yelled at him for a long time before he got out of the car.

The three of them, Ruiz, and his two young sons piled into a twenty-year-old minivan and began the two-hour drive north to Mesa. Ruiz smelled of stale beer and would fall into jags of coughing that ended with him rolling down the window and spitting. Horace sat in the passenger seat while Ruiz's two sons and Owen and Johnny sat in the back.

They were just outside the city limits when the boys began arguing over a handheld video game. Ruiz yelled at them to keep quiet and they would for a time but then slowly, after five or ten minutes, they would start up again. Ruiz's agitation grew the longer he drove and finally he pulled off the highway and stopped.

"I'm tired of this pansy shit," he yelled. His face was pale and sick and sweaty. "It's fight day for fuck's sake. You know how important fight day is? Fight day is when you save every ounce of yourself and all the months of hard work and you give it back to the ring. You don't give it to the goddamn car ride. What you don't understand is all this, everything we do is about discipline. It's about thinking through every punch, every move you're gonna make in that goddamn ring. It's about visualizing how you're going to demand respect. How you're going to win the match. Not this bullshit, not fighting over a son of a bitch video game."

He got out of the van and slammed the door. He walked into

the desert and behind a cactus Horace saw him bend over and
vomit and then stand up and then bend over again and vomit
more.

Ruiz waited for a long time before he came back to the van.
"We're stopping in Eloy for breakfast at McDonald's," he announced calmly. "But for that to happen you have to be silent
until we get there. I mean not a word. Barely a goddamn breath."
He started the van and pulled out onto the interstate, but again
he began coughing and that caused him to gag and when he did
he farted so loudly that all the boys laughed.

The Arizona Event Center in Mesa, once a country-and-western
dance hall, sat in a now forgotten strip mall. To the left of it were
two spaces for lease and to the right a western clothing store
called Botas Juarez. Next to the clothing store was a beauty college and then more vacant spaces. The event center marquee
was blank with no listings and there were very few cars parked
in front of it. Ruiz left the engine running and told Horace to
get out and make sure they were at the right venue. Horace
jogged across the parking lot to the front door to see a blurry
photocopied flyer for the championships. The door was open
so he went inside, saw the ring and a handful of people already
there, and ran back outside and waved.

Two middle-aged women were setting out folding chairs as
Ruiz and the boys entered. The women wore heavy makeup
and jewelry and jeans with crosses embroidered into their back
pockets. They knew Ruiz and said hello to him, and he flirted
with the bigger of the two before gathering the boys in a corner
of the hall.

"Get your asses around me," he said. "I know I got us here
early and we have some time to kill. But in my experience, it's

best to know the lay of the land before anyone else. It's best to be comfortable with a place, know your environment so you don't think about it anymore. Get this place to feel like your living room. We do that so when the time comes you just think about what's happening in the ring, not outside of the ring. Remember boxing is the whole reason you're here. Everything important today happens inside that ring. I want you all to walk around on your own. I want you to feel this place, check out the can, check out every corner. But if you leave this building, if you step one foot outside without my permission, I'll kill you. I'll kill you and your parents will be happy that I did. And if you get into any trouble today, any trouble at all, I'll call the cops. I'm not joking. And believe me, those sons of bitches will be happy to cart you away and put you on a chain gang." Sweat dripped down his face and his shirt was wet with it. He began coughing again and the coughing became gagging. He waved the boys off and headed for the toilets.

The event center walls and ceiling were painted black and there were no windows. Horace stood at the edge of the room as people began arriving. White farm boys and Mexican city kids filtered in with their families, who carried gym bags and large coolers with them. Everyone seemed to know each other and the room came alive with talking, kids laughing, and coaches setting up in empty corners so their boxers had places to get ready.

A concession stand opened, as did a bar and a small souvenir booth. Horace found a photocopied program on a table. The Sixty-Sixth Annual Arizona Golden Gloves Championships. Inside were articles on Hall of Fame boxers: Michael Carbajal, Tony "El Tigre" Baltazar, Rollin "The Chiller" Williams, Jesus Ernesto "El Martillo" Gonzales, Alfonso Olvera, and Jerry

"Schoolboy" Cheatham. Attached to the program was a yellow flyer and on it a list of the day's fights. Horace saw his name on bout two.

Horace Hopper vs. Purcell Jenny

There were to be two separate fights at lightweight. The winners of the preliminaries would meet later in the day for the Arizona state championship in bout seventeen. He found Ruiz at the concession stand eating a hot dog and drinking a large Coke.

"I'm listed as Horace Hopper," he said, his voice faltering in embarrassment.

"What?" Ruiz asked with a mouth full of hot dog.

Horace couldn't look at him. He just stared at the floor. "Horace Hopper is the name I was given later on, it's what's on my ID, but my real name is Hector Hidalgo. That's the name my dad has, that's the name he gave me before he got murdered."

Ruiz quit chewing and looked at Horace. "Your dad got murdered?"

Horace nodded slowly. "He got murdered in front of me when I was twelve. In the driveway of our house. He stood up against a drug cartel and they killed him for it. After that my mother was so worried she changed our name to Hopper. She made up the name Horace Hopper."

Ruiz looked at him, confused, and shook his head. His right eye was red and bloodshot while his left was normal. Even in the air-conditioned room he continued to sweat. He nodded and waved the boy off.

Horace walked around the gym, his heart racing, and then went outside to the parking lot. He shook his head as he walked. Why did he have to lie? Why did he always have to lie when he became scared or embarrassed? Was he ever going to change? When was he going to finally start acting like a man? A man with character. A man who would run into the middle of a car fire and save a baby and a dog. His hair would be burning, his hands would be bubbling, but he wouldn't care. He'd save the baby and the dog, he'd get them to safety.

Palm trees that went four stories high lined the main entrance of the strip mall. How did they get water? Did those sorts of trees need water? Were palm trees even made of wood? He should know these things, shouldn't he?

He looked across the parking lot to a McDonald's and then a Pep Boys auto parts store. He walked along the strip mall building, past the beauty college, and then across the parking lot to the main avenue. He looked up and down at strip malls and businesses lining the road for as far as he could see. Endless miles of cars passed. Every single person inside every single car had a TV, a phone, a bed, and ate chicken and got the runs. How many chickens got killed every day?

He turned away from the sprawl and went back toward the event center. He came to Botas Juarez western wear and went inside. Up and down aisles he walked until he saw a pair of Mexican cowboy boots his size. They were dark brown, and carved into the leather were two white skeletons surrounded by roses. The man skeleton wore a cowboy hat and the woman skeleton wore a red dress with white polka dots and they were dancing arm in arm. The boots were on sale for two hundred dollars. Horace tried them on and he liked the way they fit. He walked around the store in his black sweats and stopped in front of a large mirror and shadowboxed while staring at the boots.

Outside, Ruiz saw him through the window glass and came into the store red-faced and fuming.

"Jesus Christ, Hector, what in the fuck are you doing? Your fight's in twenty minutes. And do you know who you're fighting? You're fighting Purcell Jenny. He is the best boxer in the state. Maybe in the country. How many goddamn times did I tell you not to leave? How many?" There was ketchup and mustard on

Ruiz's shirt and the two clerks behind the counter stared at him as he yelled. "Already I caught Johnny eating a candy bar and drinking from a liter jug of Coke while he walked down Country Club Drive like it was the most normal thing in the world to do. He was a half mile from here when I found him. He could have been kidnapped and killed. He could have been run over."

Horace tried to apologize and took off the boots, returned them to the shelf, and followed Ruiz out of the store and back to the event center. The main room was now a third full. More kids and families had arrived and finally also spectators. Horace went to the bathroom and changed into his black boxing shorts. In Ruiz's corner of the room he put on his boxing shoes and a black tank top that read ELEVENTH STREET GYM in gold letters and began to jump rope. Ruiz then wrapped his hands and pulled him close.

"Now listen," he whispered. "Jenny won state last year, was second in nationals. They say he could make the Olympic team. So my advice is try to land one that wrecks him. He'll win on points but you could stop him. You have the power to do it, you just have to get in there to take the shot. Okay?"

Horace nodded, but he was too anxious and excited to listen. He entered the ring at exactly twelve-thirty in headgear, boxing gloves, and his mouth guard in. He was so pent up he had trouble catching his breath. Ruiz stood on the outside of the ring telling him to calm down, telling him not to jump around like a monkey, but Horace couldn't stop himself.

The announcer, a fat, red-faced, bald man in gray sweats, was ringside at a desk. He turned on the mic and said in a booming voice, "Final call for Purcell Jenny. I repeat, final call for Purcell Jenny, the lightweight Arizona and regional 2015 Golden Gloves champion. Final call for Jenny." The announcer glanced around the room one last time, waited a minute, and then hit the bell with a small hammer. "Horace Hopper will advance to the lightweight finals in bout seventeen. For bout three David Gonzales, Phoenix Boys Center, in the red corner and Marcos Villar from Fuentes Boxing Club in the blue corner. Please bring both boys to the ring. Again, David Gonzales and Marcos Villar to the ring for bout three."

The referee took the gloves and headgear from Horace, and the boy climbed down from the ring.

"You have two hours at the most. Maybe three," Ruiz said as they walked back to their section of the hall. "Don't eat too much, but get something now if you're hungry. And whatever you do, and I'm serious, don't leave the fucking building again."

Horace said nothing. He stared at the floor as they walked.

"Don't look so down, Hector. You'll get to fight soon enough. Anyway, you got lucky. Purcell is the real deal. He's on a different level than the rest."

"I could have beat him," Horace said and looked up.

Ruiz laughed and then sighed wearily. "Well, that's the right attitude to have. It's true you gotta believe in yourself. That is the main thing. But once in a while you need luck, too, and we got lucky. So eat now and then watch Owen and Johnny. 'Cause when you're not fighting you're . . ."

"Supporting," said Horace.

"Right," Ruiz said.

Horace put on his sweats and walked to the concession stand and ate the insides out of a hamburger and drank a glass of water. From a back seat he watched Johnny lose a decision in the eighty-pound weight class, and then two bouts later Owen entered the ring at fifty-four pounds. When the bell rang he sprinted toward Davey Edwards, a fourth grader from Flagstaff, and began throwing wild punches. Edwards continued to back up until he nearly fell out of the ring. But then, his face red and streaked with snot, Edwards came rushing back and began throwing haymakers and the round ended. Owen came out exhausted in the second and Edwards began to box him. He got Owen with two hard rights to the face, but with that Owen became enraged. He again threw wild punches, connecting enough that the referee stopped the fight and Owen was declared the winner.

Ruiz seemed better when Horace entered the ring at two-forty-five. The sweating had ceased as had the coughing and gagging attacks. He grabbed Horace by the shoulders, looked him in the eyes, and whispered, "Hector, you got lucky again. You saw this kid fight earlier, you saw how he struggles. He barely won his first bout. He's a white farm kid from Yuma. It's the best possible setup for you, but don't get foolish. Don't get cocky either. He looks like he hits hard but he's slow and his combinations are slower and he doesn't throw a lot of them. You got this kid. So go in there and get the goddamn job done. Okay?"

Horace nodded over and over but he was too nervous and excited to listen. And then, suddenly, the fight began.

The farm kid from Yuma came out cautious and when he did connect there wasn't much power behind his punches, and Horace's combinations were getting through. His opponent's face became covered in red-flecked snot. The kid was already fading as the first round ended.

Ruiz chewed Nicorette gum as he spoke to Horace in the corner. "You got him, Hector. Just throw combinations and remember to move your feet and keep your hands up. He hasn't hurt you but he could. And remember to move your goddamn feet. What do you have to remember?"

"To move my feet," Horace said and looked out to the small crowd.

"Are you tired?"

Horace shook his head. "I'm just getting going." He again looked at the crowd. A third of them were watching him. Ruiz gave him a drink of water and said, "Don't look out there. It's in here you have to look, inside the ring. It's that kid from Yuma you gotta focus on. This fight's just beginning."

The second-round bell rang and Horace went to work. He landed two combinations to the farm boy's face that sent him reeling. Thirty seconds later Horace landed the hardest body shot he'd ever thrown. The kid from Yuma fell to his knees and couldn't get up. The referee went to him, paused for a moment, and then called the fight over. It took nearly a minute before the kid finally got to his feet, shaky and hurt. Blood trickled from his nose. In the blue corner a man who looked like his father shook his head gravely.

The referee stood between the fighters, Horace to the left and the farm boy to the right. The announcer's voice came out of the PA so loud it began to feed back. He declared Horace Hopper the winner, and the referee lifted Horace's arm and both fighters were handed trophies. Horace's was a foot taller than the farm boy's and read ARIZONA GOLDEN GLOVES LIGHT-WEIGHT CHAMPION 2016.

Horace got down from the ring and walked past the specta-tors, the boxers, and the parents, and for the first time in his life he didn't feel like an outcast or a failure. He didn't feel like a misfit, he didn't feel off or defective. Finally, after so much work and heartache, Horace Hopper was leaving him. He was being cut away and left to disappear into nothingness. He had the trophy in his hand and the respect of the people in the room. He had won.

Owen and Johnny held the trophy while Horace went to the bathroom, cleaned up, and changed into his sweats. At the concession stand a man wearing a green suit bought him two hot dogs, Red Vines, and a Coke. Two other men sitting in the twenty-one-and-older section yelled out his name and gave him a thumbs-up.

When he finished eating he walked back to Ruiz's corner and sat down. Owen and Johnny were wrestling while Ruiz's two kids were eating popcorn and playing the handheld video game. Horace leaned back against the wall relieved and full of pride and closed his eyes.

11

Mr. Reese climbed out of his truck and walked across the parking lot to the Banc Club. Inside he passed through the aged casino and the din of the slot machines to the diner, where his oldest friend, Ander Zubiri, sat drinking a glass of wine and filling out a keno card.

"I don't see how you can drink wine at seven in the morning," Mr. Reese said and took off his cowboy hat, threw it on the booth seat, and sat down.

Ander shrugged his shoulders. He wore bifocals, a stained straw cowboy hat, dirty jeans, and a green, threadbare western shirt. He hadn't shaved in three days. "I ordered for both of us when I saw you pull in," he said and went back to filling out his keno ticket.

"The new kid couldn't take it," Mr. Reese said and put his elbows on the table.

Ander looked up. "What happened?"

"It's hard to tell exactly. He only speaks a Peruvian dialect, so I didn't have much of a way to communicate with him. He's a relative of Pedro's, that's why I hired him, but I don't think he'd ever been out with sheep. I'm not sure he's even spent much time outside a city. I don't know. . . . I was hoping he'd be a good fit and then Pedro would have a relative with him and I could buy Conklin's flock before lambing season. Double my size. But now with Horace gone, and the amount I spent on the well, I'm not sure what I'm going to do."

Ander took a drink of wine. "I don't know what you're thinking anyway," he said. "You're only two years younger than me, your health's worse than mine, and now you want to expand. You want more employees, not less. More headache, not less. And prices keep going down. You know I went to the grocery store yesterday and there was no lamb in the entire meat department."

A middle-aged waiter with greasy black hair and Band-Aids on three of his fingers came to the table. He picked up the keno ticket and the ten dollars sitting on top of it, and poured Mr. Reese a cup of coffee.

"I know," Mr. Reese said when he left. "I know you're right."

"So what happened exactly with the new kid, what's his name again?"

"Víctor. He ran away from Pedro and was hiding maybe a mile up the mountain in an aspen grove."

"Hiding?"

Mr. Reese nodded. "Horace found him and brought him back to the ranch and we put him on a bus to Los Angeles."

"Los Angeles?"

"That's where he wanted to go."

"How's Pedro?"

Mr. Reese shrugged his shoulders. "The last time I saw him he seemed all right. The dogs look good. He's moving the flock the way he should. He's shaving and eating. But I think we're on borrowed time. My gut says it's going to happen again, that he's had enough of it up there."

"It was pretty rough the last time," said Ander.

"That image of coming into camp finding him like that on

his bed naked and all cut up with the knife still in his hand. . . . That'll never leave my head."

"People go crazy being alone too long, but I'd never heard of a guy cutting himself up like that."

"Me neither," said Mr. Reese. "I tried to get him to see a doctor, and I guess he did go once and was put on some sort of medication, but I don't think he takes it. I also told him to go back home for an extended vacation, but he just clams up when I say that. He has three kids that I don't think he's hardly seen, and even so he doesn't want to go back. I gave him phone cards and got him a solar charger thinking if he called home more it would help with the loneliness."

"Maybe calling home makes it worse."

"Could be."

Ander took a cigarette from a pack on the table and lit it with a brass lighter. "Back in the thirties my dad's cousin came out from a small town maybe thirty miles from San Sebastián. From what I was told he wasn't from the mountains, not really. He'd grown up working on a boat. But like so many people he couldn't find work so he came over here. He spoke only Basque. They said he was a meek sorta kid. Maybe he was depressed or mentally ill to start out with, I don't know. And he was a distant relative. So no one's direct responsibility. They put him out near Alturas and left him with the sheep after only his second week in the States. And remember he didn't speak English, and only pidgin Spanish. A lonely boy in a country he didn't understand and then thrust into the mountains alone. They checked on him, but I don't think anyone really cared to understand how he was doing mentally. He was just a worker, another relative who needed a job. The boy grew more and more depressed. He began to let himself go, didn't shave, didn't bathe. But even so they didn't pull him off the mountain. He was out for nearly four months when they found him hanging from a tree, dead, with a pocketknife stuck into his leg."

"A pocketknife?"

Ander nodded.

"Why would he put a knife in his leg?"

Ander shrugged. "Pain? I knew of a kid down by Carson City who shot himself after eleven years with the sheep. He'd had a month off in town, he didn't have a drinking problem, he had a bank account with money in it. His month comes and goes and then he's back in the mountains with the sheep. He's there only four days and shoots himself. Why wouldn't he just quit and stay in town? Why wouldn't he just move on to a different sorta job?"

Mr. Reese sighed.

"I try never to tell a man what to do, but I've known you most of my life. First the well and now wanting to expand. It's like you're panicking. If you look at it on paper it just doesn't make sense. Soon they'll change the herding laws anyway, you'll have to pay Pedro more. And Christ, how much longer will you even be alive?"

"You know who I saw last week," said Mr. Reese and took a drink of coffee. "Roy Gifford."

Ander laughed.

"I ran into him at the hardware store with his dad. He was back for a family reunion. He told me he's running two thousand head of cattle for some big outfit in Wyoming now. In charge of the whole thing. That's a big operation. Why couldn't Cassie have married him?"

"'Cause she didn't love him as much as you did."

Mr. Reese laughed. "Both my daughters ran out at seventeen and have never come back for more than a week or two."

"Can you blame them? They're smart, good-looking, they went to college, they didn't want to spend their lives out in the middle of nowhere. My boys didn't want anything to do with the ranch either. All three didn't. I couldn't get even one of them to take it. Not even the bum."

"No wonder you drink in the morning."

"Remember you didn't want to take over your dad's place either."

Mr. Reese nodded and the waiter appeared with two plates of steak, eggs, potatoes, and toast, and set them down on the table.

"I just can't sit around and watch TV all day," said Mr. Reese.

Ander nodded and they fell silent. They ate quietly and then Ander set down his knife and fork. "What if you just ran a small cow-calf operation? Your dad ran cattle as well as sheep. You have the hayfields. You have the water. I have two good bulls. You could do most of the work on a four-wheeler. I'll give you mine. A retirement plan. Sell the sheep and start a new operation. Small and easy."

Mr. Reese nodded and kept eating.

"Why you so quiet?"

"Just thinking is all."

"What about?" asked Ander.

"Personally, I could leave, I could. You know I've wanted to, but Louise, she'll barely go to the store anymore. Last week we got in a fight because I made her go into town for a doctor's appointment. It never gets better. If she was never around people again she'd be all right about it. And she doesn't want to move in with the girls, doesn't want to travel. She never wants to go anywhere. She wants to die there, on the ranch. So what choice do I have but to keep going? I either keep trying or give up. And if I give up, what will I do all day?"

Ander nodded.

Mr. Reese pushed his plate away and set his elbows on the table. "I stopped by the ranchers' breakfast a while back. Most of them got out or retired a long time ago, most are living on social security and savings and are probably doing all right. But while I was there all they did was complain. All they did was bitch and not one of them had a truck that was older than three years. What do they have to complain about? I don't want to be like them. They don't do anything."

Again Ander nodded.

"Back to cattle, huh?" Mr. Reese said and took another drink of coffee.

"It'll be less of a headache on you. A small herd, a retirement herd."

"Jesus, I thought I'd care less about things as I got older but I don't. I care just as much. But I'm also getting tired."

"That's why, in old age, I always drink wine," Ander said and smiled.

"But you always drank wine."

He again nodded. "It got me out of two marriages." He laughed. "It's been more than a good friend."

12

The crowded Greyhound bus idled in the depot, its air conditioner struggling against the heat of the day. Everyone inside was sweating and uncomfortable. Horace sat by the window two rows behind the driver and closed his eyes. He was nearly asleep when a young pregnant woman sat down next to him holding an infant in her arms.

"Is this the bus to Salt Lake?" she asked, out of breath. She wore a T-shirt with a unicorn on it and shorts and had thin brown hair and an acne-plagued face. Her thick, sweaty leg rubbed on Horace's Levi's, and he moved as far as he could from her.

He nodded and looked at the infant.

"Don't worry, she won't cry. She don't ever cry when it's this hot out."

The driver stepped onto the bus, made his announcements, and they left the station. Horace slept in spells, the infant stayed quiet, and the day passed. When they pulled over for a scheduled dinner stop the pregnant woman pushed on his shoulder and woke him. She asked if he had enough money for a Dr Pepper. Horace sat up, rubbed his eyes, and gave her five dollars from his wallet. The passengers got down from the bus and he watched as the girl walked across the parking lot to a Jack in the

Box. He followed along slowly and stood three people behind her in line and ordered dinner. As he got his bag of food he saw her sitting in a corner seat, the baby on her lap, while she ate.

He walked back to the parking lot and had his dinner near the bus. When people began getting back on he did as well. The woman's baby bag and a small stuffed rabbit were on the seat next to him. He sat down, closed his eyes, and leaned against the window glass. The bus driver did the passenger count and stopped in front of Horace's row. He asked where the person sitting next to him was, but Horace opened his eyes and said he didn't know. The driver left the bus to look around. He came back a short time after that, shut the bus door, and they left without her.

As they headed up Interstate 89, Horace became overcome with shame and guilt. He had helped leave a woman and her baby stranded. She was probably still sitting in the same seat in the corner of the restaurant with her baby who didn't move or cry, who smelled like dirty diapers. And what was his excuse? Why didn't he speak up for her?

He got up from his seat and walked to the front of the bus. "That woman who didn't get on. She was in the Jack in the Box."

The driver looked at him in the rearview. "It's too late now. We gave three warnings over the PA. I told everyone a half-hour break."

Horace nodded and went back to his seat.

Dusk became night and the bus struggled over the mountain passes. He tried to focus on Salt Lake City, on the motel he would pick, on the runs he would take each morning, what he'd eat for breakfast, how he would ready himself for the matches, but always the pregnant woman and her baby came into his thoughts. She didn't have her diaper bag and she probably had a suitcase in the luggage hold. A broke pregnant girl with a baby stuck at Jack in the Box in the middle of the summer, in the middle of nowhere. He put his jean jacket over his head and collapsed into sleep.

The bus arrived in Salt Lake City at seven the next morning and Horace stepped down into the small terminal, grabbed his travel bag, and took a photocopied map from his pocket. He had circled the Salt Palace Convention Center with a yellow highlighter, and he walked for half an hour before he saw the glass building and its round glass tower. He sat on a bench, worked his hand exerciser, and waited for the center to open. Buses and cars passed. There was nothing around him but miles of concrete and asphalt.

He waited an hour, then got up from the bench. He was tired of waiting and he was hungry. He walked farther down the street to find Lamb's Grill and he ate at the counter: three eggs, bacon, no hash browns or toast. Afterward he kept walking. A Howard Johnson motel came into sight and he got a room on the second floor and watched TV and waited.

It was afternoon when he went back. The Salt Palace was now open and bustling. He was in line for twenty minutes before he was able to tell them his name. A black woman wearing a Golden Gloves T-shirt sat behind a table and looked through a list and put a check by Horace Hopper and he received a gift bag, an access badge, and his schedule. He moved away from the crowd, stood against a wall and thumbed through the program to find he was to fight Mickey Shrep, from Topeka, Kansas, at one p.m. the next day in ring three.

A steady stream of boxers, trainers, and families continued to come in, and with each person Horace felt his confidence crumble. He sat on the floor and leaned against the wall as boxing clubs from Boston, New York City, Los Angeles, Houston, Miami, Kansas City, Seattle, Detroit, Minneapolis, Chicago,

Cleveland, Philadelphia, New Orleans, and Atlanta entered the building. The fighters, mostly black and Hispanic, were dressed better than he was and they were in groups. None of them were alone.

As he sat and watched, a darkness began to seep in. He was nothing. A nobody. An Indian who wasn't an Indian and a white kid who looked like an Indian. He knew then, at that moment, while he watched all the other fighters, that he would never be a championship boxer. He was too slow and he froze under pressure, and the best, the elite, they never froze. Érik Morales never froze. And he wouldn't even help a broke pregnant woman and her baby. No champion would be like that. No champion at all.

The line of fighters and trainers grew: Buffalo, Cincinnati, San Francisco, El Paso, Raleigh, Lafayette, Oakland, Denver, Oklahoma City, Albuquerque, Tallahassee, and Lincoln. There were so many of them, and they were all dressed in new sweats and just-out-of-the-box Nike and Adidas shoes. They had good haircuts and every single one of them seemed at ease. Horace's mood grew darker and he decided then that he would go back to his aunt's house in Tucson. He would get his things, find a different place to live, and give up boxing for good.

He closed his eyes in exhaustion and was nearly asleep when he heard his name called. When he opened his eyes he saw Mr. Reese standing over him dressed in cowboy boots, jeans, a freshly ironed blue western shirt, and his gray felt cowboy hat.

"How you been, Horace?" he said in his cracked and tired voice.

Tears suddenly streamed down Horace's face. "I'm not sure, Mr. Reese."

"What's wrong?" he asked.

"I don't know."

"Did anything happen?"

"No."

"Did something go wrong with check-in?"

Horace shook his head.

"Everything's on the square? No problems?"

"No problems. I'm registered."

"But you're not okay?"

"I don't know."

"When's your first bout?"

"Tomorrow at one o'clock."

"Where's the Arizona team?"

"I'm not sure."

"Do you have a trainer looking after you?"

"My trainer didn't have any other boxers making the trip so he couldn't come."

"We'll get someone to be in your corner. Is that what you're worried about?"

Horace wiped the tears from his face and shrugged.

"Do you have a place to stay tonight?"

Horace looked at the other boxers in the room. "I'm staying at the Howard Johnson," he whispered.

Mr. Reese moved to the wall and leaned into it and sighed.

"Is your back still giving you trouble?" Horace asked.

"A bit," he said.

"I don't understand why you're here, Mr. Reese."

"I came to see you. Do you mind if I stay and watch your fights?"

"I don't mind."

"Do you think they still have rooms at the Howard Johnson?"

"There's an extra bed in my room."

"I don't want to impose."

"You never impose, Mr. Reese. To tell you the truth I was thinking of leaving."

"Leaving?"

"Yeah."

"Why?"

"Look at these guys. I won't win. They're all from big cities."

The old man smiled. "So that's it?"

"What?"

"You're nervous?"

Horace nodded.

"Everyone gets nervous," Mr. Reese said. "That's just a part of it. You're testing yourself. A man gets nervous when he tests himself. It's been that way since time began. . . . Are you hungry?"

"I am if you are."

"Then let's get out of here," Mr. Reese said. He took a handkerchief from his back pocket and wiped his nose. "I've never been able to get used to fake air."

"It's hard to get used to," said Horace, and Mr. Reese reached out his hand and helped the boy to his feet.

In the area designated for red corner prefight warm-ups Horace retied his boxing shoes and continued to shadowbox. A half dozen other boxers were in different parts of the room, and the sounds of laughing and talking and fists hitting mitts drowned out the announcements on the PA. Mr. Reese stood in the corner talking with a man named Link Wallace, a trainer and gym owner from Kalispell, Montana, who Mr. Reese had got to look after Horace during the tournament. An obese man dressed in white sweats then came into the room and yelled, "Horace Hopper—ring three." Link, Mr. Reese, and Horace followed the man out to the main room and waited at the edge of the ring while an announcer called the results of the previous fight. After that Horace got into the ring.

Mickey Shrep was a short and thick twenty-year-old white kid from the outskirts of Topeka. He lived in a room above a garage across the street from his mother, three half sisters, and his third stepfather. He tripped as he came through the ropes, and a handful of kids watching laughed. There were two other rings in the same hall, and a fight was in progress in each of them. Only a handful of spectators sat in the folding chairs around ring three. Mouth guards were put in both fighters' mouths, headgear and gloves were put on, and the two boxers were brought to the center of the ring.

With no fanfare or excitement, the bell rang.

Mickey Shrep hit harder than anyone Horace had fought, but he was plodding and out of shape and he didn't pressure. Luck had again found Horace. When the first round ended he had landed ten clean shots and was barely winded. The second round was the same as the first, and when it ended Link Wallace said only, "Just keep doing what you're doing but try to move more. He's slow but he's still catching you." And then a minute into the third Horace landed a head shot with such force that it sent Shrep wobbling. The referee paused the fight, checked Shrep, and then let it continue. But Shrep had lost his taste for it after that and spent the rest of the round in retreat. When the final bell rang the referee gathered the scorecards and the two fighters came to the center of the ring, one on each side of the referee. Over the PA the announcer said, "Horace Hopper advances to the second round. How about a big hand for both fighters?" A dozen people clapped, the gloves were taken off, and both boxers exited the ring.

Horace changed to his street clothes and found Mr. Reese standing in line at the concession stand. They ate lunch and watched three hours of fights and then left the Salt Palace. Mr. Reese took a handwritten list from his wallet, and together they went through it and bought Mrs. Reese boxes of candles, five one-thousand-piece puzzles, a heating pad, headphones for her radio, a new toaster, two different size nonstick pans, and four sets of white bath towels. At Home Depot, Mr. Reese bought a new Sawzall, an assortment of blades, five pairs of gloves, a cordless drill, two sets of bits, and a dozen assorted boxes of nails and screws. They ate an early dinner and were in bed with the lights out at nine o'clock.

At two in the morning Mr. Reese woke to Horace rustling in the bed across from him.

"You can't sleep?" the old man asked.

"I guess I'm just nervous. Did I wake you?"

"No," Mr. Reese said and coughed. "I wake up a half dozen times every night."

"Is your back hurting?"

"A bit."

"I bet it's 'cause you're not used to the bed," said Horace.

"That's part of it, I think," the old man said. The sound of a TV came through from another room and the hum of the AC unit kicked on. Mr. Reese pulled the sheets up tight on top of him, rolled over, and closed his eyes.

"I don't know why I have to fight so early."

Mr. Reese opened his eyes. "Eleven-fifteen. You're right, that is pretty early. But there's a lot of fighters to get through."

"The guy I'm fighting is named Modine Moffin. He's a black kid from Detroit. He was third in the nation last year."

"I know, I saw him fight, too. I was sitting right next to you."

"He's fast, isn't he, Mr. Reese?"

"He seems like it."

"I'm going to get destroyed."

"Don't say that."

"It's true."

"You have to think positive. You have to think like a champion. That's what you've always told me, and if there's any time to think like a champion it's now."

"But it's hard to."

"I'm sure it is. It's difficult to put yourself out there. That's why most people don't try things that are hard or that scare them."

"Have you ever put yourself out there, Mr. Reese?"

"Me?"

"Yeah."

The old man paused and then said, "I suppose so."

"What was it?"

"You don't want to hear about my life."

"I'd like to hear about your life, Mr. Reese. I would."

"Well," he said quietly, "I always wanted to be a pilot."

"Like an airline pilot?"

"Maybe. . . . Since I was a boy what I wanted from life was to live by the ocean and be a pilot. Two pretty big things, especially knowing I was born on a ranch in Nevada. Ambitious but not unattainable, at least that's what I thought. So I joined the Air Force after I finished high school and I liked it. Even the bad things about it I didn't mind. But I washed out of flight school 'cause I have poor eyesight. I didn't wear glasses back then 'cause I didn't want anyone to know my eyes weren't right, but of course they weren't right and so, by default, I was let go from pilot school. I was stationed outside of Bakersfield, California, and I was there for the rest of my stint. Only a couple times did I get to ride in a plane and I never flew one. I had thought just by being in the Air Force that I would get to see parts of the world, but it wasn't the case. That wasn't my job. My job was to fuel planes. I drove a fuel truck and never left the base outside of Bakersfield. It was the first big setback in my plans, but I did my stint and got out and moved down to La Jolla. Do you know where that is?"

"No."

"It's near San Diego. I guess now it's considered a part of San

Diego. I worked in a machine shop and rented a one-bedroom house right near the ocean. Every morning before work I'd get up and go swimming in the sea."

"You did?"

"I did."

"Did you learn how to surf?"

"No," he said and smiled. "Surfing wasn't as popular as it is now. Living by the beach in that little house was one of the highlights of my life. But you know when I first got there I didn't know anybody and that was hard. I was tested. I worked in a concrete building with only a single window and I was there nine hours a day on a drill press. That's difficult for a kid who's used to seeing the sky all day and the openness of things. Plus, I'd never been alone. Not ever really. Not even in the Air Force, where I always had roommates. But when I got down to La Jolla I didn't know a soul and I hardly ever saw the sky and I lived by myself. Solitude. I had to live with my own thoughts, and that can be hard. But sure enough I got used to it and I got to be by the ocean. One of my dreams had come true. And then I met a woman."

"Mrs. Reese?" asked Horace.

"No," he said. "This was before I met Mrs. Reese. I was only twenty-three. I met a woman 'cause her sister's husband and I worked together. We all became friends. The co-worker, his wife, and his wife's sister. We'd have Chinese food or Italian or Mexican. You have to remember I had never eaten out, not really. My mom's cooking and then the Air Force's cooking were pretty much all I knew. It might not seem like much, but all of that was pretty exciting. And also finally, after a long time of being alone, I had friends. And then the woman and I became closer. We started dating. We'd go to the movies and have fires together on the beach. We'd go swimming. Sometimes we'd drive down to Rosarito, Mexico, with her sister and her sister's husband and go swimming, night swimming even. When I look back at it, it seems like we were always swimming."

"What did she look like?"

"She had the bluest eyes I've ever seen on a woman. She had blond hair, a California girl, I guess. The kind they talk about in songs."

"Why did you leave?"

"My dad had a heart attack. He had the sheep up past Horse Canyon and he was by himself. He died. He was only fifty-two. My sister called me at work and told me the news and with that phone call my life in California ended. I had two sisters still in school. I had my mother, my aunt, and my grandmother. They all lived on the ranch. They all depended on it to get by. So right then, that day, I had to quit my job. I left with a paycheck in my pocket and never set foot in that machine shop again. I remember I went to the little house I had near the ocean and started crying. Crying for my dad, of course, but also crying 'cause I'd never get to see the ocean like that again. I had held my dream in my hand but now it was over. I took my things out and called the landlord and left my keys on the kitchen table. And then I had to go see the woman. She worked at the local newspaper. I went there and told her I had to go back. For as long as I live I'll never forget having to walk into that huge brick building and tell her. Even after all these years it's still hard to think about."

"She didn't follow you?"

"She visited once. We were engaged, you know? But she was from La Jolla and she would have had to live in a house with five women. She'd be surrounded by nothing but sagebrush, a thousand sheep, a half dozen horses, a half dozen dogs, dozens of chickens, a handful of pigs, and a bunch of barn cats, and nothing but dirt and my family breathing down her neck every day."

"But she didn't at least try?"

"She wanted to but I told her I'd get through life a lot better thinking about her by the ocean, and not taking the ocean from her. She had spent her whole life in San Diego, she was happy there, and I didn't want to be the reason she lost that. I've always loved the ocean more than anything else in the entire world. So why would I take something I loved so much from the woman I was in love with?"

"What was her name?" asked Horace.

"Alice Hampel."

"Whatever happened to her?"

"I don't know exactly, probably lived her life. Had a family and children. At least I hope she did."

Horace rolled onto his side. He looked in the dark toward the old man. "Then how did you meet Mrs. Reese?"

"Her dad owned a place up by Pony Springs in Lake Valley. He was a cattleman. She had two brothers and a sister. Mrs. Reese grew up in what I'd call a house of abuse. Her dad beat up on all of them. And all of them have struggled in life because of it. Both her brothers died young and her sister long ago disappeared. When Louise was fifteen she married a man and escaped. But that man . . . It's not my place to say but after a couple of years she was abandoned without a dime in Chicago, Illinois. She was in a hard spot and was forced to go back and live at her folks' ranch. Her father shunned her for her marriage and her mother did as well. And you know how nice Mrs. Reese is. It's awful how they treated her. So she got taken on as a cook for a ranch up by Pritchard's Station just so she could move out. I met her then and we became friends and then after a while we got married. She liked my family and my family liked her and our life went on together. A few years passed and then my grandmother died and my sisters graduated from high school. They moved to California together and both married and started having kids. So my aunt and my mother moved in with them to help out. Suddenly I was thirty years old living on the ranch alone with Mrs. Reese. She was maybe twenty-three or twenty-four at the time. And she was happy to be there. I'd always thought of leaving, but Mrs. Reese was against it. I think 'cause of all she'd been through she liked the solitude of the high desert, the ranch, and the stability and peacefulness of our life. And then we had our kids so we just stayed."

"I'm sorry about the ocean, Mr. Reese."

"The reason I told you about that is to let you know that you have to give it a shot. You have to try and get what you need to get by in life. It makes you a better person to try. I got a chance and it didn't quite work, but it almost worked. It was close to working. But if I didn't go down to La Jolla in the first place, I'd never have La Jolla in my heart. And now I have La Jolla in my heart for as long as I want it there. You're the Arizona Golden Gloves Champion because you had the guts to move down to Tucson and try. No one can take that away. Not ever, not for your entire life. And today you got the best of Mickey Shrep, and he came all the way from Topeka, Kansas, to try and be a champion. And tomorrow you're against Modine Moffin, and you're going to show up and try as hard as you can, and if you do, you'll beat him."

"He's pretty fast, though, Mr. Reese. I'm not good against speed."

"But he hasn't been hit by 'The Machine Gun' yet, has he?"

Horace laughed. "No, Mr. Reese, I guess not."

Horace stood in the same corner of the Salt Palace warm-up room as he had the day before while Link Wallace looked over his wrapped hands. Mr. Reese stood in the back leaning against a wall when the obese man came through the doors in the same white sweats as the day before and yelled out, "Horace Hopper—

ring one." Fewer spectators were there than the day before, and Horace, Link Wallace, and Mr. Reese walked toward the ring as a featherweight match ended and the winner was declared.

Modine Moffin was a dark-skinned black man, five feet, eight inches tall with a shaved head. His muscles shone under the lights. He wore new black boxing shoes, shiny black shorts, and a black tank top that read DETROIT BOXING in gold writing. A large bald man in a T-shirt that read DETROIT IS MY HOME put Moffin's headgear and gloves on.

"Just do what you did yesterday," Link said to Horace. "But remember to move your feet." He put in Horace's mouth guard and stepped from the ring. The referee checked both boxers' gloves and led them to the center. A bell rang out and the fight began.

All the waiting, the tossing and turning, the going to the bathroom a half dozen times throughout the night, the walking the streets of Salt Lake City at five in the morning, the trying to eat but not being able to eat, the ordering of two separate breakfasts, the forgetting midsentence of what he was trying to say, the near inability to comprehend what someone was telling him, the desire to run away but begging for the fight to start all at the same time was now over. In an instant, the ring of a bell, Horace was getting hammered by a blur of quick combinations from the Detroit boxer.

Modine Moffin's punches came out of nowhere. They seemed as fast as light. There were times in the first round when Horace became so overwhelmed that, like always, he fell into the ropes and froze. He didn't move his legs or his head. He just stood motionless with his gloves covering his face.

When the round ended Horace went to his corner in a daze. He said to Link, "He's so fast I don't know what to do." His nose was dripping snot with traces of blood in it and he was out of breath.

"It doesn't look like the kid's got any sort of power, so just start throwing punches. When you want to cover up, don't. Just start working combinations. Do his punches hurt?"

"No," Horace said. "Not really."

"Then that's what I'd do," said Link, and round two began.

Moffin again came hard. He threw combination after combination and his point lead grew. But Horace began taking punches to throw punches. He found openings from odd angles. He got Moffin in the face with a right hook that caused Moffin's nose to bleed instantly. And then he got him again in the stomach with another right hook. He followed with a body shot that knocked the wind from Moffin. The Detroit kid had never been hit so hard. With twenty seconds left in the round, he fell to his knees. He was hurt and he struggled to get back to his feet. The referee looked him over and okayed the bout to continue. But as Horace moved toward him the round ended.

Moffin came out in round three and pressured even harder. He backed Horace into the ropes three separate times and gathered more points. But the third time the freeze broke and Horace landed two serious body shots, the last nearly stopping Modine Moffin for good. The kid from Detroit's legs turned to rubber, his nose bled in a stream, and he waited out the round in retreat barely able to breathe.

The final bell rang and the referee gathered the scoring cards, glanced at them, and handed them to the announcer. He then brought both fighters to the center of the ring, Horace on his left and Moffin on his right. They waited a minute until the announcer's voice rang out into the room. Modine Moffin's name came through the speakers as the winner. The referee lifted the Detroit kid's arm and it was finished and decided. The referee took the gloves off both fighters and Link helped Horace down from the ring, took the headgear from him, and said, "I really thought you had that one." Horace nodded and remained silent. He thought if he spoke he would cry. He shook Link's hand, muttered a thank-you, and never saw the man again.

At the Howard Johnson, Horace stood in the shower crying as quietly as he could. Why did Mr. Reese have to see him lose? Why couldn't Mr. Reese have just left after he beat Mickey Shrep? He would have thought Horace had talent then, that he was smart for moving to Tucson.

When he shut the water off he could hear the sound of the TV. He dressed and came out into the room, where Mr. Reese sat upright on the bed with his back against the wall.

"I always forget how many stations there are nowadays," the old man said.

Horace looked at the TV, sat on his bed, and put on his shoes. He looked at the carpet. "There's a bus leaving at seven p.m.," he said. "I guess I'll take that."

"You're going back to Tucson?"

Horace nodded weakly.

"Are you going to continue to work at the tire shop?"

Again he nodded. "I'm gonna go pro now," he whispered.

"You're going to become a professional boxer?"

"Yeah."

"Are you sure?"

"I know if I had more rounds I would have knocked him out. Don't you think I would have knocked him out?"

"I just don't know, Horace," Mr. Reese said and shut off the TV. "I would have thought that, but I just don't know that much about boxing. And also I don't know much about Modine Moffin."

"You don't think I can do it, do you, Mr. Reese?"

"It's not that I don't think you can do it, I just think it's gonna take a lot out of you to find out."

Horace began kicking at the carpet.

"And I'm not the right person to ask. I don't want you to get hurt, Horace. You're more than a boxer to me. You're pretty damn important to both me and Mrs. Reese."

"I don't care about getting hurt," Horace said and looked at the old man. "A real champion doesn't care about getting hurt. So I'm not going to care about getting hurt."

Mr. Reese nodded slowly. "Why don't you come back to the ranch and think it over for a while? We sure could use the help."

Horace shook his head. Thoughts were coming and going so fast he could barely breathe. It felt like a weight was dropping on his back the longer they spoke. "I have to become a champion, don't you see? I have to prove that I'm someone before I come back. I'm not anything right now, Mr. Reese. I'm nothing but a failure. You must see it. You must see it every time you look at me."

"No," Mr. Reese said, suddenly becoming uneasy. He moved his feet off the bed and sat just across from Horace. "I don't think that at all. I've only ever thought the opposite."

"Well, I can't go back. Not until everybody knows, even my mother and father, that I'm the best. That's when I'll come back and I swear then I will come. But I can't right now, don't you see? I'm sorry, I really am, but that's the way it has to be. I'm going to go back to Tucson and train harder. I'm going to train harder than anybody's ever trained."

"When did you say your bus was leaving?"

"Seven."

"Well, let's check out of here and get a late lunch," Mr. Reese said and tried to smile. "I want Chinese. That's one type of food Mrs. Reese can't make at home. Then I want to take you shopping. We can get you some new training clothes and shoes. Mrs. Reese knew you wouldn't come back. She's smarter than me. Anyway, she told me, made me promise, that I would buy you some new clothes."

"You don't have to do that."

"If you don't let me then I'm gonna be in real trouble. Mrs. Reese will throw me down a mine shaft."

Horace looked up at the old man and suddenly laughed. "Remember that guy, Lucky?"

"Sure, I remember him."

"When he ran the tractor into the side of the barn you told him he'd better pack up his things and get out before you threw him down a mine shaft. You say that every time you get upset."

"He was a bad hire, that's for sure. Mrs. Reese saw it a mile away, but I didn't."

"He's the only guy I've ever seen who gargled with vodka in the morning," Horace said and again laughed.

The old man stood up. "We've known each other a long time, Horace. Mrs. Reese figured you were fourteen years and seven days when you came out for that first summer and took the room upstairs."

"I like that room."

"It's still there," Mr. Reese said. "And the trailer is, too, and we could also do what we've talked about, building you an apartment in the main barn."

"Thank you for saying all that, Mr. Reese."

"But only come back when you're ready and if really you want to."

"I want to come back someday," Horace said. "I love the ranch more than anything. I just can't do it right now."

Mr. Reese nodded. "Chinese food, clothes shopping, and then if we have time we'll have a second meal and I'll take you to the bus."

"Just so you know I don't wear small-town clothes anymore."

"Get whatever kind of clothes you want," Mr. Reese said and put on his boots.

"And maybe we should get Mrs. Reese a gift."

"We should, you're right."

"For starters we should get her a few boxes of See's candy," Horace said. "Dark chocolate though, and nuts and chews only. Those are the ones she likes. Did you remember to bring your cooler?"

"I did," Mr. Reese said.

"Did you bring it for the See's candy?"

"Yep," he said.

13

Mr. Reese stopped at a service station in Wendover. As he got gas he noticed his truck's rear-right tire was low. He moved the truck to the edge of the station, in near darkness, and filled the tire from a coin-operated air compressor. After that he went inside, bought a cup of coffee and a donut, and got back on the road. He listened to the radio and jumped stations as the night gave them and took them away. Interstate 80 led to 93 and soon he was on a desolate desert road where no traffic passed.

An hour outside of Ely he felt movement in the bed of the truck and pulled to the shoulder and parked. From the glove box he took a flashlight and got out. He checked the tires and then looked underneath the truck, but everything seemed normal. As he stood back up he saw the taut canvas tarp covering the bed move. He unfastened one of the tailgate corners to find two boys lying flat surrounded by his supplies.

"What are you two doing back here?" he said, startled.

"Nothing," one of the boys said.

"Both of you get out of there now," Mr. Reese said and unclasped three more hooks and pulled back the canvas. The boys stood up in the bed and then jumped down onto the side of the road. The bigger of the two was holding a dog, a medium-size black mutt, in his left arm and set it on the ground. A choke chain hung around its neck and a rope ran from it to the boy's belt. The mutt sat on the dirt and began licking at its right paw.

Mr. Reese ran the flashlight over them. The bigger of the two looked to be in his late teens and was tall and heavy. The other boy seemed younger and was too thin and even in the poor light he looked anemic, his face sallow. Both had scraggly beards and wore cutoffs and thin black T-shirts. Mr. Reese looked in the bed of the truck and saw two backpacks with sleeping bags attached to them.

"Where you two trying to get to?"

"Mexico," the bigger of the two said.

"Where in Mexico?"

"Los Mochis."

Mr. Reese shook his head. "How did you know which way I was going?"

"We didn't. We were just sick of waiting."

"Don't you know you could get shot doing something like this?"

They just looked at him.

"How much water do you guys have?"

"Half a gallon maybe," the bigger said.

Mr. Reese again shook his head. "It's supposed to be over a hundred tomorrow and there's nothing out here, no shade of any sort. Did you think of that?"

The two kept silent.

Mr. Reese paused and then kicked the ground. "I can't see you two getting a ride this late and who knows about tomorrow so I'll give you a ride as far as Ely and then you're out, okay?"

The two nodded.

"Get in the bed the way you were and I'll put the canvas back."

The bigger boy grabbed the leash and yanked the dog off the ground by its neck, choking it, until he pulled it into his arms.

The smaller boy got in the bed of the truck, took the dog, and then the bigger boy got in. They both lay flat and Mr. Reese re-hooked the canvas tarp and got on the road again.

In Ely he parked at the Silver State Restaurant and un-clasped the canvas cover. The smaller boy jumped down first and the bigger handed him their backpacks and the dog. Mr. Reese looked over his supplies, glanced inside the cooler, and when he was satisfied nothing had been taken, pulled the canvas back over the bed.

It was past midnight. The two boys stood looking around. The smaller of the two said in a stuttering voice, "Wha . . . Wha . . . What's the nearest town . . . af . . . afte . . . after here?"

"There's not much," Mr. Reese said and took off his glasses and cleaned them on his shirt. "You're pretty far away from any-thing. But if you're heading south I'd say Las Vegas. It's three or four hours away, depending."

"Is . . . Is . . . Is it hot in Las . . . Las Vegas, too?"

"This time of year it's hot over the entire area, and it will be for a while." Mr. Reese looked at the dog where it stood next to the bigger boy. There was goop in its eyes, it wasn't putting weight on its front right paw, and he could see its ribs even in the darkness.

He looked back to the boys. "Are you two hungry?"

They glanced at each other and nodded.

Mr. Reese pointed to the front door of the restaurant. "I'll buy you guys some chow if you want."

The older of the two tied the dog to a bike rack near the en-trance and they went inside. The restaurant was empty but for a fat, middle-aged waitress, who led them to a rectangular table in the middle of the room. The boys leaned their backpacks against the edge of the table and sat opposite Mr. Reese. Un-der the fluorescent lights they looked even worse. Their clothes were dirty and threadbare and their hair was cut crudely, long in places, short in others. Both had acne, some pimples red and bursting, others scabbed over. They smelled. The smaller of the two chewed his nails and sat hunched over as the waitress brought water and menus. They both ordered full turkey dinners and Cokes. Mr. Reese ordered a cheeseburger and a cup of coffee.

"So what are your names?" he asked after the waitress left.

"People call me Captain and he's Bob," the bigger of the two said.

"Why aren't you in school?"

They both shrugged their shoulders.

"What's your dog's name?"

"N . . . N . . ." Bob tried.

"Knife," said Captain.

"What's wrong with his paw?"

"He cut it on something."

"What about his eyes?"

They again both shrugged their shoulders, and the waitress came back with their drinks.

Bob looked at Mr. Reese. "He's . . . He's got worms. . . . Worms coming out of his ass."

"All he does is scratch all night," Captain said and drank off his soda.

Mr. Reese put sugar in his coffee. "Do you have any idea how bad you both smell? You can shower in truck stops. They have showers and laundry facilities at most of them."

The two boys looked at each other and smiled.

Mr. Reese took a drink of coffee. "Why are you going to Mexico?"

"Why do you care?" said Captain.

"I'm just curious more than anything," Mr. Reese said. "I'm just trying to understand. I figure I gave you a ride, didn't leave you stranded, didn't call the police, and I'm buying you dinner. The least you could do is answer a few questions."

"We . . . We . . . We know some people there. We can live on the beach," Bob said and again chewed his nails.

"But isn't Los Mochis nine or ten hours from the border?"

They shrugged.

"You don't know?"

Neither said anything.

"What kind of work can you get down there?"

"We ain't going down there to work," said Captain.

"How you gonna eat?"

"You don't have to work to eat," he scoffed and then got up from the table and walked to the bathroom. Bob kept his head down and drank sip after sip of soda until he had finished it.

"Where'd you get all those tattoos?" Mr. Reese asked.

"Lo . . . lots of diff . . . different places," he said. On his left hand was a black pistol and three crude *X*s around it. On his right were four *X*s and a red and black cardinal that seemed the only professional tattoo. On his wrist was a rudimentary cross and above it read "R.I.P. JO 9–23–15."

"Do you understand Spanish?"

Bob shook his head.

"How about your friend?"

He shrugged.

"They only speak Spanish in Mexico and they use different money down there."

"Different *money*?"

Mr. Reese nodded. "They use the peso. How old are you?"

"Six . . . Six . . . Sixteen."

The waitress came then, set the food down, and Bob began eating. She refilled his soda, and Captain came from the bathroom and sat back down.

"She already got you another one?" he asked.

Bob nodded and Captain took his glass, drank it in two swallows, and began eating.

Mr. Reese watched the boys as he ate. "I know you don't want to talk to an old man, but out of curiosity I have to ask, what sorta plan do you guys have for your future?"

They looked at him but didn't answer.

"Don't you want to have your own place to live in? Get a car, have your own money, a family someday?"

The boys looked at each other, again smiled, but said nothing. They just kept eating. Bob finished half his plate and pushed it away, so Captain took it, scraped the remains onto his own plate, and began eating them. The waitress came and refilled both of their drinks again.

"Are your families worried about you?"

Captain just shook his head.

"My . . . mom's worried," Bob said.

"But his mom's so fat she can't even get out of her bed. She's so big she's stuck in there. People have to come just to help her use the can."

Bob nodded timidly, and the waitress set down the bill. Captain asked for another refill on his soda and the waitress came back with a full glass and Mr. Reese paid her. When Captain finished the drink, they left. Mr. Reese followed the boys outside and watched as they put on their backpacks.

"I have a proposition," he said and took out his billfold. "I want to buy your dog off you for fifty bucks." He held the money out so they could see it. "He's in rough shape, you must have noticed that. He can't stand on his right paw and his eyes are infected. He's underweight and you said he has worms. And you won't be able to get him across the border. Most likely they won't let you. Even if you can it'll be harder for you to catch rides with a dog. My wife and I live on a ranch. He'll have a good life with me."

Captain looked at Mr. Reese. "How about you throw in the cooler, too?"

"I can't do that," he said. "No, fifty is what I have to spend. Fifty is the offer."

Captain didn't look at Bob or the dog. He only nodded. Mr. Reese gave him the money, and Captain unhooked the leash from around his belt and handed it to the old man. "How about you give us a ride to Las Vegas?"

"I can't do that either," Mr. Reese said. "I'm not going that way."

Captain shook his head and without saying anything the two of them began walking away.

14

Horace sat outside El Maida Shrine Auditorium. Even after a shower and a change of clothes, he was still sweating in the evening heat. His face was swollen, his nose was busted, and both his eyes were black. Ruiz said it wasn't a bad break, not bad enough for an emergency room visit, but still it was bleeding and it wouldn't stop.

El Paso seemed to Horace a never-ending sprawl as he looked out toward the lights of the city. He'd been so nervous as they drove in that he remembered nothing of getting there and nothing of the parts of the city he had seen.

Cheering rang out from inside the hall and cars came and left from the parking lot, and finally, after he'd waited a half hour, a cab appeared in the distance and he walked toward it waving his hands back and forth.

When he had gotten home from Salt Lake City, Horace had declared to Ruiz that he wanted to go pro. He told him he knew he needed work, but he was certain that if he started slow, started with a few easy fights, then it wouldn't take long before he'd be prepared to take on someone real. Ruiz was sitting on an orange plastic chair outside the back of the gym, in the alley, chewing Nicorette gum and looking at his phone while Horace spoke.

"I'm not sure about you going pro," he said as he continued to stare at his phone. "I don't think that's such a good idea, but I'll see what I can do," and with that the conversation ended.

It was nearly six weeks later when, after a session, Ruiz took Horace aside. "I'm afraid the only way I can get you a fight is gonna cost you money."

"Cost me money?"

Ruiz nodded. "I can get you a fight next week, a four-rounder against a kid from Mexico. His opponent just got popped for a bad green card and got deported. They called me today asking if I knew of anyone. Most likely I can get the fight but it'll cost you three hundred and fifty dollars."

"How much do I get if I win?"

"Nothing. It's just the way things work now. You do this to get in the door. You do this so the next time you get paid. It's modern boxing."

Horace shook his head. "So win or lose it's going to cost me three hundred and fifty dollars?"

Ruiz nodded. He looked tired and bloated and had stains on his shirt. He coughed. "I've told you time and time again to find someone else. I'm not a promoter. Look, I'll help pay expenses, gas and food and all that. But you'll have to pay the three fifty up front. It ain't much of a deal so it's your call."

Horace came back the next evening with the money. The gym was empty but for two middle-aged women in matching work-out tights standing next to each other, trying to hit the speed bags. He handed the cash to Ruiz and Ruiz put the money in his shorts pocket.

"So who's the guy I'm fighting?" he asked.

"Edgar Samaniego," Ruiz said. "He's seven and O, a street kid from Oaxaca. People say he's a good prospect. They say he's fast, has a good chin, and is a true warrior, but they say that about every kid out of Mexico. He's never fought over six rounds and he ain't fought anybody good yet."

"How many rounds is it again?"

"Four."

"You think I got a chance?"

"You are one hard-hitting son of a bitch. He'll definitely find out what El Paso is like."

"El Paso?"

"That's where the fight is."

"How are we going to get there?" Horace said, beginning to get worried.

"I'll drive you. I have to pick up a couch there. We can stay at my friend Russell's house."

"I've never been to Texas."

"Texas is just a line in the dirt. It's all the same anyway once you get hit."

Horace woke up at five a.m. every morning for the next five days. He did his run, sit-ups, and push-ups. He jumped rope and worked on his combinations in front of the mirror and then after work he did night sessions with Ruiz. But there wasn't enough time to train properly, and he'd been sliding. He'd been eating at McDonald's and KFC and there was a half-eaten quart of chocolate chip ice cream in the freezer. And worst of all he'd been drinking soda, he'd been drinking it every day, sometimes up to four Cokes between lunch and dinner.

The truth was he'd been lazy. He hadn't improved since he came back from Salt Lake City. He hadn't worked on his craft like he was supposed to, like he told Mr. Reese he was going to, and now he was going to pay the price.

When Saturday morning came he walked to Ruiz's house,

exhausted. He had been so worried he would be late that he couldn't sleep. He arrived an hour before he was supposed to and waited in the carport. At eight he knocked on the front door to find Ruiz missing. He hadn't come home the night before. It was two hours later that Ruiz finally drove up. His wife stood in the driveway yelling at him in Spanish.

"*¡Eres un borracho!*"

"Goddamn it," he cried. "I just got home."

"*¿No podrías incluso llamarme por teléfono?*"

"I tried," he mustered and went inside.

Horace sat on the couch watching Ruiz's sons play video games on the TV while Ruiz and his wife continued to argue. She screamed in Spanish and he yelled back in English. This went on, back and forth, until Ruiz stormed into the bathroom. He was in there for forty-five minutes. When he came out he went into his bedroom, put together a travel bag, and he and Horace left.

Ruiz's eyes were bloodshot and he gagged and spit and farted as he drove. He stopped first at an In-N-Out Burger and then pulled over two hours later at a Burger King. Both times he spent long periods on the toilet.

They arrived at El Maida Shrine Auditorium with less than two hours until Horace's fight. A group of old men in Shriners' caps played Ping-Pong in a side room, and in the back parking lot another group were loading go-carts onto a flatbed truck. The carts were red and had names on their doors: Fritz, Gary, Dotty, Lloyd, and Jerry. The main hall was small, with a capacity of five hundred people. Workers unfolded chairs and moved tables around the ring, and Horace watched until Ruiz led him to a small meeting room to change. In the corner he lay down on the floor, closed his eyes, and tried to visualize the fight. When he opened them a group of men were on the opposite end of the room. All the boxers were there, but only one was warming up. A Mexican. His hair was short, nearly shaved, and he wore green sweats and spoke in Spanish to a gray-haired man who held mitts. Horace figured it to be Edgar Samaniego.

Ruiz had disappeared, so Horace went outside behind the building and warmed up alone by the garbage cans. Then he grabbed the thin cardboard box from his travel bag. He opened it and took out the red trunks with the gold waistband and embroidery. He looked at Mrs. Poulet's stitching: "Hector" written in large red cursive letters on the front, the embroidered Thompson machine gun on each leg, and on the back "Hidalgo" in cursive with an embroidered Thompson machine gun on each side of the name. He put on the trunks and waited for Ruiz to wrap his hands.

The room was half full and no one clapped when Horace entered the ring. He was so nervous and excited he couldn't think. His eyes were everywhere and he couldn't stand still.

"Calm the fuck down and get over here, Hector," Ruiz yelled from the corner. He snapped his fingers in Horace's face. "Come on. You have to focus now. You have to keep your mind in the ring. Not outside of the ring. You have to concentrate on round one. And here's what I want you to do. Are you listening?"

"I'm listening," said Horace.

"I want you to throw combinations, but I want you to stay out of a brawl. I want you to get the lay of the land in this first round, stay careful, and then we'll see where we're at. Okay?"

Horace nodded, but he was too distracted. The spectators were talking and yelling and there was loud music playing on the PA. His mind was chaos. Edgar Samaniego came into the ring, and the referee, a tall, thin white man wearing blue latex gloves, brought them together. And when he did, it suddenly all stopped. The whole place grew quiet and the bell rang.

Samaniego came out stalking. He was even faster than Moffin, and he landed shot after shot for the first minute. Horace was hardly able to throw a punch. But Samaniego didn't have power and he didn't have the chin they said he had, because near the end of the first round Horace got him with a body shot that hurt him, and followed with a right hook that blew Samaniego's mouth guard out. Samaniego survived the round but he was shaken.

In the second, Samaniego pressured with a series of combinations and Horace froze against the ropes as he always did. He was pummeled. Punch after punch came unchecked and unstopped and his nose was smashed, his eyes began to swell, and his lips were cut. Samaniego landed everything he threw and seemed barely winded.

But in the madness of it Horace's mind somehow cleared. He found himself accepting the punishment without anxiety or fear. The freezing dissipated and he could finally think and take control of his body. He moved to the center of the ring and Samaniego followed and Horace got him with a left hook and the round ended.

In the third, Samaniego came out with a series of combinations, one of which caught Horace's right eye and blurred it completely. He could only make out streaks of light and darkness and the eye watered continuously. But he moved to the center of the ring and got off a single combination to Samaniego's body that had such power it dropped Samaniego to his knees and the kid from Oaxaca was done. He couldn't get up. There was a minute left in the third when the referee called the fight.

Hector Hidalgo, victory by KO.

Inside the Shriners' kitchen was a bathroom and Horace sat on the toilet, his nose broken and bleeding in a constant stream.

The skin around his eyes was swelling and turning black. He held a towel underneath his nose as Ruiz set it and then shoved gauze into the nostrils. He told Horace to keep his head back until the bleeding stopped and left to watch the next fight. Horace sat that way for twenty minutes and then showered. His entire face hurt, as did his side where Samaniego had hit him with a dozen clean shots. Even in such a short fight he'd taken a lot of punishment. He'd been hit by ten times as many shots as he'd landed. He stayed in the shower for what seemed like an hour. He dressed in the corner of the room, in near darkness, and then Ruiz and a tall Mexican man in a cowboy hat came in. They didn't see him. The man in the cowboy hat took an envelope from his coat pocket and handed it to Ruiz. Ruiz opened it, took the money from it, counted it, put it in his wallet, and they shook hands and left.

Horace couldn't believe what he had seen. He finished packing his gym bag, and went out to the auditorium to find Ruiz drinking in the bar, talking in Spanish to a broken-faced old man in a brown suit.

"You need some food money, Hector?" Ruiz drank from a rum and Coke.

Horace shook his head.

"You can have some of these onion rings if you want. Can you chew?"

"I can chew," said Horace.

Ruiz stood up, drunk, and put his arm around him. "You did good tonight. I told you that son of a bitch from Oaxaca would take a beating. How's your nose?"

"It's okay," he said.

Ruiz inspected it. "It looks like shit, but no worse than it did an hour ago. I think you'll be all right. Your first pro fight, first broken nose, first win. Quite an evening. We'll be leaving with this old man, Russell, after the last fight. You should have seen him back in the day. Fast as a cobra and mean as a badger. He'll put us up in his trailer."

Horace nodded.

Ruiz finished his drink and smiled. "Why do you look so goddamn sad? You just beat a kid who's had seven pro fights, a kid people were saying might be something. You're an undefeated professional boxer."

"I guess my head and my nose just hurt," Horace said, but he couldn't even look at Ruiz.

"That Oaxaca son of a bitch got in more than a few. You're the type of fighter who's going to take a lot of punishment. Russell and I were just talking about it. But people love a brawler. They love a brawler, don't they, Russell?"

The old man nodded vaguely.

Horace looked around the room and without thinking it through said, "I just want to let you know I'm going to catch my own ride home."

"Your own ride home?" Ruiz said.

"I have some friends here. Is that okay?"

"Do what you need to do." Ruiz pulled out his wallet. He took two hundred dollars from it. "This money is for your expenses. I won't be leaving until tomorrow midday, that's when I have to pick up that couch from my sister-in-law. Call me if you change your mind. And cheer up, you did good tonight."

Horace nodded and put the money in his pocket, and walked to the opposite side of the auditorium and watched the next fight. He tried to push the image of Ruiz taking money from the Mexican man out of his mind, but he couldn't. Maybe he was mistaken about what he had seen but he didn't think so. Ruiz had received money for his fight, because there was no way Ruiz would give two hundred dollars away so easily. Ruiz had lied to him. Ruiz had gotten money for the fight and swindled him. The main event started and Horace watched it from the edge of the room but grew more depressed the longer he was there and left.

When the cab dropped him off at the downtown El Paso Greyhound station, the doors were locked and the lights were off. What was he going to do now? And why had he told Ruiz he was getting his own ride home? Why couldn't he for once just use his head? Even if Ruiz did take his money, he could at least have gotten a free ride and a free place to stay, couldn't he? Now he had nothing.

He walked down the sidewalk. He came to a karaoke bar and could hear people inside singing. He walked three more blocks and in the distance saw an open Church's Chicken. In the bathroom he checked his nose for bleeding, and put a handful of toilet paper in his pocket. He ordered an extra-large Coke, two chicken and cheese sandwiches, an order of mac and cheese, an order of mashed potatoes and gravy, an order of fries, and two apple pies. He sat at a table and slowly ate the mac and cheese, the fries, and one of the sandwiches. He nursed the Coke until a middle-aged woman in a Church's uniform told him and the two other men on the opposite side of the restaurant that they were closing.

He walked for an hour more—block after block of closed stores—and ate one of the apple pies. He went past a clothing store named Los Dos Hermanos and another called Sexy Jeans. He passed a shoe store, a furniture shop, and an abandoned building. Under the awning of a Dollar Tree store he saw a man sitting on a sleeping bag. Next to him slept a fat woman. The woman wore a dirty white blouse and red sweats that had been cut off at the knees. She had a walking cast on her right foot. The man drank from a quart of beer and was propped up against the building wall.

"Where you going in such a hurry?" the man asked. He was Indian and heavy, with short black hair. He wore blue sweat-pants and a Dallas Cowboys T-shirt and had a red bandanna wrapped around his neck. He had no teeth.

"I'm waiting for the bus station to open," said Horace.

"It's closed until six," the man said. "What time you got now?"

Horace looked at his phone. "It's one o'clock."

"You got a long five hours, man. . . . You ain't Mexican, are you?"

"No," said Horace.

"Where you from?"

"Nevada."

"What are you, a fuckin' Paiute?" the man said and laughed.

Horace nodded.

"Why do you dress like a spick?"

"How am I supposed to dress?"

"That's a good question. You're pretty smart for a Paiute."

"What are you?"

"What does it matter to you, you a cop?"

"I ain't a cop," Horace said.

"I'm just joking around with you, bro. I'm a Paiute, too. We're brothers. What did you do, get into a fight?"

"I'm a boxer. I had a fight tonight at the Shriners'."

"At the Shriners'? The guys with the little hats?"

Horace nodded.

The man laughed. "Did you win?"

Horace nodded.

"You want a drink to celebrate?"

"No," said Horace. "I don't drink."

"Good. You being a Paiute you'd probably drink the whole bottle and then spit in the bottom." The man laughed and then sighed and took a drink from the quart. "Indians have always been the best fighters. Always. You know about Henry Armstrong? That son of a bitch was a fighter."

"But he wasn't Paiute."

"How the fuck do you know?" the man said, his voice suddenly booming. "Were you in there watching his mother get it on night after night? Everybody knows the only good Indian in the sack is a Paiute. Didn't they teach you anything in school?"

Horace laughed and the laughing sent shocks of pain through his face and nose and he let out a soft cry.

"It hurt bad?"

"A little," said Horace.

"What about Ernie Lopez?"

"Who?"

"You don't know Ernie Lopez?"

Horace shook his head. "I've heard of Danny Lopez."

"Ernie was his brother. They called him Indian Red. They say he was a Ute but there had to have been a Paiute that jumped over the fence one night when the husband was off licking cow balls like all Utes do. No, he was Paiute all right. I know things. I can tell who is and who isn't in the first thirty seconds I meet them. And I saw him fight four times and he fought like a Paiute."

"He was a good fighter?"

"They say if it wasn't for Nápoles he would have been a world champion. That's how good he was. His brother, Danny 'Little Red' Lopez, was a world champion. But I liked Indian Red better. He was a Paiute with red hair and freckles. A gringo Indian. An Indian that needed sunblock." He laughed and took another drink from the bottle.

"But the Mexican guy beat him?"

"No, Nápoles was Cuban. You probably don't even know where Cuba is!"

"It's an island down by Florida," said Horace. "So what happened to Lopez?"

"He fought Nápoles twice and lost both times and then he went crazy. I think he fought three more times but lost them all." The fat woman next to him began talking in her sleep. The man put his hand on her leg and rubbed it.

"Why did he go crazy?"

"Who?"

"Ernie Lopez," Horace said.

"I don't know. Maybe Indian Red got his brain rattled. Punch-drunk maybe. Boxers always go nuts, or usually anyway. Maybe he just couldn't handle losing. Most people can't. But whatever happened, Lopez couldn't make it after the second loss to Nápoles and then his wife split and shit went south. But that's always the way it is. When you're going down people jump ship. Most don't even say goodbye."

"So what happened to him after that?"

"Who?"

"Ernie Lopez."

"He became a drifter. He gave up on everything and became a bum. Rode the rails, all that sorta shit. What's your name anyway?"

"Horace, Horace Hopper."

The man laughed for a long time. "That's one hell of a Paiute name. What kind of name is Horace?"

"I don't know. My mom's grandfather was named Horace."

"What was he, some sort of sea captain?"

"I don't know what he was."

The man looked over to the sleeping woman. She had rolled on her side. A tattoo of a snake holding a red flower in its mouth ran up her calf. Her large right breast fell out of her blouse, and the man took it in his hand and pushed it back inside the shirt and covered her with a blanket. Next to her was a green leather purse. He took a pack of cigarettes and a lighter from it.

"Is that your wife?"

The man shook his head and lit the cigarette. "Shit no, I've been married enough." He blew the smoke out and smiled. "But I've been with her seven, maybe eight, years. I think in most states you'd say we were married. But I'm not divorced from my last wife so maybe not. In some states I guess you'd say I'm a polygamist, but in most states I think you could just say I'm fucked." He again laughed.

"How many times you been married?"

"Twice."

"What's your name?"

"Billy Malachowski."

Horace laughed.

"What are you laughing at?"

"That ain't much of a Paiute name either."

"My grandfather was Polish. I forgot about that." Billy grinned. "My father was Irish and Mexican and Polish but my mother was a Paiute. A hundred percent if there is such a thing. What do you have in the bag?"

"Church's Chicken," Horace said. "You can have some if you want."

"Sit down."

Horace sat across from him. Two hard-shell suitcases were next to them and a pair of new basketball shoes sat beside Billy's arm. Horace took a chicken sandwich from the sack and handed it to Billy, who opened it, looked at it, and set it next to the woman. "I can't eat that 'cause I don't have teeth. What else you have?"

"An apple pie."

"I'll take that." He set the lit cigarette on the concrete next to him and took the pie.

"You always lived in El Paso?"

Billy shook his head. "Hell no, I'm from Los Angeles. I had a good job there for a long time. I had a company car and an expense account. I lived in Oxnard in a three-bedroom house that if my ex-wife still has is probably worth a half million dollars. You ever been to Oxnard?"

"No," Horace said.

Billy finished the apple pie and put the cigarette back in his mouth. "It's not a bad place. I was a rep for an auto parts company. I hit twenty stores a day. Just driving and talking. I had five guys working under me. Fourteen years I put in there. I got paid good but we could all sense the company was going down. Our days were numbered. At the same time, I could tell my wife was getting tired of me. I'm not sure why she was, but she was. I never cheated on her, never went out. I only drank three beers a night. Never more, never less. But I knew in my guts she didn't love me anymore. The woman and the job both went south at the same time. So one day after work I didn't go home. I drove the company car all the way to the main headquarters in Miami. You know where Miami is?"

"In Florida," said Horace.

He nodded. "Florida, the opposite end of the country. The car had twenty thousand miles on it when I started. When I got to Miami it had almost thirty. I had it washed, detailed, and left it in the parking lot of the main headquarters office. I put the keys under the mat, called my boss in L.A., told him where it was, and that was it."

"What about your wife?"

"I called her a few times but I never went back."

"You really never went back?"

Billy nodded and took a drink.

"What did you do?"

"A lot of shit but nothing. I worked as a bartender at a sports bar in Vero Beach for a few years. Worked day labor when I had to. Was a cabdriver."

"But you don't work anymore?"

The woman again talked in her sleep. He nudged her and she opened her eyes. "I'm hungry, Poppa," she said.

He handed her the chicken sandwich. She stayed on her side and began eating it. A car stopped across the street and two men got out and began yelling at someone farther down the block, and then ran after him. In the quiet, Billy lit another cigarette. When the woman had eaten half of the sandwich, she put it down and closed her eyes.

"You ever see your wife again?"

"Sure. Seen my kids, too."

"How many kids you have?"

"Three." He looked in a yellow plastic sack near his feet and took another quart of beer from it. He took an opener from around his neck and opened the bottle.

"Was your wife mad at you?"

He nodded. "Sure, for a while. But she remarried. My kids hate me. My two daughters are more worried than mad but my son hates my guts. He thinks I'm a bum. And he's right, I am. At least I have one smart kid." He laughed. "Mona," he said. "Mona." The woman opened her eyes and looked at him.

"What, Poppa?"

"We're sitting with a Paiute boxing champion."

"Okay, Poppa," she whispered and closed her eyes again. Billy looked at her for a moment, glanced out across the street, and then looked at Horace.

"What else you got in there to eat?"

"Mashed potatoes and gravy. You can have that if you want."

"Real food," Billy said and smiled.

Horace took the container from the sack, gave him a plastic spoon, and Billy started on it.

"How did you get a second wife?"

Billy finished the mashed potatoes and took a long drink of beer. "I was working in a warehouse. This big-ass Lakota worked in the office at the same place. She found out I was Paiute, and she was all over me after that. She was an Indian freak, everything had to be about being Indian. We always had to go to powwows. Every fucking weekend it was something. She had a roommate but kicked the roommate out. She was a big woman, but I like big women. She had a temper. I don't mind tempers as long as there's no hitting or knives. No forks either." He laughed. "I was in Cleveland with her for five years, married. When she wasn't mad or moody she had a good sense of humor. But she was a drunk, a bad one, too, and finally, because of it, she found Jesus. She got sober and after that we didn't last long, maybe a year. She was no fun then. Without booze she had no sense of humor. Just a big fucking tree up her ass. So I moved to Colorado and got a job as a bartender in Durango and goddamn it if my wages didn't start getting garnished 'cause my Christian wife defaulted on a car loan and on some credit cards that she put in both our names. I moved to Denver and mowed lawns under the table for this white guy named Sid. I stayed for a couple years. I ran a truck and a crew of three guys. One guy who showed up for a while, Rob, had been in and out of prison. He used to huff gas and thought that Mexicans had different intestinal organs than white people." He stopped, laughed, and took a drink. "I went to a family barbecue of his and met his sister who'd just gotten out of rehab. That sister is Mona and she's the one sleeping right here. We lived in Denver until her mom got sick and then we moved down here to El Paso and took care of her. Then her mom died and it turned out there was a bunch of tax liens on her house and she owed a bunch of people a bunch of shit. So we put all her things in a storage locker, moved out of the house, and took her 1978 Chrysler Cordoba and drove to

Houston, where Mona knew a bar owner, and I bartended there. But the place went under. We came back to El Paso to get the things out of storage and then Mona broke her ankle coming off a sidewalk. We were laid out flat then. She had to have surgery. I couldn't work a straight job either 'cause my teeth got all fucked up and my face swelled. I looked worse than you. It was hard to just walk down the street without people staring. We ran through the money we had, I got my teeth pulled, and she had to have a second surgery on her ankle. Then the Cordoba's radiator blew. Not a big deal but I left it on the street and didn't deal with it 'cause I got an infection in my mouth and was bedridden. When I finally went outside, the car was gone. They'd towed it and we couldn't get it back 'cause they wanted a grand and the car wasn't even ours. The title was in her grandmother's name."

"So what are you gonna do now?"

"My sister runs an Applebee's in Omaha. But she's in AA and won't have drinking in her house. Once I get my new teeth, which is in two days, I'll hit her up for bus fare and we'll move out there. She can get me on washing dishes and then I'll move up until I'm bartending. I'm a good bartender. I've been successful wherever I've worked." He took another drink and Mona started talking in her sleep again and Billy rubbed her arm until she fell quiet. "When's your next fight?"

"I don't know."

"What's your name again?"

"Horace Hopper."

Billy broke out laughing again. "That's a hell of a Paiute name. I'll keep my eyes out for you." He finished the beer. "I'm going to have to crash out now. Good meeting you and thanks for the grub."

Horace stood back up. He took a hundred dollars from his wallet and handed it to the man.

"That's a lot of money," said Billy. "You should keep it."

"I don't need it," said Horace.

"From one Paiute to another," Billy said and laughed. He put the money in his sweatpants pocket, moved next to the woman, and lay down.

15

Mr. Reese's phone rang as he drove into Tonopah. It was his third trip to town in five days, all because of the tractor. Each time he left NAPA Auto Parts he was certain he had everything he needed, but always he drove back to the ranch to either break another part or find one thing he had forgotten to put on his list.

It was late afternoon and over a hundred degrees and the old truck had no air-conditioning and there were no clouds nor any breeze. He pulled the truck to the side of the road and shut off the engine next to a boarded-up, long-forgotten store. The phone continued to ring. He took off his cowboy hat, set it in the seat next to him, and wiped his forehead with a red handkerchief he kept in his back pocket. He cleared his throat and answered.

"Is that you, Cassie?"

"I was hoping I'd catch you, Pop. I got lucky."

"I think I'm the lucky one," he said. "I want you to know a day doesn't go by where I'm not thinking about you."

"You always say that," she said and laughed.

"That's because it's true," he said and looked out the driver's side window. A large motor home pulling a car passed going the opposite direction. The license plate said Louisiana. The man driving had a small dog on his lap, and the dog had its paws on the steering wheel. Mr. Reese could just make out a woman in the passenger side seat wearing sunglasses, her bare feet on the dash. "I think I know why you're calling. I appreciate it and, in her own way, Mom appreciates it, too."

"Both Lynnie and I are worried about her again."

The old man again wiped his face with the handkerchief. "I'm sorry you are. I know you've both had hard talks with her on the phone lately."

"I hate putting you in a spot, Pop, but we both think she's getting worse."

"That might be the case from where you're sitting, but in my estimation she's about the same." He paused and took a deep breath. "What I've come to realize is that your mother's moods are built more or less on a cycle. I have a notepad in the shop and I keep track of the good times and low times. We're just in a low spot right now, that's all."

"I didn't know you kept a record of it," she said.

"I guess more than anything it's an attempt to make sense of it. I do know that in the last thirty years she's been in the same sorta state ten or twelve times during the month of September. I think my first September entry is 1981."

"I'm sorry, Pop."

"Don't be sorry," he said. "That's just a part of who she is. It's harder on her than us."

"Is she leaving the house at all?"

"She feeds the dogs, the donkeys, and the chickens, and of course looks out after the barn cats. But what you mean is, does she go into town? Does she see people?"

"That's what I mean."

"I took her to a doctor's appointment a month ago and we did the shopping together and ate lunch at the park."

"Really?"

"More or less," he said. "I'll let you know if you should worry, but right now I don't think it's time to worry."

"All right," she said and paused. "And your back?"

"My back's fine. Almost better."

"All of a sudden?"

"No, it's been a process, but it's okay now."

"I can't help worrying."

"I know."

"I love you, Pop, but I have to say this: Mom just seems different this time. . . . Even on the phone. I can feel it."

"That's probably true. Your mom is about where she was when you left and again when Lynn left. But she pulled out of it each time and look what happened. We visited you in college. We visited Lynn in college. We visited the babies. She's just going through a gully right now. I think a lot of it has to do with Horace leaving."

"How is he doing?"

"To be honest, I'm just not sure."

"I woke up the other night thinking about my old boyfriend, Roy Gifford."

The old man laughed. "I've thought about him over the years, too."

"I'm sorry I didn't want to marry him, Pop."

"You weren't cut out for ranch life," he said.

"Maybe. . . . You know I want more than anything for the ranch to stay alive."

"I know you do."

"You really think Horace will come back?"

"I'm certain of it."

"I hope so," she said.

"He's a good boy."

"I'm so glad you found him, Pop."

Again Mr. Reese laughed. "I'm glad he found us. He helped us keep things going when we were getting tired of keeping going. And he's taught me a lot of things. Taught your mom things, too. He can get you inspired, that's for sure. You should have heard him talking to your mom about being her own champion, about building her own boat, and being the best she could be. He's read a few self-help books, that's for sure."

Cassie sighed. "I guess I just woke up this morning feeling guilty."

"You shouldn't feel guilty. I knew by the time you were eleven you would move on."

"You did?"

"Yep."

"How did you know?"

"You were bright and curious, and most of all because you had maps of the world taped to the walls of your room. That's a pretty big hint that you might not want to spend your life on a small-time ranch in the middle of Nevada. And remember your sister was the same way, too. You both had bigger plans, and I'm just glad that you did what you wanted to do."

"And you think Horace really will take over?"

"That's my plan. He's young, but ranching is in his blood. I can feel it. He's a natural for it."

"I hope you're right, Pop."

"Me, too. Anyway, how's Scott?"

"He's fine," she said.

"And the boys?"

"Everyone's good."

"And work?"

"It's the same old thing here. I guess I just woke up worried today."

The old man looked at the closed-down store. The plywood

that covered the windows had been tagged with spray paint, and part of the awning was hanging low and broken. On the side of the building were dozens of pallets, and an old table leaned against the wall. "I can hear it in your voice," he said. "Look, you guys want to change some things. I appreciate that. You want us to move in with you. I hear that. But Mom's not there yet. I don't know what else to say about it. The good news is the ranch is in fine shape, my back is better, and if I give Horace a year or two to sow his oats I'm certain he'll come back. So don't worry too much about us."

"Okay," she said and let out a long breath. "You're a better liar than Mom at least."

He laughed.

"Please come visit."

"One of these days I'll just get her in the truck, kidnap her, and we'll head your way like we just robbed a bank."

16

Horace drank from a gallon jug of water and stared at the sidewalk. He was upset with himself over his worsening discipline with food. For the last six nights he'd finished his workouts by running to Lucky Wishbone, where he ordered the Pop five-piece chicken dinner with garlic toast, fries, and a side order of coleslaw. It was too much food and it wasn't good for him, but even so each time he ate the entire meal and refilled his fountain drink at least once with Coke. The two girls behind the counter flirted with him, and no other women in Tucson ever flirted with him. He had even asked one of them out on a date, a skinny, long-haired Mexican girl named Mariana. She told him she had a boyfriend, but after that she only charged him for the three-piece, not the five-piece dinner, and never again made him pay for his drink or side dish.

As he walked home the same questions came into his head over and over as they did every night. Why couldn't his favorite food be something good for him, or at least be Mexican food? And why did Mexican food have to be spicy? And why did it have to be so hot in Tucson? And why was Spanish so hard to learn? And were the Reeses okay? Was Mr. Reese really going out to check on the sheep alone? Why didn't he use a four-wheeler like everyone else? And why did he insist on riding Slow Poke? The horse was old and cataracts had blurred his vision. And why couldn't the Golden Gloves matches have been four rounds? He would have won if they had been four rounds, wouldn't he? And why, even after six weeks, was his nose still bleeding all the time?

He went through the chain-link gate and walked alongside the carport until he came to his old-lady guesthouse. He unlocked the door and went inside to be engulfed in heat. He turned on the AC unit and sat at the kitchen table and became more depressed. He never liked coming back to that house. It only reminded him of his mother and her family and it always smelled of old-lady air freshener. He changed into shorts and a T-shirt, grabbed his CD player, and left. He walked for miles and, in a moment of weakness, went to Zia Records and rebought Slayer's *Reign in Blood* on CD. He was ashamed for buying it, but he couldn't help himself, and he listened to it over and over as he walked around the city. It was past midnight when he grew tired enough to go back to his house. He slept under the AC unit until five, and then he got up, put on his running clothes, and did his morning workout.

That afternoon while he changed tires on a white Yukon with tinted windows and custom Tuff rims he got a call from Ruiz about a fight in Monterrey, Mexico. The bout was in four days and was a preliminary six-rounder.

"Why so sudden?" Horace asked as he sat on the shop floor.

Ruiz was short of breath as he spoke. "One of the fighters got in a motorcycle wreck and broke his collarbone. The guy you'd be against is using this fight as a warm-up for a bigger fight in November. He just needs the rounds. The problem is I have to know right now if you can do it or they'll give it to someone else."

"I have to decide now?"

"Yeah."

"Who will I be fighting?"

"The kid's named César 'El Clavo' Jiménez."

"Is he any good?"

"I don't know anything about him except he's twelve and O."

"What's 'El Clavo' mean?"

"The nail."

"How much will I make?"

"I'll have to do some negotiating, but I can probably get you three hundred. Did you get your passport like I told you?"

"Yeah."

"Good," said Ruiz. "Look, I have to go. You want me to take it?"

"I'm not sure," said Horace, suddenly nervous. "What do you think I should do?"

"It's risky. We don't know who this guy is and he's twelve and O. He's a local kid, too. From the area. None of that is good 'cause you're green. But it's a fight and fights are hard to come by."

"How will I get down there?"

"We'll worry about the specifics later. But one thing to know is you'll need a day to get there and a day after to get home. Three days off work at the minimum. This isn't a great opportunity, it's just the only thing that's come my way. What do you think?"

"I'm not sure," said Horace.

"Want me to tell them you won't take it?"

"No. . . . Well, maybe I should do it."

"You're sure?"

"I guess so," he said and hung up.

Horace wasn't in the best shape but then he wasn't in bad shape either. He'd been training four nights a week with Ruiz, and for the last three weeks he'd been running every morning. He was getting better, even under pressure he was. The time had come to take the chance.

His grandmother used to collect self-help books. She'd go into long spells of melancholy and visit Whitney's Bookshelf on Main Street and go through their self-improvement section and leave with a half dozen books. It's how Horace found *The B.O.A.T.—Building the Champion Inside of You: Believe, Overcome, Aspire, Triumph.* It was in a stack next to the TV, and every day they watched TV. It was a book he read over and over and the only book he brought with him to Tucson. In the third chapter it said a champion had to be careful and precise, but there were also times when a champion had to take a chance to get to the next level.

Test your boat, test yourself. Let the bricks (built with honesty, integrity, hard work, and service) protect you. Let them surround you during the ongoing war of life and lead you to the next horizon. Let them get your ship through the storm to success.

He found his boss watching TV in his office and asked if he could have the days off. Benny took a can of beer from the fridge and got on the phone with his nephew, who said he would cover the shifts. It was set. Horace worked that evening until seven and then changed into his running clothes and took off down the road. He went past his normal five miles and kept running until his legs were shaking and he had trouble standing.

After work the next day Horace went to the library and looked on YouTube for fights with César "El Clavo" Jiménez but couldn't find any. He trained that night with Ruiz, worked the next day until five, and then with a small travel bag and his passport walked to the bus station and took the night bus to San Antonio, Texas.

It was morning when he arrived. He'd slept nearly five hours in the half-empty bus and felt rested. He washed his face in the bus station bathroom and called a number on the piece of paper

Ruiz had given him. An hour later a thin Mexican man with greased-back black hair came into the station dressed in shiny red sweats and black tennis shoes. Horace saw the color of the sweats, got up from his seat, and walked toward him.

"Are you Diego?"

"That's me," the man said.

"I'm Hector," said Horace and put out his hand.

The man shook it and smiled. "You hungry?"

Horace nodded.

"Can you make weight if you eat?"

"I can make it."

"Was the bus ride all right?"

"It was okay."

"We don't have much time. We'll stop at Cracker Barrel, is that okay?"

"I don't know what that is."

"It's a restaurant," Diego said and they began walking. "They have everything, you'll like it. After that we'll drive nonstop. It'll be five hours, more or less. If we get lucky you should get a few hours to rest before the fight."

Diego led him out of the station into the morning heat. Horace's shirt grew wet with sweat as they passed through the deserted parking lot and got into a twenty-year-old red Toyota Corolla.

"Why is it so hot and wet here?"

"It's the humidity."

"The humidity?"

"You know what humidity is, right?"

Horace nodded, but he wasn't sure he knew. He'd never felt anything like it, he knew that. It was as if they were walking around in a hot bathtub. He buckled his seat belt, and Diego started the car.

"Ruiz told me you train a boxer who's fighting tonight."

Diego nodded.

"Where is he?"

"He went down yesterday. If I can help it I don't like my guys sitting in a car the day of a fight. Ruiz should have had you come earlier."

"He didn't say anything about that."

"He probably just wanted to use the free ride with me."

"So it's okay that it's free?"

Diego smiled. "Don't worry, I'm not a tightwad like Ruiz. How did you meet that guy anyway?"

"I moved from a ranch in Nevada. He was the only trainer in Tucson I could find when I looked online."

"So you're a ranch kid?"

"Yeah."

"Like cows and horses?"

"Sheep."

Diego laughed. "How did you get into boxing?"

Horace shrugged his shoulders.

"You from a boxing family?"

"Not really. I guess I've always just liked it," answered Horace.

Diego nodded. "Me, too. My dad always liked it, but man I loved it." He turned on the radio and they left.

Horace leaned against the passenger side door, closed his eyes, and couldn't help but think of Arnaldo. He had met the man through his grandmother when he was thirteen. Arnaldo was small and wiry with thick, dyed black hair and he was a bartender at the Banc Club casino. He told Horace he was raised in Italy but he had no accent of any kind. He also said he had fought in sixty professional fights as a flyweight but Horace could never find any of his bouts on the Internet, no listings for him at all. But his face and nose were those of a battered boxer. He looked like he'd been hit a thousand times and run over after that.

Horace remembered the afternoon he came home from school, beat up and barely able to walk. He'd been cornered by a football player from the high school, a huge white kid named Lester. The kid gave Horace a black eye and broke one of his fingers. He also cracked his ribs, or at least it felt that way as it hurt just to breathe. His grandmother wanted to call the police but Horace begged her not to. So she had Arnaldo come over and teach him how to box. They had been working together for three months when it happened again.

Behind Barsanti Park, Horace was jumped. Lester had nearly killed him that time. He was six feet tall and over two hundred pounds. Horace had fought back. He broke Lester's nose and gave him a busted lip. He had power in his punches, even back then he did. But Lester began throwing wild swings, and under the volume of them Horace fell apart. He wasn't sure why he froze but he did. Lester threw him to the ground, got on top of him, and began pounding Horace's head into the dry park grass.

"Fucking faggot hippie powwow Indian motherfucker," he remembered Lester saying. There were four of them standing around and then one of them pulled Lester off Horace. "You better watch out," the kid had said. "You're going to kill him pretty soon."

Horace missed three days of school from the beating, but he didn't mind the pain. He wasn't bothered by getting hit either. It wasn't that he liked it exactly, he just didn't mind it. He remembered as he lay on the grass and dirt, bloody and in pain, all he thought about was the fight. His combinations were solid, his jab was improving, and he had power. Lester weighed nearly a hundred pounds more than he did, and even so he'd held his own for a little while. The front of Lester's shirt was covered in blood, and Horace knew Lester's nose would swell and that some of his body shots had connected. He'd hurt the white son of a bitch.

Horace opened his eyes and turned to Diego. "How I really started fighting was because there was a white guy, a lineman for the football team in my town. He had it out for me 'cause I had long hair at the time and I'm Mexican. He was huge, maybe six-three. But I had been training with this old guy, Arnaldo. The football player was tough but he was slow. I'm not the fastest but I'm pretty fast. Faster than a white guy anyway. So I just picked him off punch by punch until his friends made me stop. After that Arnaldo got me a small and big bag and we set them up in his garage and started taking things seriously. We used to watch old fights on the Internet together and he'd give me advice. He cooked for me, helped me with my homework. I spent almost every night there. I guess you could say he was like my father and my coach wrapped into one."

"He still around?" asked Diego.

"No, he died when I was in high school. He got lung cancer. I was with him, though, at his bedside until he quit breathing. Even at the end he was giving me advice, helping me."

"I'm sorry to hear he passed," Diego said. He grabbed a container of Tic Tacs from the dashboard, put a few in his mouth, and handed the box to Horace.

He took three and again leaned against the window glass and closed his eyes. The truth was Arnaldo had a vicious temper. He was mean to Horace and mean to his grandmother. He was a drunk who threw things, whose moods were always erratic. It was just after Christmas break when Horace went to Arnaldo's house for a training session to find Arnaldo gone for good. His grandmother said he had been deported back to Italy, but the people at the Banc Club said he ran off, that he'd been stealing out of the till, embezzling somehow. His car and clothes had vanished, but everything else was still there. No one changed the locks or turned off the power or moved into Arnaldo's house for nearly six months. So Horace continued going to his garage to work out. He hadn't liked training with Arnaldo anyway, as all the man did was yell at him to hit harder. "Hit harder, Horace. Goddamn, hit harder, hit the fucking bag harder." And worse than that Arnaldo forgot most of their training sessions and when he did show up he was usually drunk and just wanted to watch TV.

At Cracker Barrel they ate breakfast and then they got back in the car and passed into Mexico at Nuevo Laredo. They stopped only once, at the halfway mark to Monterrey. It was a small roadside convenience store with nothing around it. Horace got out of the car but was too nervous to ask the clerk if she spoke English, and Diego had to buy him a bottle of water and point to where the bathrooms were.

It was late afternoon when the outskirts of Monterrey appeared, and soon they were trapped in bumper-to-bumper traffic. Horace looked out at the sprawl: houses, apartment buildings, construction sites, and gigantic industrial complexes. It was the biggest city he had ever seen, and Diego said there were more than four million people in the area. An hour passed in gridlock and then Diego turned off the main highway. He drove side streets for a half hour and then parked in front of a blue building with a metal awning. Above it, in art deco red neon, it said COLISEO.

Men were breaking up the sidewalk with a jackhammer across the street and a group of women passed directly in front of them as they got out of the car. The signs were in Spanish and all the people they passed spoke Spanish and Horace realized, for the first time, that he really was in a different country and he'd never been in another country.

They walked under an overpass and went by a dozen shops until they came to Hotel Victoria, a weathered and run-down two-story hotel. Inside Diego spoke Spanish to a clerk and received a key. He took Horace upstairs and opened the door. Inside was a twin bed, a desk, a dresser, a small bathroom, and a TV. "This is your room," said Diego. "The promoter is paying for it. In the future you should tell Ruiz that you want to stay in a nicer place."

"Are you staying here?"

"No way," Diego said and laughed. "We're staying at the Hilton." He looked at his phone. "You can stay here and rest for an hour or you can come with me now and check out the arena."

"I'll go with you," Horace said.

Diego handed him the room key and they walked back to the Arena Coliseo. It was four in the afternoon and the place was deserted. They saw a red ring in the middle of the main room. Tecate beer banners hung from the base and the ring was surrounded by blue chairs and farther back bleacher seats rose up on all sides.

"Will the place be full?" asked Horace.

"I'm not sure of the numbers," said Diego. "But it'll be mostly full, I'd imagine. The main event, Moreno versus Rivera, should be a decent draw. I'll show you your dressing room and I'll look after you during the fight. I owe Ruiz a favor so I'll be in your corner. Do you know anything about the guy you're fighting?"

"No," said Horace.

"Nothing?"

Horace shook his head. "Do you?"

"Supposedly he hits like a sledgehammer," Diego said and smiled. "I guess that's why they call him 'The Nail.' But you never know what to believe. . . . Anyway, after you're done, I'm afraid you're on your own. I'll have my hands full."

"Don't worry. Ruiz already told me."

"Did he give you the bus times to Nuevo Laredo?"

Horace nodded.

"From there they have a few buses a day to get you to San Antonio, and after that you have the return to Tucson."

"I have the schedule in my bag."

"Good," Diego said. "Then I'll see you later."

It was past midnight and the streets alongside the Coliseo were crowded with traffic, and music poured out of cars and from clubs on the main avenue. Horace made his way down the sidewalk, past streams of people, and walked slowly back to the Hotel Victoria. He unlocked his room door and struggled to lie down on the bed. He thought maybe his ribs were fractured, but Diego said he didn't think so, although he also said there wasn't much they could do if they were. His nose was again broken and his right eye was swollen shut. There was a cut above his right eyebrow that had been taped, and again no matter what he did, his nose kept bleeding. Diego said some fighters broke their noses and some didn't. "You have a great chin and a weak nose," he had told him. "That's called luck."

When the bout started Jiménez had come straight at him, and he hit harder than anyone Horace had ever fought. The first round came and went in a haze and he was hammered by dozens of brutal punches. He landed nothing himself. In his corner Diego yelled at him to move, yelled at him to throw punches, yelled at him to protect himself, but Horace couldn't focus on anything. It all washed over him. Everything was a blur.

The second round started and finally Horace began to settle down. He took three hard shots to the face but landed a solid combination. Jiménez countered and pushed Horace into the ropes and let loose a severe series of shots to the body and Horace's ribs were injured. But then Jiménez backed off and Horace countered with two good shots, the round went on, and what he realized toward the end of the second was that Jiménez was already beginning to tire. The bell rang, the round ended, and Horace was barely winded.

As he sat down on his stool Diego gave him water and told him to work the body. He said it over and over until Horace finally listened. The third round came and he did what Diego asked. He concentrated on Jiménez's body and with twenty seconds left in the round he dropped Jiménez to his knees with a shot to the kidneys. The crowd booed and cried out. The Coliseo was now three-quarters full with more and more people entering. They screamed for Jiménez and he got off his knees wobbly and unfocused and hung on until the end of the round. In the fourth Jiménez came back. He put Horace against the ropes and broke his nose, cut him above his right eye, and the eye blurred completely. Horace took nothing but punishment the entire round, but he wasn't tired and he didn't feel hurt. When the bell rang, he sat down on the stool, and Diego yelled over and over, "Defense, Hector, defense." The bell rang again and the fifth started. Jiménez came out pressuring and again put Horace against the ropes. He threw punches at will until he became visibly tired. He then backed up, and when he did Horace hit him with a body shot that staggered him. He followed with a combination to the head with such force that it dropped Jiménez instantly. The Mexican was laid out flat on his stomach. He didn't move for twenty seconds and then finally, with the help of his trainer and a doctor, he sat up.

Diego hugged Horace and talked loudly as he helped get him out of the ring and back to the dressing room. He beamed. "Motherfucker you hit hard. You hit as hard as any kid I've seen in a long long time. You walk into punches but man oh man do you have power."

Diego helped Horace sit down in the dressing room, half

blind and bloody. "I gotta go but an old man named Pancho will fix you up. Okay? I've already paid him so don't worry about that. And he's a good guy and knows what he's doing. More than I do anyway. Again, good job tonight, and congratulations."

Horace nodded and Diego left. He got himself undressed and showered but by the time he got out he could barely dry himself. It hurt his ribs just to breathe let alone move his arms. The old man, Pancho, knocked on the door and came in. He said a few things in Spanish that Horace couldn't understand and then he sat Horace in a chair and turned his attention to his wounds. He set his nose and stopped the bleeding. He wrapped Horace's ribs in an Ace bandage, and taped the deep cut above his eye, which was now swollen shut. He helped him dress. When he got him to his feet he led Horace to the top level of the Coliseo and left him in the VIP section.

The people there, dressed up and wealthy-looking, congratulated him. They said things in Spanish and smiled. Men shook his hand. Diego's boxer Adolfo Venegas won a split decision, and afterward people booed and threw things into the ring because he'd beaten a local fighter. Horace made two trips to the buffet and drank three Cokes before taking a seat at the end of a row to watch the main event. By the time it was over and he saw Diego he couldn't get up from his chair.

Diego laughed and helped him stand. "Your ribs?"

Horace nodded.

"That's real pain," Diego said, smiling easy. "To me that's the worst pain there is. You gonna be okay?"

"I'll be okay," Horace said as he winced.

Diego took an envelope from his pants pocket and handed Horace nine hundred U.S. dollars and thirteen hundred pesos.

"That's about seventy dollars in pesos if you didn't know. That'll get you breakfast, lunch tomorrow, and a bus ticket back to Nuevo Laredo. Did you eat?"

Horace nodded and looked at the money. "Ruiz said it would be three hundred dollars."

Diego laughed. "Ruiz wanted me to give you the three hundred and give him the rest, but it's your money. I don't want to get involved in any sort of bullshit, and Ruiz is the king of bullshit."

Horace put the money in his pants pocket.

"You did good tonight," Diego said. "But you got lucky, too. His punches were hard but he was out of shape. I heard he hates working out and likes smoking weed too much. You need to work on how you respond to pressure. You're right. That's your main weakness."

"Do you think you could fix it?"

"I could get it better, but you live in Tucson."

"If I moved to San Antonio could I train with you?"

Diego put his hand on Horace's shoulder. "I'm overextended as it is. But I could help you. You'd have to find your own place to live and a job. And you'd have to pay me. Let's talk about it some other time, okay?"

Horace nodded.

Diego took a card from his wallet and handed it to him. "I like you, you're a good kid, but you're the type of fighter who'll end up taking a lot of shots. Especially when they get film on you. Once guys get footage on you, you'll be in some trouble. And listen, getting hit as much as you'll get hit changes you. It changes your brain, it changes the way you think, how you respond to things, your moods. It changes your future. I'm gonna be honest with you, you're not a good boxer, you're a brawler, and you'll pay the price for that."

"I don't mind paying the price," said Horace.

Diego laughed. "Every kid I know says that without even thinking about what I just said."

"But I've thought about it."

"You're really sure this is the life you want?" asked Diego.

Horace nodded, but for the first time since he left Tonopah he felt as though he might be lying.

When he woke the next morning he couldn't get out of bed. He leaned on his side and took two codeine tablets from the package of ten Diego had given him. He washed them down with water and looked at the clock on his phone. It was six a.m. and very quiet. He closed his eyes and waited for the pills to take effect. He was now a two-and-O professional boxer. He'd fought in Mexico and won. He'd beat two undefeated fighters on short notice. He should be elated and relieved but instead he felt lonelier and more depressed than he ever had.

It seemed the closer he was to what he wanted the more lost he became. The sinking feeling that had plagued him his entire life wasn't going away. It was getting worse. And why did Mexico have to frighten him so much? How could he be Mexican when he couldn't learn the language and he was scared to even be in the country? Mr. Reese had told him that life, at its core, was a cruel burden because we had the knowledge that we were born to die. We were born with innocent eyes and those eyes had to see pain and death and deceit and violence and heartache. If we were lucky we lived long enough to see most everything we love die. But, he said, being honorable and truthful took a little of the sting out of it. It made life bearable. Mr. Reese said liars and cowards were the worst people to know because they broke your heart in a world that is built to break your heart. They poured gas on an already cruel and barely controllable fire.

As he lay in the small, dingy room Horace tried to find a position on the bed where his ribs didn't hurt but he could find none. The minutes crawled by. Why weren't the pills working? He was tired of thinking and his ribs seemed to hurt worse the

longer he was awake and his nose was again bleeding. He moved
to his side and took two more codeine tablets, put fresh Kleenex
up his nostrils, and thought of Mariana at Lucky Wishbone. He
concentrated on her and his nerves slowly eased, the pain sub-
sided, and he closed his eyes.

He woke next at nine. He tried to sit up but was unable to
and rolled to his side and worked his legs off the bed until they
reached the floor. He used the nightstand as support and with
great effort stood up and made his way to the toilet. He looked
in the mirror and saw one of his eyes still swollen shut and the
other black. His nose looked awful, horribly swollen and discolored. He took a long shower, got dressed, and walked down the
steps to the front desk. The clerk understood English and called
a cab, and the cab took him to a bus station where he bought a
ticket back to Nuevo Laredo.

From there he took a bus to San Antonio, where he had
a two-hour layover. He asked a lady at the Greyhound ticket
counter if San Antonio had a Church's Chicken and she looked
on her computer and found one. He took a cab there and ate
fried chicken, coleslaw, fried okra, and macaroni and cheese
and got back just in time for the bus to Tucson.

17

Mr. Reese sat on the carpet in the living room watching a DVD called *Yoga Therapy for Back Pain*. The sun had come over the Monitor Range and was streaming through the windows into the old ranch house. He wore faded gray sweats and moved and stretched along with the young woman on the TV. Mrs. Reese, who was in the kitchen making breakfast, came into the room from time to time to watch.

"Is it helping?" she asked.

"I'm not sure," he replied.

"They say it takes awhile."

"You know all this makes me think of my dad."

"How so?"

"My mom and aunt used to have to roll him out of bed sometimes he'd get so tight. He probably never stretched a day in his life."

"Like father like son."

"He'd be laughing at me if he saw what I was doing."

"He'd be happy you were taking care of your health," she said and moved closer to the TV and squinted. "She sure has a nice figure."

"She does."

"I wish I had a figure like that."

"I do, too," he said and smiled.

She pushed on his shoulder and went back to the kitchen and he continued to follow the routine. When the DVD ended he got up from the mat, turned off the TV, and changed into his work clothes. They ate oatmeal in the kitchen while listening to the radio. Afterward Mrs. Reese cleared the plates and Mr. Reese, Little Lana, and the black mutt he'd bought from the two boys, whom Mrs. Reese had named Ely, went outside.

Inside the barn were the two Massey Ferguson 399 tractors. Morton's, now a parted-out relic, sat in the far corner. Mr. Reese had rebuilt his engine and had scavenged the good parts off Morton's and was now nearly done. He put Morton's cab on his, replaced his tires with Morton's new ones, and attached the AC unit. A small radio sat on the workbench, and both Ely and Little Lana rested on horse blankets and watched as the old man worked.

At noon Mrs. Reese rang the same bell that had always hung from the porch awning. She began bringing lunch down to a picnic table in the front yard. Mr. Reese washed up in the barn sink and made his way toward the old cottonwood tree that gave shade to the table. The dogs trailed behind him, panting in the midday heat. They ate turkey sandwiches, carrot sticks, potato chips, and drank iced tea. Afterward Mrs. Reese rubbed heat lotion on Mr. Reese's back, and he took three ibuprofens and went back to the barn.

It was late afternoon when he came up the porch steps and knocked on the front door.

Mrs. Reese opened it.

"I'm too dirty to come inside but I want you to put on your overalls, grab two beers, and meet me outside."

She smiled and shut the door. Little Lana and Ely were next to him on the porch. "Down and stay," he said gently, and the dogs lay down on the porch. He went back to the barn and started the tractor. He drove it out of the barn and up to the front porch steps, where Mrs. Reese came from inside holding two cans of beer and dressed in a pair of paint-stained overalls. He helped her inside the tractor cab, she sat on his lap, and he drove them down the gravel drive away from the ranch.

"How did you do it? How did you get it to run?"

"A lot of trips to the auto parts store," he said and smiled.

"And now it even has a cab," she said. "You won't get beat up by the wind and sun all day."

"We got lucky. Morton's transmission was shot, Eddie didn't take care of the engine either, but he sure put the bells and whistles on her. He even put on new tires four or five years back."

"See, kids do some things right," she said and opened the cans and handed him one.

"And I have a present," he said.

"What is it?"

"Are you hot?"

"I'm frying like an egg," she said. "Why can't you open the windows?"

"I want you to hit that." He pointed to a black button.

She hit the button and cool air came from two vents in front of them. "It even has air-conditioning?" she exclaimed.

"Yep," he said.

"Did Morton rob a bank?" she said and laughed.

"He might have," Mr. Reese said and put his right arm around her waist. "You steer and I'll do the pedals."

Mrs. Reese laughed again.

"Jesus, I love to hear you laugh. It's been a long time."

Mrs. Reese kissed him, took a drink of beer, set the can in a holder to the right of the seat, and put her hands on the steering wheel. "Where should we go?"

"How about Hawaii?" he said.

18

As the weeks went on Horace spoke to people less and less, and then Benny went on vacation. He left Horace in charge but the customers that came mostly spoke Spanish. Even when they spoke English, Horace had begun to lose his already feeble ability to talk to strangers.

He got up each morning and did his workout and went to Máximo's. Three nights a week he ran to Ruiz's gym for sessions, but that left four nights and two full weekend days alone. Sometimes on Saturday and Sunday he would just lie in his house in front of the AC unit and watch TV. He'd get up only to eat, use the toilet, and in the evening, when it had cooled, go to Food City for groceries or to Lucky Wishbone, where he'd get dinner and try to talk with Mariana behind the counter.

He figured this loneliness was also a test. A test of stamina and courage and fortitude. The quest to be a champion, he supposed, was a lonely quest. But what he also began to understand, which he hadn't thought of before, was that loneliness was also a sort of disease. It wasn't that he was just tested by loneliness, he was infected by it. He began not picking up the phone when Mr. Reese called, and once when his aunt invited him to eat Mexican food, for no reason at all he told her he couldn't go.

When Benny came back from vacation Horace realized that

he hardly spoke to Benny anyway. And Benny seemed to have no real interest in him. At the beginning it had been Horace asking questions, Horace starting the conversations and asking about Benny's life. But slowly he'd quit and when he did there was nothing left but silence.

With Ruiz Horace just played the part of a boxing student, and during their time together Ruiz never once asked how he was doing in Tucson, or where he lived, what his workday was like, did he have brothers and sisters, did he have a mom still alive or a dog or a cat?

Horace was alone in the city and he realized that being alone in the city was worse than being alone on the ranch. Because when he was alone on the ranch he had the dream of the city, the dream of what he would become in the city. But now he was there and he was still alone. He was just himself in another place.

Two months passed when Horace came to the gym to see Ruiz throw a towel across the room and wave him over. His face was red and bloated, and deep bags were under his eyes. He coughed. "I've thought more about our conversation last night, and I have to tell you, Hector, you've upset me. You go behind my back with Diego and now you're in a fight that could get you killed. I know your eye still gets blurry and we both know your ribs still hurt. The whole thing looks bad for you, and it also makes me look like I don't know what I'm doing, that I don't take care of my fighters, that I put my fighters in bad situations. I thought we had an agreement, and the agreement was that I was to represent you."

"Diego called me yesterday," Horace said. "He offered me the fight. I said yes because he needed to know right then. But the second I hung up I called you. It happened that fast, and I told you that, over and over I did. I don't know why Diego didn't call you. I wasn't going behind your back. He asked if I was working with you, and I told him I was. Anyway, you're the one who always says you're too busy to find me fights."

Ruiz saw Horace was becoming angry. He could see his feet tapping on the worn concrete floor. He could see his hands becoming fists. He sighed and shook his head. "Diego's the real son of a bitch here, Hector. That's what's going on." He spit on the floor and his voice grew quiet. "But I gotta say I really don't know why I do this anymore. All the goddamn backstabbing. I've been thinking more and more about selling the gym. I could work for my brother-in-law in heating and cooling. Then everyone would get off my back and I'd just show up for work and make money. An easy check. I put my heart and soul into this place, and for what?" He shook his head and again spit on the floor. "Look, Hector, I'm just not sure I can work with you anymore."

"But I need help with the fight. I need help bad."

"I don't know."

"Please," said Horace. "This is the biggest fight I've ever been in. It's eight rounds."

"And who are you fighting?"

"His name is Vicente Salido. He's fourteen and two, but I guess the record doesn't tell the truth. The first loss was a split decision. Diego was there and said he was robbed. The second was his last fight. It was in Las Vegas. He won but was disqualified for using cocaine. So really he's sixteen and 0. Diego says people think he could be a champion, but he drinks and does coke and gets into fights at clubs. Plus, he's already broken his hand three times. Diego said fans like him 'cause he once fought with a broken jaw and a busted hand and still won."

"When is it again?"

"Seven days."

"Seven days?" Ruiz shook his head.

"Diego said he could give us a ride there 'cause he has a fighter in a four-round opener."

"Diego this and Diego that," Ruiz barked. He put a piece of Nicorette gum in his mouth and let out a long sigh. "I'll help you, Hector, but I'll help you as your official manager or not at all. What's the fee Diego told you?"

"Two thousand."

"Then thirty percent of that."

"So that would be"—Horace said and closed his eyes—"six hundred dollars?"

Ruiz nodded vaguely.

"And you'll go with me to Tijuana and be in my corner?"

"I'm not going to Tijuana. I hate it there. I've always hated it there. Anyway, my wife's cousin is getting married next weekend. But I'll train you."

"Diego said he'd charge two hundred to be in my corner. So thirty percent of eighteen hundred is . . ." Horace again closed his eyes and worked out the figures. "Five hundred and forty."

"I ain't gonna nickel-and-dime with you," Ruiz said, and his anger erupted. "This is what I'm talking about! This is what I mean when I think I should just hang it up. I don't haggle and I won't scavenge. Do you want my help or not?"

"I do."

"Then it's six hundred."

Horace kicked at the concrete. "All right," he said. "It's a deal."

They arrived at the Tijuana Marriott in Diego's red car the morning of the fight. Diego and his boxer, Juan Pablo Martinez, checked into one room and Horace another. They ate in the hotel restaurant and then Horace went back to his room and lay in the biggest bed he had ever been in. He set the AC unit to high and got under the clean sheets. The room smelled of flowers and fake ocean spray.

Diego knocked on his door at four p.m. and they took a cab to the Auditorio Municipal, a large white building with palm trees surrounding it. Horace and Juan Pablo were put in a small, windowless dressing room, and Diego disappeared to find the promoter. Juan Pablo plugged in a boom box and listened to rap music while shadowboxing in front of a full-length mirror. Horace sat watching him for a time and then walked the long corridor to the auditorium main floor. Tecate banners hung from all four sides of the red and white ring. Chairs sat twenty deep, and after them, bleachers. He found a seat high in the rafters, watched the workers, and waited.

When the fight finally came and his name was announced Horace stepped toward the center of the ring in his red and gold trunks to nothing but boos. Diego had told him it was to be expected. "They're all stupid and drunk," he said. "They don't know anything about you, they just need to yell at something and they want the local guy to win. It's that simple and they're that dumb."

Vicente Salido entered to unruly hometown applause. He nodded his head toward the people in their seats and waved his arms. He was tall and handsome and wore a rhinestone-encrusted green robe and turquoise trunks. The Auditorio Municipal was two-thirds full and a constant stream of people continued to come in and find their seats. There was one more preliminary bout after theirs and then the main event. Horace

watched the crowd around him in a near trance until Diego
yelled at him. "It's in here, Hector, in the ring."

"But there's so many people," Horace said nervously. "He
must be really good."

"He's not that good," Diego said. "And he's not the reason
people are here. Remember anybody can get beat, anyone.
You're just as tough as he is. And don't worry about outside the
ring. There's nothing you can do about it. Anyway, forget it all
'cause shit, man, it's about time to start rocking." Horace looked
at the referee, and finally, after waiting all day, and worrying all
week, the bell rang.

As Diego had said would happen, Salido hit Horace at will
for the first three rounds. The shots didn't hurt but they began
to add up. His ribs ached and his damaged eye began to swell.
But what both he and Diego soon realized was that Salido didn't
like to get hit, and most of all he was distracted. His mind wasn't
on the fight.

"You'll have to take five to get one," Diego said excitedly after
the third round. "But the one might be enough. He doesn't look
right. I can't put my finger on it, but he doesn't. You'll have to
pressure him and you'll pay for it. But you have to go after him.
You'll have to cut the ring off and take the shots and get in,
but if you can, you can beat him. He already looks like his best
rounds are over. How do you feel?"

"I'm not tired yet," Horace said, trying to breathe as deep
as he could. His nose was dripping blood and his right eye was
half-swollen shut and his lips were cut. "He doesn't hit as hard
as I thought he would."

In the fourth and fifth rounds Horace took dozens of shots to
the head, stomach, kidneys, and ribs. Diego cringed throughout
the two rounds and halfway into the fifth thought seriously of
stopping the fight, but it was then that Horace connected three
hard shots to Salido's body and his opponent began to fall apart.

"It's time for you to take an even bigger chance," Diego cried after the fifth. "Keep your defense up but press harder and then harder after that." Horace's right eye was now nearly shut and his lips were bleeding into his mouth.

"I'm not scared of him," he said, trying to catch his breath. A small stream of blood leaked from his nose and covered his lips as he spoke. "I'm not scared of him at all."

The sixth opened to Salido connecting with three combinations to Horace's face. Horace countered with a left hook to Salido's kidneys that dropped him. Salido got up but there was nothing left in him, and the only way he made it through the round was clinching and backing up. In the seventh Salido came out sluggish and Horace went after him. He took a series of hard shots to the ribs and face but finally found an opening and hit Salido with two more kidney shots and Salido went down and he didn't get up for nearly three minutes.

In the small, empty dressing room Horace sat alone, exhausted and hurt. Juan Pablo had already left the building. He had been knocked out in the second round and had taken a cab back to the hotel. Horace couldn't get his eyes to focus. His vision was all blurs and streaks and his right eye was swollen shut. He showered and dressed, but when it came time to put on his shoes, he couldn't. Like after the fight in Monterrey it hurt to breathe, it hurt to button his shirt, it hurt to move at all.

Diego came into the room full of excitement. He gave Horace two codeine pills, helped him finish dressing, and they went into the now sold-out arena. People everywhere cheered and yelled in Spanish for the boxers in the ring. Horace ate two hot dogs and drank two Cokes, and stood in the back and watched Iván Morales fight a boxer from Argentina. The place erupted with every Morales punch.

But as the fight continued, the pain in Horace's ribs grew worse, and in the seventh round he went back to the dressing room to find the door locked. He hobbled farther down the long corridor to another dressing room that was open. He lay on his back on a bench seat and closed his eyes.

When he woke he could no longer hear the sound of the crowd. He had to roll himself off the bench to stand. It was hard to walk. The auditorium was now quiet and most of the people were gone. He found Diego near the entrance talking to three old men.

"Where have you been?" Diego said. "You missed Érik Morales."

"*Érik Morales was here!*"

"He saw your fight."

"He saw me fight? He really did?"

"He said Vicente Salido had never been hit so hard."

"Really?" Horace's beat-up face broke into a smile and the pain in his ribs eased.

"He also said Salido was seen getting drunk two nights ago and has been mixing heroin and cocaine lately. So don't get too big of a head yet." Diego laughed and then handed Horace a manila envelope. "I found this at a souvenir booth. It's an eight-by-ten promo picture of Morales when he was young. He even signed it for you. 'For Hector, who punches as difficult as concrete, *Buena suerte*, Érik Morales.' I told him you didn't know Spanish so he wrote it in English. I think he meant '. . . who punches as hard as concrete.' But you get the idea. You feel good enough to get some food and celebrate?"

"I think so," Horace said, still staring at the photo.

"Are you sure?"

"My ribs hurt pretty bad."

"They'll hurt no matter what you do. Take two more codeine pills. Once we get them flowing in your system you'll feel better." Diego took the pills from a package in his coat pocket. Horace washed them down with a sip of Diego's beer.

"Your eye looks bad, but not any worse than it did the last time I saw you. At least he didn't break your nose. Also there's this." Diego handed Horace another envelope.

Inside were eighteen one-hundred-dollar bills.

"I already took my two hundred out."

Horace took another hundred from the envelope and handed it to Diego. "Here's for gas and for tonight."

"Tonight?"

"If you wouldn't mind ordering for me and paying for it. I can't understand anything anybody says here."

Diego laughed and put the money in his wallet.

"Is Juan Pablo coming with us?"

Diego shook his head. "He's in the hotel, sulking. He should have had a few local fights before trying anything real. But he wouldn't listen. He thinks he's a lot tougher than he is, and he does the worst thing a boxer can do, he quits. He gave up at the end of the first round when he got hit with an uppercut that rattled him. If he had any guts at all he lost them when he took that shot. He should have at least stayed and watched the fights and learned something, but he's not that sorta kid. Anyway, let's go have some fun. You earned it."

Outside they met a middle-aged man with a boxer's face dressed in black jeans and a black dress shirt. He was smoking a cigarette and Diego introduced him as Javier Hernández. He spoke broken English and Diego waved for a cab and the three were driven to the red-light district of Tijuana and dropped off in front of a restaurant called Kentucky Fried Buches. Its sign was white with red letters, and below it read, DESDE 1963. Around them music blasted out of buildings and apartments, cars honked, and drunk people walked in the middle of the road. It smelled of broken sewer lines, grilled meat, exhaust, and urine.

"You said you like Southern cooking, right, Hector?"

Horace nodded.

"This place has nothing but fried chicken necks."

"Fried chicken necks?"

"Don't look so scared." Diego laughed and put his hand on Horace's shoulder. "You'll like them. Everybody likes them. We'll just get a few as appetizers."

Inside was a small room and they ordered at a white-and-red-tiled counter. The necks were served with tortillas and salsa, and the three of them stood at a chest-high table and ate. Afterward they walked down the bustling street to a restaurant called Birriería Guadalajara.

"This place has the best goat stew you'll ever have in your life," Diego said, and they sat at a corner table in the crowded restaurant. Diego looked at Horace and laughed. "Don't look so worried all the time, Hector. You're Mexican and you're in Mexico. You should feel relieved, not worried. Everyone around here is like you. Finally you don't have to be around white people all the time. So lighten up." A waitress came and Diego ordered beers and bowls of *birria* and began talking in Spanish with Javier. When the food came Horace ate as much as he felt he had to so that Diego wouldn't make fun of him. But he didn't like the taste or how spicy it was. He drank a beer and then Javier ordered shots of tequila and he had one. Afterward Diego took them to a pharmacy and got Horace his own packet of codeine pills. They kept walking. They passed Americans in sailor uniforms, white college kids, street bands playing Tejano and rock music, an old woman sitting on a milk crate making tacos on a Coleman stove, street dogs, and prostitutes of all ages.

They passed a line of lowrider cars. As Horace stared at

them he felt a growing dread. He didn't even like lowriders. The more tires he changed, the more he wished that all cars and trucks stayed stock. Like Mr. Reese always said, why put so much money into things that don't matter? Big rims and skinny tires and hydraulics didn't even make sense.

Javier took them to a burgundy-colored building where a neon sign Horace couldn't understand hung above the door. Inside a bouncer in a black suit stood behind a counter. Diego gave him money and they were taken past the main room with its three stages and three naked women dancing, to a second room, where there were fewer people, and only a single girl danced on the stage. There were four more girls standing near a small bar that was backlit in red neon light. The bartender wore a tuxedo.

"Here are the youngest and best-looking girls in TJ," Diego said to Horace. A cocktail waitress in a red dress came, and Diego ordered tequila and beer for the three of them. "These girls aren't used up. It costs more, but everything good costs more. I'll need extra money if you want me to set you up with one. And remember to use a condom. These girls are young but you still have to be safe."

The waitress brought the beer and tequila. They toasted to Horace, and he forced himself to drink the shot. He began to feel drunk, and the pain in his ribs lessened. Diego and Javier again spoke in Spanish. Horace watched the girl dancing for two songs and then tapped Diego on the arm.

"Do you think I have what it takes to become a championship boxer?" His face was still swollen, and his bad eye was still nearly shut.

"You're pretty good," Diego said and then turned in his chair and faced Horace. "But you have a lot of work to do. First you should get away from Ruiz. He's not a good trainer and he's not a good person. You won't go anywhere with him. I have to say

I was surprised how tough you were tonight. I underestimated
you. You can take a lot of punishment. But you know, I haven't
seen a guy get hit that much in a long time. And I see fights
every week. You get hit way too much, way too much. But on
the flip side, I can't believe how hard you hit. That's something
in your favor, and that's something real." He stopped and took
a long drink of beer and looked briefly at the girl dancing. "But
you have to remember you caught Vicente Salido on a bad night.
That's a fact. He has the natural gifts, but he doesn't take his
craft seriously and tonight it caught him. He thought he was
better than he was, and that did him in as much as what you did.
The reality is you have some serious faults, and like I said the
last time I saw you, when they get film on you it's going to get seriously bad. Already you seem to run into punches, and it'll get
a lot worse when they know your style. I guess I just don't know
how far you could go. I know it'll hurt to find out. But you hit as
'difficult as concrete.'" Diego laughed and finished his beer. He
patted Horace on the shoulder. "But let's not talk about boxing.
Let's just have fun and celebrate your success, okay? You were a
true warrior in the ring tonight." He went back to talking with
Javier and ordered them more beer and tequila. All the while a
girl, who looked fifteen, danced on the stage.

Horace drank the next shot and beer that was set in front of
him and by then he was drunk and he forgot about his swollen eye and face, his cut lips and hurt ribs. Diego asked him
for another hundred dollars and Horace gave it to him without
question. Diego got up from his seat and began talking with
the bartender. He came back with three more beers and three
tequilas. They drank the tequila together and Diego put a beer
in Horace's hand and led him to the edge of the room where
two young girls stood in school uniforms. Diego took one by the
hand and said to Horace, "I've already paid for you. All you have
to do is follow her to the room."

Diego walked up the flight of stairs and disappeared. Horace looked at the girl standing next to him. She was just over five feet tall, skinny, and very young and beautiful. She wore shiny black shoes with white stockings and a plaid skirt. Her bare stomach showed and she wore a thin white half shirt and a black sweater over it. She took his hand and walked him up the same flight of stairs.

The room was small with a TV in the corner. There were snapshot photos on the far wall near a desk, but he couldn't make out what they were of.

"¿Habla inglés?" he asked.

The girl looked at him shyly and shook her head. She was too young, and he didn't want to touch her. He wanted to leave but wasn't sure he should, and then she stood in front of him and took off her clothes. She undid Horace's pants, pushed them down to his feet, and dropped to her knees. He didn't want her to do it at first, but she put her mouth on him and before he knew it he had come.

The girl was unready and stood up, gagging. She walked quickly to a sink, spit it out, and washed her hands and face and brushed her teeth. He couldn't tell if she was upset or not. He stared at her: her small ass and thin legs, her little breasts. He watched her dress and put on her high-heeled shoes and stumble in them like a kid would.

"Mi nombre es Horace," he said.

She nodded, smiled, and then took his hand and led him back down the stairs to where Javier sat with a beer and a shot of tequila. Diego came down a half hour later and they ordered another round of drinks. When they left the streets were even more crowded, drunken, and wild. They walked for half a mile and stopped at a taco truck, where Diego ordered Horace three *pastor* tacos and a *horchata.*

"The *horchata* will calm your stomach and help with tomorrow's hangover," Diego said. Horace ate the tacos and drank the *horchata,* and when they were finished they said goodbye to Javier, and Horace and Diego took a cab back to the Marriott. In the lobby Diego gave Horace a hug and told him they'd be leaving the next morning at nine.

In his room, Horace collapsed on the bed and tried to sleep, but sleep wouldn't come. He thought of the skinny girl and wondered how old she was. As he lay in the king-size bed, he realized that every day while he trained and put tires on cars and ate at Lucky Wishbone she was spitting out come into a dingy sink.

An hour passed and his stomach hurt from the food and his mind became engulfed in a tirade against himself. "You said you wanted to be a champion, but a champion doesn't do that. A champion doesn't take advantage of a street girl. And tomorrow in the car don't blame Diego. He didn't make you go up those stairs. He didn't force you. A real champion thinks for himself. A real champion builds his own boat and travels his own way. A real champion stands up and says, 'This isn't right!'"

He looked at his phone. It was two-thirty in the morning. Why was the night going so slowly? He wanted to get up, but he didn't know where to go and he was too scared to walk outside alone. If they had a gym he would work out, but his ribs hurt worse than they ever had, and he thought his stomach might burst from all the food. He held it with his hands like a pregnant belly: two hot dogs, four Cokes, two chicken neck tacos, a bowl of goat soup, three *pastor* tacos, a *horchata*, six beers, and five shots of tequila. He rolled off the bed and stood up. His ribs burned with just his breathing. He began to pace.

He wanted nothing more than to get back to Tucson, where at least he could understand the language, where at least he knew what he was eating and which faucet he could drink from. And the second he got back he'd move out of his aunt's house, and he would get his own place. He would call the Reeses and tell them that he missed them. He would rebuild his boat. Brick by brick, and row by row. He would make up for who he was.

He continued to pace and the night wore on. At five a.m., his nose began to bleed, and at five-thirty he got the runs. At half past six he threw up, and that caused such pain to his ribs that he dropped to the bathroom tile, where he stayed until his alarm went off at eight-thirty.

19

Mr. Reese pulled into the turnout at Canyon Mine and shut off the engine. He nursed a cup of coffee, ate a peanut butter and jelly sandwich, and listened to the radio. From the truck's glove box, he took out the weathered laminated sign—THIS TRUCK BELONGS TO THE REESE RANCH. PLEASE DON'T VANDALIZE! WE'RE A MOM-AND-POP OUTFIT—and put it on the dash. He finished the coffee and got out of the truck. He went through his yoga stretches, and then unloaded Slow Poke and Honey, and tied them to the side of the stock trailer.

In the dawn light he took a vial of Valium from his shirt pocket, broke one in half, and swallowed it dry. He took the supplies from the bed of the truck and loaded Honey's panniers, tightened both cinches, and then walked the horses up the narrow, washed-out mining road until he came to a stump on the side. He stood on it, brought Slow Poke beside him, put his foot in the stirrup, and got on the horse.

For the first hour he felt all right. Louise had rubbed his back with heat lotion before he left, and Slow Poke's plodding, methodical pace had a rhythm that eased more than hurt. The old man swayed with every Slow Poke sway, concentrated on his breathing, and time passed without incident.

He had gone up three thousand feet when the narrow

canyon walls opened to the first plateau. Acres of meadow grass appeared and the struggling creek grew, and groves of aspen trees quaked alongside it. Mr. Reese needed to urinate and the horses needed a rest, but when he tried to dismount he found he was unable to. His back was stuck and the pulsating pain that had begun earlier was now worse. He pulled the vial of Valium from his shirt pocket, took out a full pill, and swallowed it. He waited for ten minutes but the pain seemed only to worsen.

He took Slow Poke's lead from around the saddle horn and pulled his right leg from the stirrup and then his left. He pushed his cowboy hat down as far as he could and wrapped his arms around the neck of the horse, then slowly rolled off Slow Poke until he fell into the grass. The horse didn't spook, only looked tired and hot in the midday sun.

The pain worsened as Mr. Reese tried to stand. He broke down crying. He got himself upright, hunched over and stuck, while Honey stood listless next to Slow Poke, her eyes half closed in sleep. He grabbed both leads and moved the horses to the shade of the aspens, tied them to trees, and urinated. He grabbed his lunch and water bottle from Honey's panniers, he loosened both horses' cinches, and collapsed on the grass. He tried to find a position that was comfortable but there was none. The pill didn't seem to be working so he took another half, and then finally the pain eased. He grew drowsy and fell asleep.

It was dusk when he woke. He stood up disoriented and sore, but the spasms had stopped. He looked at the darkening sky. It was too late to make it to Pedro's camp. He'd have to wait until dawn. He decided not to unsaddle the horses for fear that he wouldn't be able to get the saddles back on the next morning. He apologized to Slow Poke and Honey and led them to the creek to drink before bringing them back to the aspen grove and hobbling them. He took a small tarp, an air mattress, and his sleeping bag and laid them out. He ate a turkey sandwich in darkness.

The breeze grew cool, and he pulled off his boots and took drinks from a flask. In the distance he could hear yips from coyotes and above him the stars shone and he could make out satellites passing in the vast sky. He got in the sleeping bag and fell asleep.

The horses woke him before dawn, startled by something in the night. The small air mattress Louise had bought him helped, but the fact was that he was so tight he wasn't sure, when morning came, if he would be able to stand.

He thought of his father's death alone in the mountains. Would that be such a bad way to go? He wouldn't mind dying alone, away from people. He didn't think he would be more scared that way than any other. Maybe less somehow. But then Louise would be frantic. She wouldn't call the police or the BLM, she'd just call Ander, and Ander, now seventy-four, would try to get on a horse and look for him. In the end a half dozen people would have to search, and the sad thing was one of them would find him just like Ed Morton had found his father. He supposed then he'd rather die in bed at home. It would be the least amount of work and worry for everyone involved.

He looked at the starry sky above him and thought of his daughters and then of Horace and wished he had Little Lana to keep him company. He closed his eyes and again drifted off. He woke next at sunrise, took half a Valium, waited for it to take effect, and then slowly got himself out of the sleeping bag. He did the stretches he could and rubbed heat lotion on his lower back. He put his sleeping gear away, ate a peanut butter and jelly sandwich, and switched out of his cowboy boots into a new pair of running shoes that were easier on his back. The horses stood next to each other quietly. He tightened both cinches and together they began the walk toward Pedro.

It was late afternoon when, in the distance, Mr. Reese heard the bleats of the sheep. He rose over a small ridge to see his flock nestled in a bowl-shaped meadow and a blue tarp in the far corner, half hidden in a grove of aspens.

Little Roy came to him first, but Mr. Reese's back was so tight and sore he couldn't bend down to pet the dog. The border collie walked beside him as he headed toward camp, and soon he made out Whitey and Jip and then Wally and Tiny. Everyone was okay. He high-lined the horses next to Myrtle and took the saddle off Slow Poke. He unloaded the supplies from Honey and took off the panniers. He brought his personal pack into the grove of aspens and found Pedro lying facedown, naked, on his sleeping bag. The camp was in disarray, with discarded cans of food near the fire. A fifth of rum was three-quarters empty by Pedro's head.

Mr. Reese called to Pedro a half dozen times and then kicked on his foot with his running shoe. Pedro was breathing but wouldn't stir. The old man moved to the other side of the spent fire pit, laid down his tarp, the air mattress, and sleeping bag, and collapsed. He slept until dusk. When he woke he had to roll onto his stomach and push himself upright. He took half a Valium and put heat lotion on his back.

Pedro still hadn't woken. Mr. Reese fed the dogs and started a small fire. From inside a nylon cooler he took two steaks. He washed two pans and looked through Pedro's supplies and found potatoes, onions, and garlic. He chopped them and set them in a frying pan on the Coleman stove. Night came and Mr. Reese again called out to Pedro, and finally his worker rolled over and sat up. His eyes were wet and bloodshot. He saw Mr.

Reese, nodded, and then stood up, unsteady, and found his clothes.

They ate, watching the small fire. Wally sat next to Pedro and Tiny and Little Roy next to Mr. Reese. They didn't speak and the fire died and they went to sleep. When dawn came Mr. Reese opened his eyes to see a fire again going in the pit. Pedro was up and coffee was brewing on the stove. The old man opened his sleeping bag and rolled onto his stomach. He was so tight it was difficult to stand. In his underwear he put heat lotion on his lower back. He stretched as Pedro watched from where he sat on his sleeping bag.

Pedro didn't eat breakfast. He only drank coffee and sat next to the fire.

"We need to talk," Mr. Reese said as he finished a peanut butter and jelly sandwich.

Pedro nodded.

"Do you still have your phone?"

"*Sí.*"

"Do you have minutes left?"

"*Sí.*"

"When you've finished your coffee show me where I can get reception and I'll call Louise and tell her I'm staying. We'll have Ander meet us with supplies. If we head down Corral Canyon, we'll save two weeks. We'll get the sheep to my place from there. We'll be a month early, but I have the hay. I'm not going to leave you alone up here anymore."

Pedro kept his eyes on the fire.

"In your head, what's happening?"

Pedro just shrugged.

"You won't tell me?"

Pedro kept still.

"I think it's time you went back to your wife and family."

Tears suddenly leaked down Pedro's face.

Mr. Reese took a drink of coffee. "You've been alone up here for more than twenty years. Ten with the McGill ranch and ten more with me. That's a long time in the mountains."

Pedro nodded.

"Either way, I'm done," said Mr. Reese and sighed. "I can't ride anymore, and Horace is gone. I'm having a hard time finding help. I have to face the fact that it's over." He paused and looked at Pedro. "Can you make it a couple more weeks?"

Pedro nodded.

"Is there anything you want to talk about? Is there anything I can help you with?"

Pedro shook his head and looked at the ground. Mr. Reese took a last drink of coffee and threw the rest on the fire.

20

For weeks Horace was too hurt to do anything but go to work and walk home. He didn't see Ruiz, and spent his nights alone watching TV and taking walks through the city. He tried to save money by eating at home, but he grew to hate the food he cooked and he was tired of making it. He began going to Lucky Wishbone four nights a week, and Mariana continued to flirt with him, even when his face was so visibly beat up.

"Does it hurt bad getting hit?" she asked him.

"Not exactly," Horace told her. "Not when it's happening. It does later on though."

"It looks like it hurts now."

"It does hurt now," he said and smiled.

"I've never been to Tijuana," the girl said. "What's it like?"

"It's crazy there," he said.

"And dangerous?"

"I guess so. It seemed like it was."

"Were there a lot of people at the fight?"

"Thousands," he replied.

"And you won?" she said, excited.

Horace nodded, and as hard as he tried he couldn't make himself tell her that he had only fought in a preliminary bout. That the people weren't there to see him or cheer for him.

"My older brother's in the Marines," she said. "He used to box, but not professionally."

A customer came in and stood behind Horace.

Mariana rolled her eyes and shrugged. "Don't worry about paying," she whispered and then said, "Do you like movies?"

"Yeah," he said.

She went to the register and pushed a button and a blank receipt came from it. She tore it off and had him write down his number. "I still have a boyfriend, but I'll go see a movie with you if you can go during the day."

"Which day?"

"I see a movie every Wednesday," she replied. "And I always see the twelve-thirty or one o'clock showing."

"Okay," he said.

He met her the next week at the movie theater dressed in his newest jeans and newest long-sleeve shirt. He even bought new running shoes and wore them. His right eye was no longer swollen, but the skin around it was discolored, and it often blurred and watered for no reason at all. His ribs, on the other hand, still hurt in everything he did. It was hard for him to just sit, and painful to even roll over in bed.

He paid for his ticket and went inside the lobby to find her looking at framed movie posters on a wall. She wore a black dress with thin straps and white tennis shoes. Her hair, which he'd only seen held back in a ponytail, was down. She wore red lipstick and mascara.

"I thought about it and realized you'd never seen me without my uniform. I was thinking you wouldn't recognize me."

"I'd recognize you no matter how you were dressed," said Horace.

"And I don't smell like that place," she said and laughed.

Horace smiled. "Do you see a lot of movies?"

"Wednesday is one of my days off so I see movies on Wednesdays if I can. It's too hot to do anything else and there's always too many people at my house anyway. Is your boss okay with you taking the afternoon off?"

He nodded.

"When are you boxing next?"

"I'm not sure."

"My dad's favorite sport is boxing."

"And you live at home?"

"Yeah, but I'm gonna move out soon. You know the girl I work with, Camila?"

Horace nodded.

"She and I might get a place. My two younger brothers and two younger sisters, my grandma, and my mom and dad and me all live in a two-bedroom house. It's supercrowded. You have to wait an hour just to get five minutes alone in the bathroom." She rolled her eyes and smiled. "Your face looks better."

"It's mostly just my ribs that hurt now," he said.

"You must be really tough. I don't like it even when I get a cold or cut my finger."

"I'm not that tough."

"You're probably even tougher than my brother and he's in the Marines. Have you seen the other Hunger Games movies?"

"I don't know anything about them."

Mariana smiled and then, like she'd done it a million times, took his hand and they went inside the theater. Only three other seats were taken, and she led them to the back corner. She gave him a piece of gum, took one herself, and ten minutes into the movie she reached over and kissed him. By a half hour into the film all they did was kiss. When Horace stopped her to ask about her boyfriend, she only whispered, "I don't want to talk about him. He's really boring and lives in Texas. I don't like him anymore anyway." They kissed more, and when the credits ended and the lights came up she whispered, "I wish it was just starting."

They walked out together into the lobby. "Just so you know, I'm gonna leave by myself in case one of my relatives drives by. I'm related to everybody in this town so it's easy to get in trouble. But I had a nice time, Hector. I'm not going to give you my number 'cause it's my home number and if you call, my mom will think something's up, and she likes my boyfriend. I had a cell phone but I dropped it in the toilet of all places and I have to wait until I get paid to get a new one. But come into the Wishbone and I'll give you a free dinner tomorrow night. Okay?"

He nodded and watched her walk out of the theater and he felt better than he had since he could remember. He walked to the counter, got a Coke and a package of Red Vines, and bought a ticket to the same movie. He went back in and sat in the seat she had been sitting in. He began to watch the film, but even alone he couldn't concentrate. He'd been given a gift, a chance to make up for Tijuana. Make up for failing, for drinking beer and tequila, for the girl, for always being scared in Mexico, and for being depressed and lazy afterward. He would be different now. He would be the best man she'd ever met. He'd make her life easier and he'd make her laugh every day. He'd kiss her better than she'd ever been kissed, and he'd take her to the movies as often as she wanted. And when he wasn't with her he would train harder than he ever had. He would make real money as a boxer and move out of his aunt's place. He'd get his life back on track. He'd right his boat.

Each Wednesday after that Horace met Mariana at the movies. They kissed in the back, and by the third time, and all the times after, she took his hand and put it between her legs and inside her underwear. When the movie ended they would walk out to the lobby, and she would leave by herself, and he would again watch the movie alone.

She began to write him love letters and gave him free dinners with extra sides each time he came to Lucky Wishbone. She would call him on the work phone sporadically during the week. But she never let him call her, they never met outside of the movie theater, and she never broke up with her boyfriend.

Horace's ribs healed enough that he began training again, although now he wasn't as certain about his future in Tucson. Diego was right, to be a real boxer, he would have to leave Ruiz, he would have to leave Tucson, and he was just beginning to find his way there. Even his aunt seemed to like him better. She invited him to a small work party she was having at her house. He helped her clean up the carport and front yard and bring up a table and chairs she had stored in the basement. When the party began she even introduced him to her co-workers. She wasn't exactly nice and he could tell she didn't really want to know him, but it was getting better. If he did leave he would have to move to San Antonio and begin again alone. He'd have to find a place to stay, get a new job, and he'd be even farther from everything he knew.

He began to think he would ask Mariana to go out with only him. But each Wednesday came and passed and he said nothing. He was scared that if he said anything she would stop seeing him. That it would put too much pressure on her. He couldn't chance that. So in the end he kept quiet.

At work, he just did what Benny asked. Shipments would come in, they would be swamped, and then it would again slack off. He'd have days with no real work. He convinced Benny to let him paint the outside of the building, paint the office and bathroom, and do odd jobs to keep his hours up. He also began taking Wednesdays off entirely. And then one evening af-

ter work he walked to Lucky Wishbone to find that Mariana
had quit. The girl who worked with her, Camila, said she didn't
know why, and when he asked for Mariana's number Camila
said she didn't have it, although he knew she did. After that
he couldn't sleep and could barely eat. He didn't know what to
do. He didn't know where she lived or how to get ahold of her.
When the next Wednesday came he went to the same theater
and waited in the lobby. He sat nervously on a chair near a fake
fireplace, and when he looked up she was there.

She wore a yellow dress and the same white canvas shoes she
always wore. She had on dark red lipstick and black eyeliner.
She smiled at him, but as she did tears welled in her eyes.

"Camila said you quit," Horace said.

"I had to," she whispered and sat across from him. "I'm pregnant, Hector. I never told you this but my boyfriend is in the
Marines, too. He and my brother are stationed in Texas and
they're best friends. They were on leave months ago, before I
met you, and he stayed with us. It happened at a party we all
went to. I was going to break up with him but now I'm getting
married to him and moving to Texas."

"You're moving to Texas?"

She began crying uncontrollably.

Horace watched her as she cried, and then she looked at him
and wiped her tears with her hands. "But can we still see the
movie today?"

"I want to if you do," he said.

She nodded slowly and tears continued to stream down her
face.

In the theater they sat in the back, in their usual seats, and
the movie played. They held hands and kissed, but every time
they did she cried. "I'm the stupidest person in the entire world,"
she whispered.

"Maybe you could just stay with me," Horace said.

Mariana shook her head. "Everybody in my family already knows. We're really, really Catholic and so is he. I get married next week and I move to Fort Bliss at the end of the month." She kissed him again and he held her in the darkness and then finally the movie ended and they walked out to the lobby.

"I won't forget you, Hector, and I'll follow your career. I think I love you and I will always watch for your fights on TV and maybe someday, somehow, we'll be together again."

His heart raced as she spoke. He wanted to tell her his real name, tell her about himself, but he knew it was the wrong time to do it. So he just told her he loved her back, they said goodbye, and she left.

That evening Horace called Mr. Reese.

"You sound like something's troubling you," the old man said.

"I met a girl," Horace admitted.

"A girl?"

"Yeah."

"What's her name?"

"Mariana."

"What's she like?"

"She's moving to Texas," Horace said and lay back on his bed on the floor. "I guess we were sorta dating for a while but she has a boyfriend."

"She has a boyfriend?"

"I feel bad about it, Mr. Reese. But I liked her. And she's the only girl I've met here that liked me."

"That's hard."

"We met every Wednesday at the movies."

"That sounds nice."

"But she can't be a very good person if she's marrying one guy and making out with another, right?"

"She might be a good person. . . . She just sounds like she's confused. Who is she marrying?"

"She has to marry her boyfriend in the Marines 'cause he got her pregnant. But she told me she doesn't really like him. He's just a friend of her brother's and it went too far."

"How old is she?"

"Nineteen."

Mr. Reese sighed. "She's young and it sounds like she's got herself into some trouble."

"Are girls in cities always messing with two guys like that, Mr. Reese?"

"No," he said and laughed. "As you get older you'll get better at stopping things that can hurt you before they start. You'll see farther down the line."

"What do you mean?"

"Well, for instance the next time a girl you meet has a boyfriend you might just walk the other way. Simple logic goes a long way, but logic's hard when your heart's involved. And you're a romantic so it will be harder for you."

"A romantic?"

The old man laughed. "You're trying to be a Mexican championship boxer. That can be seen as being romantic."

"I never thought of it that way."

"And remember your girlfriend in high school, Mandy?"

"Sure."

"Before her and her folks moved away you two were going to get married and you were what, sixteen?"

Horace laughed.

"Look, everyone struggles with things like this. And people get lonely, and lonely people tend to make bad decisions. I've made mistakes, too. That's how you find out about these things. Paying attention to actions over words can sometimes save you a lot of heartache. . . . What's your girl's name again?"

Horace sat up on his bed. "Mariana."

"That's a nice name."

"I guess her action was that she was cheating on her boy-friend."

"I have a question to ask," said Mr. Reese. "Did the boyfriend know about you? Was it okay with him that you were seeing her?"

"No, he didn't know."

"Did she take you to meet her folks and all that sorta thing?"

"No," Horace said, his voice suddenly saddened.

"I guess those actions say some things," said Mr. Reese.

"I guess they do," Horace whispered.

"But remember you got to see a movie every week with a girl who liked you, right?"

"I did."

"And now you remember that it hurts when it doesn't work out. So next time you'll be more careful."

"But still I don't think she's a horrible person."

"I don't think so either. She liked you, didn't she?"

"I think so."

"Then she couldn't be all bad."

"And she did give me free dinners at the place she worked."

The old man laughed. "I'm sorry you're down, Horace, but it'll get better with time."

"You think so?"

"I'm pretty sure."

"I'm going to get off the phone now."

"Okay."

"And don't tell Mrs. Reese, all right?"

"I won't tell her."

21

The weeks after Mariana left, Horace isolated himself even further. Besides Benny, an occasional customer, and the sessions he had again started with Ruiz, he spoke to no one. He quit going to Lucky Wishbone and again began cooking at home to save money so he could move to San Antonio. He decided he would leave in two months.

He also made a new pact with himself, and every night he turned off the TV and again focused on listening to his Spanish-language CDs. He put stickers on every bowl, plate, mirror, table, and lamp with the equivalent Spanish word. And each morning he put gel in his hair and walked out the door the way he thought a Mexican boxer would walk and he held himself that way all day long. When he was around people he didn't know, at a store or restaurant, he spoke with his version of a Mexican accent.

He trained four nights a week with Ruiz, who had just separated from his wife and moved into the basement of the run-down gym. He slept on a couch that Horace helped him carry down into the small, windowless room. During training, Ruiz would fall into long speeches about personal robberies and swindles, missteps and lost opportunities. He gained more weight and his breath smelled always of Nicorette gum and potato chips.

And then, one Saturday morning at home, two months after Horace had last heard from Mariana, he received a call from Diego.

"How you been, Hector?"

"All right," Horace said and shut off the TV.

"Healed up?"

"Pretty much."

"You still training?"

"I've been working out on my own every morning and I go to Ruiz four nights a week."

"So you're still with him?"

"I don't know what else to do here. But I am saving my money to move to San Antonio."

"San Antonio?"

"To work with you."

"That's right," Diego said and paused. "I'm spread pretty thin, Hector, but I'll help if I can. Let's talk about that another time. The reason I called today is to let you know there's been a cancellation in a preliminary fight at the Desert Diamond Casino in two weeks. That's not far from Tucson. It's in your area. The main event is Contreras versus Ochoa. Ochoa used to be the WBA featherweight champion. He's a legend in Arizona. You ever heard of him?"

"No."

"You should look him up. He's over the hill now, but he was great for a while. The fight they're trying to fill is against a lightweight named Raymundo Figueroa. You ever heard of him?"

"No."

"He went to the Olympics for Mexico. He didn't make it far, but he's good. He turned pro a couple years ago and now he's thirteen and O. He was supposed to fight a guy from the Ukraine, but the guy tore his bicep and canceled. It's eight rounds. He's out of your league at this stage, but I'm making calls to see if I can find someone and I was at the *H*s and I thought I'd see where you were at and how you were doing. So how are you doing?"

"Pretty good, I guess."

"Have your ribs healed?"

"More or less."

"How about your eye? Is it focusing?"

"For the most part. Is Figueroa really that good?"

"I think so."

"How much money is it?"

"Five thousand dollars. Figueroa is a good draw all over the Southwest, and Mexicans love him. The promoters think thirty percent of the ticket sales are because of him. He's on all the promotions, too, so they don't want him to cancel. At this point they're just looking for a body and they're running out of time. No one they've tried is willing to take him on such short notice."

"So you didn't call just to see how I was doing?"

Diego paused. "I don't know what I was thinking exactly, but the more I think about it the more I realize Figueroa is too much for you right now. He isn't like Vicente Salido. He's been trained as a technical boxer since he was a kid, but he's also a brawler. He's a devout Catholic and they say he's never had a drop of alcohol in his life. People think he could be a champion someday. He's not going to be distracted like Salido, that's for sure."

"He'll be a champion someday?"

"People always say that, but in this case he might have a shot. But he's the wrong kind of fighter for you. I hadn't thought things through when I first called. So let's forget about it."

Horace got up from his bed on the floor and began pacing. His chest tightened and he grew short of breath.

"Are you still there?" asked Diego.

"I'm still here."

"Do you want me to see if I can get you tickets?"

"I'll take the fight," Horace whispered.

"What?"

"I'll take it," he said louder into the phone.

Diego let out a long sigh. "Are you sure?"

"I am."

"Ruiz won't like it."

"He doesn't like anything."

"Give Ruiz fifteen percent and he'll be okay. I'll take twenty-five as a finder's fee. Ruiz will want to be in your corner, but he isn't much of a cut man."

"Could you be in my corner?"

"If he can't do the fight I'll do it. But ask him first. Hector, just so you know, you'll most likely lose. Maybe it'll be good for you to lose, I don't know. But Figueroa has one of the best trainers in Los Angeles working with him. He's got a whole team behind him. Right now he's just building up his record. You'll only be a number. I'm telling you this 'cause I always try to be honest. He's just in a different league than you are."

"But didn't you say that no one is superhuman or always successful, that anybody can be beat?"

"I said that to build your confidence when I could tell you were sweating it in Tijuana. But I'm not sure I even believe that. You're tough. You hit as hard as anyone, but you're green and you have some serious flaws. You're just not at the same level. Maybe someday, but I don't know. And he's quicker than anything you've seen, he's a great technical boxer who's had over a hundred amateur fights as well as the thirteen pro ones. He's the worst kind of fighter for you."

"I'm not scared."

"Maybe you should be."

"Then why did you call?"

Diego was silent.

"I might as well find out what it means."

"It's going to hurt to find out."

"I've had the shit kicked out of me enough to know I don't mind it."

Diego breathed heavily into the phone and coughed. "I'll make the call and see if they'll go for it. They'll want to find a more well-known fighter, but there's not much time. If they get desperate they might take you. Call Ruiz and then get on You-Tube and watch all you can on Figueroa. If you see the footage and don't want the fight, call me. Until then, I'll try and get it."

A week passed and no call came from Diego. Even so each night after work Horace ran to the library and watched You-Tube clips on Raymundo Figueroa. From the moment he woke in the morning it was all he thought of. He printed out photos of Figueroa and wrote "B.O.A.T." on top of them. He put a copy next to his bed and one in the shop bathroom. When he told Ruiz about the possibility of the fight with Figueroa, Ruiz was both excited and angry. He talked about the deceit of Diego and his outrageous finder's fee, but also of his own chance, hopefully, to meet the higher-ups working for Figueroa and for once in his life get a break. During their sessions he gave no real advice to Horace except for saying, "He'll kill you if you go toe to toe with him. Just don't do it and you may have a chance to last the eight rounds."

Horace's phone rang near midnight five days before the fight. He was half asleep when he heard Diego's voice telling him he had it. When he hung up he felt groggy, but as soon as he fell back into bed he was wide awake. He didn't sleep the rest of the night. For the next four days he slept poorly, and when he ran to and from work he did so in a free-fall panic. He felt as though he was always one step behind, catching his breath.

The morning of the bout, he threw up, and when he looked at his hands he could see that they shook. He took out the thin box he kept underneath his bed and lifted the red boxing trunks from it. He stared at Mrs. Poulet's embroidery and then wrapped the trunks in a T-shirt and carefully put them in the bottom of his gym bag.

The ride to the casino took less than an hour, and Ruiz dropped him at the front entrance and then left to pick up his kids from school. The casino's auditorium was a large oval room, and workers were there arranging chairs and hanging Tecate banners around the blue ring. Horace sat for a long time watching and then walked to the casino's coffee shop for lunch. As he sat waiting for the fried chicken special he watched an Indian busboy walk past him. The busboy looked the same age as Horace. He wore new basketball shoes and his hair was short and he looked like he lifted weights. He pushed a cart around and then spoke to a waitress who was also Indian. She was pretty and had long black hair that was curled slightly. Her fingernails were painted pink and they sparkled under the fluorescent lights. The two laughed, and then she set her hand gently on his back and whispered something in his ear before going back to work. Horace wasn't sure what tribe they were from, but seeing them together made him feel even more uneasy than he already did.

When the waitress set down his food it tasted like sand. He put forkfuls into his mouth, but he had trouble swallowing. He felt as though he was slowly falling from a cliff. When the waitress came by again he ordered a Coke, and he asked her to refill it twice before his appetite came back and he finished his meal and left.

In his dressing room he drank water and cursed himself for drinking the three Cokes. His mind battled back and forth, so he turned off the lights and moved to the corner of the room and collapsed into sleep on the floor. When he opened his eyes next the bright overhead lights were on and Diego stood hovering above him.

"Nerves of steel you have," he said. "Sleeping when most men would be shitting their pants."

"How long do I have?" Horace said and got up.

"Maybe an hour at the most. You should be warming up. Where's Ruiz?"

"I don't know," said Horace.

"Well, I better leave before he comes. He'll blow a gasket if he sees me. He called two days ago, drunk, and forbid me to be around you today." Diego laughed. "So I won't see you after the fight, but I'll call you soon. Good luck, Hector. Don't go toe to toe with him. And start warming up, okay?"

Horace nodded and Diego left the room. He used the toilet, dunked his head in the sink, did a long series of stretches, and began shadowboxing while looking in the mirror. He broke a sweat and then changed into his trunks and put on his boxing shoes. A few minutes after that Ruiz came into the dressing room.

"I've been looking all over for you," he said out of breath.

"Don't say that. I've been right here," Horace said.

Ruiz had spaghetti stains on his shirt and he smelled of beer and garlic. "We don't have a lot of time and we have a lot of work to do." He opened a satchel with his supplies. "You know there's no parking close to the casino. I had to walk half a mile. You'd think they'd have special parking for us but they don't. I bet you Figueroa's people got a stack of parking passes." Ruiz began taping Horace's hands. "You nervous?"

"Some."

"You'll be all right. Just don't get wrapped up in a brawl with him and it'll be a good fight."

"I won't."

"Did you eat?"

"A couple hours ago."

"Good," Ruiz said. "You're a tough kid. Raymundo Figueroa is gonna get his head handed to him a few times."

"You really think so?" Horace said.

"Sure," Ruiz replied. "He'll find out."

When he walked into the auditorium it was nearly full. People were coming and going from their seats and music boomed from the loudspeakers. He entered the ring and no one seemed to notice or care. Minutes later, Raymundo Figueroa entered wearing a glittery black robe with silver trim. People cheered and yelled things in Spanish. His hair was short and black, he was dark skinned and handsome, and he wore black and silver trunks. He kneeled in the corner of the ring, crossed himself, and prayed. Ruiz put in Horace's mouth guard, and Horace began bouncing around.

"Calm down," Ruiz yelled from the corner. "Hector, you gotta calm down."

But Horace couldn't calm down. His heart raced with more adrenaline than he could ever remember having. And then Raymundo Figueroa's cornerman put in his mouth guard, the referee called the boxers together, their names were announced, and the fight began.

Within the first minute Horace was against the ropes getting hammered with combinations. Figueroa's punches came with such speed that Horace couldn't see them, he could only feel them. He tried to get away but couldn't, and when he attempted to counter he'd miss and Figueroa would nail him in the opening. The round went by in a flash. It was too much. But what became clear as Horace sat on the stool was that Raymundo Figueroa's punches didn't hurt, he didn't have power.

The second round came and again Figueroa pressured. He hit Horace with a half dozen clean body shots and then connected four hard shots to Horace's face, reinjuring his right eye. But Horace continued to move and tried to counter. And then finally, with thirty seconds left in the round, he got off two combinations that surprisingly shook Figueroa. The whole auditorium erupted.

The bell rang and Horace walked back to his corner, his right eye closing and his ribs again hurting. Raymundo Figueroa's punches didn't bother him one by one, it was just that he threw so many of them, and so quickly. It was already taking its toll. Ruiz stood over him, yelling and putting Vaseline on his face. He gave him water and checked his injured eye, all the while chewing Nicorette gum.

The third round began and again Horace was overwhelmed. Two minutes in he'd only thrown six punches, all of them missing. Figueroa cornered Horace and attacked his head. But Figueroa was growing sloppy and overconfident, and Horace caught him with a kidney shot that was as hard a punch as he'd ever thrown. Figueroa stumbled back and Horace pressured and landed two more in the same area, and with those he could feel Figueroa starting to slow, he could feel Figueroa becoming wary of him.

In the fourth, Figueroa caught him with a hard shot to his bad eye. Horace took the punch and countered with a body shot that nearly dropped Figueroa. In the fifth he took nothing but punishment and Figueroa's punches began to hurt. In the sixth Figueroa cornered Horace and unloaded a barrage of combinations, but Horace didn't freeze, he just got himself out of trouble and waited, and then got Figueroa with two hard body shots, and Figueroa barely survived the round. In the seventh he took nothing but shot after shot and he couldn't find an opening anywhere. Even Ruiz thought of ending the fight. Horace's right eye was nearly shut, and the referee said if he didn't start throwing punches he'd call the bout.

Ruiz screamed at him when he sat down before the eighth. "You're gonna lose this fight if you don't knock him out! Goddamn it, Hector, you can do this!"

The eighth began and he took more shots, always looking to counter. Figueroa hit him continuously and always he went after Horace's damaged right eye. Horace felt his nose break again and then he felt something go wrong inside his hurt eye, but still he waited and countered and finally caught Figueroa with a shot to the head that was so hard Figueroa suddenly crumbled to the ground. With ten seconds left in the fight Figueroa stood up, wobbly and unsteady. He was dead on his feet. Horace pressured him, and Figueroa covered and retreated. But it was too late. The fight ended.

When the old white referee came to the middle of the ring, Horace could barely see. His right eye was nothing but blurs and streaks of light, and his left eye wouldn't focus. The two fighters stood on each side of the referee and the winner was announced. Raymundo Figueroa by unanimous decision.

Horace was led to his dressing room and examined by the ring doctor, who called for an ambulance. Ruiz chewed Nicorette gum and sweat poured down his face. Diego came into the room and spoke briefly to Horace and then took Ruiz aside and they split the money. Ruiz took Horace's cut and put the twenty-five hundred dollars into Horace's duffel. Diego left and then Ruiz assisted a near-blind Horace into the shower. He helped him dry off and dress, and they walked out a side door to the waiting ambulance.

"You're as tough as any fighter I've ever seen. I'll meet you at the hospital," said Ruiz. "I have to get my car but I'll be right behind you."

Horace lay on his back and the ambulance rushed down the highway to Tucson. He was now completely blind, his head wrapped in bandages across his eyes. His whole body began to hurt, the pain in his ribs flared with every bump and shake of the road, his shattered nose bled down his lips, his right hand seized in pain, and he had a growing worry that he had lost his vision forever.

In the hospital there were long moments of waiting and then the rush of a doctor and then more waiting. When Horace woke in the morning he was in a room by himself. He was told he had a broken nose, a fractured cheekbone, three fractured ribs, a fractured right hand, and a detached retina in his right eye. He was scheduled for surgery that afternoon. The day passed and Ruiz came, visited for an hour, and then left.

Horace came out of surgery to find they'd been unable to re-attach the retina properly. It was too damaged, and most likely he would lose at least some sight in his right eye. He was told by the doctor that he wouldn't be able to fight again because of it. After that he collapsed into sleep. It was late in the night when he woke. He lay by himself and cried for a long time before a nurse came into the room.

"Will the tears make my eye worse?" he whispered to her. There was a thick patch over his damaged eye and tears streamed down from his good one.

"No," she said. "Don't worry about that, Hector. Do you need anything?

"No," he said.

"How would you rate your pain on a scale of one to ten, ten being the worst?"

"I don't know," he said.

"So not much pain?"

He shook his head slowly. "I have to admit something."

"What's that, Hector?" she asked.

"It's hard to admit."

"What is it?" she asked.

"I'm a liar," he whispered. He looked at her. "I'm not Hector Hidalgo. I'm not even Mexican. My real name is Horace Hopper."

Ruiz visited the next day and stayed watching TV and talking. He wore dirty sweats and looked haggard and hungover.

"I almost stopped the fight three times," Ruiz said as he rubbed two-day stubble on his chin. "Now I know I should have."

"I wanted to keep going," Horace whispered.

"Of course you wanted to keep going. But I should have known better. I just thought you had him, and you almost did have him. Another minute and you'd have flattened that son of a bitch."

"Maybe."

"It was a great feeling to be back in that situation. In a real battle between two warriors. I haven't been to a fight like that in a long time. I bet you Figueroa won't be able to get out of bed today. I bet he'll be pissing blood for a week." Ruiz laughed and kept his eyes on the TV. "Remember, Hector, you'll heal. In no time at all we'll be back at it. Healing and patience, that's all it takes. You know I used to be so goddamn impatient about healing that I always fought hurt. I remember this one time I had a fight in Tulsa, Oklahoma. I was driving by myself and had my car in the parking lot. But I got so beat up during the fight that the doctor had someone take me to the hospital. I'd fractured my wrist, busted my nose and cheek. But worst of all I couldn't see straight. I got throttled about two dozen times in the melon, and this guy, a black spick from Detroit, hit like a bulldozer. He won that night, but he didn't put me down. Not even close. I was at the hospital all night waiting to get patched up, and then finally I did and afterward I got a ride back to my car. It was five in the morning. I had a cast on one hand, my whole face was swollen, and I was getting these dizzy spells. I got the car started and I was about halfway through downtown when I realized I couldn't see anything. Everything was hazy. So I pulled over and parked and fell asleep. I woke up a few hours later and got out of the car and found a restaurant. My head was pounding like someone was whacking it with a sledgehammer. I hurt all over. My ribs were about what yours are probably. Like someone's squeezing you with barbed wire every time you move. I went in and ate and everyone there stopped and looked at me 'cause of two strange things: I'm Mexican and I'm all beat to hell." He laughed and put a piece of Nicorette gum in his mouth. "But luck was with me. I sat at the counter next to these two homeless-looking hippies. Each one of them had a suitcase and one had a guitar. They were trying to get to California and I told them I'd get them as far at Tucson if they drove. They agreed, and so I sat in the back and drank beer and popped painkillers. My head felt like it was in a vise for days and my eyes were seeing tracers and bolts of light all through Texas and New Mexico, but they drove good, and the one guy could play pretty decent guitar."

Ruiz continued to ramble, and Horace fell in and out of sleep, half listening. The next day came and Ruiz picked him up in the minivan. Horace had a bandage and patch over his right eye, a swollen and discolored nose, black eyes, wrapped ribs, and a cast on his right hand. They drove through town in silence, and Horace realized that Ruiz had been up all night and was still drunk.

"Stop by when you get healed up," Ruiz said when he'd parked outside Horace's aunt's house.

"They say my eye will never get better," Horace admitted. "That I won't be able to fight again."

"You can't believe any of their horseshit," Ruiz said, and coughed, then drank from a bottle of Coke. "They always told me that, but I kept going."

Horace nodded and got out.

Ruiz smiled. "Call me after you get rested up."

Horace nodded again and shut the car door. He carried his gym bag over his shoulder and made his way to the guesthouse.

He never saw Ruiz again.

22

Three semitrucks came in the early morning and loaded 1,210 ewes in three stock trailers. The sheep, nervous and worried, bleated in a constant chorus, and the dogs barked and paced outside the holding pen. Whitey and Jip, the Anatolians, stayed locked in a horse stall in the barn, unseen but barking continuously, and Mrs. Reese stood on the porch watching, tears streaming down her face.

Over twelve hundred sheep soon loaded and gone.

Ely and Little Lana sat at Mrs. Reese's feet watching obsessively as Tiny, Wally, and Little Roy went back and forth around Mr. Reese. It was past ten a.m. when they finished and Mr. Reese was handed the paperwork. He shook the men's hands and watched as the three trucks drove off, leaving a trail of dust a quarter mile long behind them.

Mrs. Reese came down from the porch and met him in the drive and held his hand.

"It's a hard feeling," he said quietly.

"It is," she said.

"I don't know what to do now."

"You'll figure it out."

He took off his cowboy hat and ran his hands through his hair. "I was thinking maybe we should go into town. Maybe eat

Mexican and have a beer or two. Maybe a margarita. I have a feeling I'll be nothing but glum if we don't get out of here for a bit. Try and make a celebration out of this."

"I can make burritos here if you'd like," she said.

He nodded slowly and looked at her. "Let's go somewhere, even if we just dip our feet in Pine Creek. Let's just get out of here."

She squeezed his hand. "Why don't you just go? I'll make your favorite dinner tonight, chicken piccata and roasted potatoes. I'll even make ice cream."

He nodded again. "I'm not going to argue with you and I won't force you, but you're sure? Just for an hour or two."

She nodded.

"Well, all right."

She squeezed his hand, waited a moment, and then said, "Where are you gonna go?"

"I'm not sure yet."

"I'll make you a lunch."

He nodded, and Mrs. Reese, Little Lana, and Ely disappeared back into the house.

The old man went across the drive into the barn, and Wally, Tiny, and Little Roy followed behind. He filled the water trough, threw each of the horses and donkeys a flake, checked on Whitey and Jip, and then walked back to the porch to see Mrs. Reese with a paper sack lunch and a small cooler.

"You know what sounds good to me for dinner?"

"What's that?" he said as he climbed the steps.

"Brook trout."

He smiled. "You figured out something for me to do."

She nodded and winked. "I don't want you to come home unless you get enough."

He took the sack and a small six-pack cooler, and kissed her goodbye. He set the cooler in the cab, the lunch in the toolbox in the bed of the truck, and grabbed his fishing gear from the barn, and for the first time since they were pups, Wally, Tiny, and Little Roy were let in the cab: three dogs as passengers. Mr. Reese got in after them, started the truck, and left.

As he rode down the drive he turned on the radio and Buck Owens came through the old speakers.

"At least they're playing a good song," he said as he leaned over and opened the cooler on the floor next to him and found a beer. He opened it, took a long drink, and sighed.

Pine Creek campground was empty and Mr. Reese parked at the edge of it. He and the three dogs walked for nearly a mile into the mountains along the strong-flowing creek. They came to a deep pool surrounded by boulders on one side and aspen trees on the other. It was a place that he and his father had fished, he and his daughters, and most recently he and Horace. The dogs stood next to him impatiently, always looking at him for instructions. As he tried to tie a hook to his fishing line, they bumped into his legs and walked around his feet.

Mr. Reese looked down at them and laughed.

"I'm sorry," he said and finished tying the hook. He leaned the fishing pole against a tree, and picked up his lunch and cooler and found a small patch of meadow grass and slowly and painfully sat down.

"Well, things are changing," he said to the dogs as they stood in front of him. "First off, we're just friends now. What that means is you'll be spending your nights in the house. Mrs. Reese will throw a fit at first, but you guys deserve it. In the summer we'll put you on the screened back porch, but in the winter you'll be inside next to the woodstove. You've all earned that. You'll also get to ride in the cab if you want from here on out. The downside is you don't get to work anymore. That's gonna be hard on all of us. It will take adjusting for both you guys and me." He called for Wally, and the dog moved right next to him and Mr. Reese began to pet him. "Also, we're gonna be more affectionate from here on out. No more business. We're retired. So it's all fun and easy times now. Wally and Tiny, you're only a couple years away anyway, but, Little Roy, you'll have to figure out how to be retired as a kid. I hope you're able. I'll try and keep us as busy as I can, but I won't be able to promise anything and I'm sorry about that." He then called for Little Roy and hugged and petted him and soon all three were in his arms.

Mr. Reese took another beer from the cooler and opened it. He took a drink and then found a stick and threw it in the creek's pool. Little Roy went after it first and jumped in. He was followed by Wally, and only Tiny stood at the bank, unwilling to get wet. She barked and paced back and forth. Wally brought the stick to Mr. Reese and he threw it again and laughed as they all chased it, this time Tiny running too fast and unable to stop in time. She slid on the dirt until she fell off the bank into the cool water.

23

Inside his house, Horace closed the blinds, turned on the AC unit, and slept. When he woke it was afternoon and he called Benny and told him what had happened and that he couldn't work. Benny said he would get someone to cover his shifts until he was better, but Horace told him he was quitting, that he was leaving town and not coming back. Benny didn't say anything after that, he just hung up the phone. Horace tried to call him again and explain but Benny wouldn't answer.

He didn't leave the house for three days, but then his food ran low. It was evening and nearly dark when he walked to Food City and bought canned soup, milk, Coke, bread, and cheese. He spent four more days in front of the TV eating grilled cheese sandwiches and soup. Mr. Reese called twice but Horace didn't answer either time. His aunt knocked on the door once but he turned the TV off and acted like he wasn't there.

On the eighth day he felt good enough that he packed what he wanted into his duffel and got rid of the rest. He busted his Spanish CDs and threw away his Spanish dictionary and phrase book. He cleaned the bathroom and kitchen and put things back the way he remembered them. With a broken hand he wrote a barely legible note to his aunt.

Aunt Briana

Thanks for letting me stay here. I know I have two months prepaid on rent but I'm leaving. You can keep the money. I know we didn't get to know each other very good, but maybe someday we will. I've left twenty dollars on the counter. I broke a mug that said "San Diego" on it. I looked for a replacement in some thrift stores but couldn't find one. Maybe you could find one online. Also I used three bars of Ivory soap but I couldn't find that brand so I replaced it with Dove. I hope that's okay.

I apologize if I've left anything the way you don't like it.

Horace

The next morning, after she left for work, he slipped the key and note through his aunt's mail slot. He walked slowly, his ribs stinging with each step, toward downtown, where he caught a bus to Las Vegas. He decided even though he had failed as a boxer and was a nobody, he would go back to the Reeses' and live his life on the ranch.

It was evening and cool when he arrived, the lights from the casinos brightening the black sky. The small bus line that went to Tonopah was down the street from the Greyhound station, and he found there was a bus leaving the next morning. He was stuck the whole night there. He carried his duffel and walked aimlessly for hours under the canopy of Fremont Street in Old Town Las Vegas. Hundreds of people walked by, and always the lights of the casinos shone down. A half dozen times he nearly called Mr. Reese to let him know he was coming back, but somehow he couldn't dial the number. The evening wore on and he grew tired and the pain in his ribs sharpened so he got a room for forty dollars at the Golden Gate Hotel.

That first night he was so exhausted and hurt that he didn't even turn on the TV. He just slept on the queen-size bed straight through until dawn. When he got up he dressed and walked to the bus station. But no matter how hard he tried to convince himself to, he couldn't buy the ticket to Tonopah. Outside the small station he paced back and forth and back and forth, but he couldn't go inside.

The bus came and left and he spent the day walking in and out of casinos. He paid for another night at the same hotel, ate at a Chinese buffet, and watched TV in his room. The next morning he again went to the station. This time he bought a ticket to Tonopah, but when the bus arrived he just stayed on a metal bench seat, his feet tapping up and down nervously. He watched as five people boarded, the driver closed the door, and the bus left the station.

As it disappeared down the street Horace's heart sank. He knew then that he could never go back to the ranch. He had been kidding himself to think he could. Because if he did he would live the rest of his life in embarrassment. Every time he saw Mr. Reese, the old man would see him for what he was: a fool. The Reeses knew too much about him and that was the problem. He had been foolish enough to think he could be Mexican and foolish enough to think he could be a championship boxer. Why had he done any of it? He would have to start new and start alone. The next morning Mr. Reese called but Horace didn't answer even though he was in bed, awake, watching TV. He stayed in his room at the Golden Gate for three more days, only leaving to get food and pay his daily room bill. He slept sporadically, and always the TV was left on.

The morning of the fourth day he woke to another call from

Mr. Reese. In the darkness of the room he watched the phone ring, but he didn't answer it, and when it finally stopped he turned off the phone. He watched TV for hours and then grew restless enough that he left to look around. But like it was when he first arrived in Tucson, he became overwhelmed by the number of people in Las Vegas. All the casinos and buildings and tourists. And knowing his mother was there in a suburb of North Las Vegas with her husband and their kid made it even worse. He didn't want to see her exactly, but no matter how hard he tried not to, he looked for her in every car that passed. If he saw her, then what? She wouldn't want him back at her house even though she would invite him. If he did stay there, when her husband came home and they'd be in bed together late at night they would worry about how long Horace would stay and what his real motivation was. They would lie in the dark whispering about him. They'd talk for hours about how to get him out of their lives and then in the morning they'd smile at him and act like everything was normal while they all ate breakfast. He almost threw up thinking about it. Las Vegas was the last place he wanted to be, but somehow he couldn't leave.

A week passed where he did nothing but walk in and out of casinos. He spoke to no one but waitresses and clerks at the stores he went to. One afternoon in an alley behind a casino he broke down crying in loneliness. He sat in front of a dented roll-up door and sobbed, and in that moment of desperation he again decided he would try to go back to Tonopah. Embarrassment and shame had to be easier than being alone in a city every day.

The next afternoon he took a cab to Boot Barn and bought new work clothes. Three plaid long-sleeve western shirts and two pairs of Wranglers. He went back to his room, packed, and waited out the night watching TV. But when morning came and he looked at himself in his hotel room mirror, dressed in his new creased clothes with the patch over his eye and the cast on his hand, the certainty of the previous day vanished. This time he couldn't even leave his room for the station.

All the days of idleness had caused him to spend his money too quickly. He paid daily for his room, ate out each meal, and rented movies every night on TV. He knew if he stayed in Las Vegas he would have to get an apartment and a job. So he woke up the next morning and began searching. He looked for three days and then came to a dreary single-story studio apartment complex a mile from Old Town. It was a poorly built ranch-style building from the 1950s. There was no yard or shrubs of any kind. The siding was yellow vinyl, and each unit had a front window and a white door. On one of the doors was taped a For Rent sign. Horace called the number on it and soon a middle-aged man emerged from an end unit. He was red faced with blue veins on his nose and he wore a Hawaiian shirt, white shorts, and flip-flops. He showed Horace the open unit, a single room with a bed, a couch, a dresser, and a kitchenette.

"As you can see, it comes furnished," the man said. He turned on the faucet in the kitchen to show it worked. In the bathroom he flushed the toilet and turned on the water in the stained plastic shower stall.

"How much a month is it?" asked Horace.

"Six hundred dollars. First and last and a six-hundred-dollar security deposit. Eighteen hundred to move in."

Horace looked at the run-down room, and not knowing what else to do said he would take it. He filled out the paperwork and then walked to the bank and got a money order for the eighteen hundred dollars. When he received the key he walked back to

his hotel and that last night there he tried to make a plan for his
future, but no matter how hard he thought about it his life made
no sense in Las Vegas.

He woke up at dawn the next morning and packed his duffel
and left the Golden Gate Hotel by eight o'clock. He walked outside to an alley, where a series of Dumpsters were lined in a row.
He set his phone on the asphalt, jumped on it, and destroyed it.
Tears welled in his eyes as he took his hand exerciser, the au-
tographed photo of Érik Morales, a jump rope, running shoes,
sweats, boxing shoes, the shirts he didn't like, and the red and
gold boxing trunks Mrs. Poulet had made him, and threw them
all in the trash.

24

Mr. Reese pulled into the Banc Club casino. It was winter and there were traces of snow on the ground and the sun hadn't yet come over the mountains. He walked through the parking lot dressed in long underwear, jeans, a thick flannel shirt, a canvas coat, his felt gray cowboy hat, and new running shoes. His glasses fogged from the cold as he walked into the casino.

Seated in a booth in the corner, Ander Zubiri filled out a keno ticket. A half-empty glass of red wine sat before him.

"How long you been here?"

"Not long," Ander replied, still looking at the ticket. "I ordered for us when I saw you drive up."

"What if I change my mind one of these days?"

"You always order the same thing no matter how hard you try not to."

Mr. Reese laughed, took off his hat and coat, and sat across from him. "I hate when it gets this cold."

Ander nodded. He had a brown felt cowboy hat leaned back on his head, and wore a light-blue western shirt with faded wine stains on it. The left pocket was missing its snap and a pack of cigarettes sat in it. He looked at Mr. Reese. "When did you get the fancy shoes?"

"A while ago. I've been getting massages and the gal there

thought a bit of my problem might be my boots. So I got the kind of running shoes Horace wears and now I feel better."

"Your back pain is gone?"

"No," he said. "But it's better."

A heavyset, blond, middle-aged waitress came from the kitchen with a pot of coffee and poured a cup for Mr. Reese.

Ander looked up from his keno ticket. "So are you going to start going on vacations now?"

"Vacations?"

"Now that you've sold the sheep. Now that you're free and you have money and time. For most people that would mean a vacation."

Mr. Reese shook his head. "What about Louise?"

"What about her?" Ander said and took a drink of wine.

"She won't even go to the store let alone visit Cassie or Lynn. How am I going to get her to go on vacation?"

"You go and I'll move in with her."

Mr. Reese laughed and shook his head.

"You know, I heard something."

"What's that?"

"Your man Pedro hired on with an outfit out of Wyoming. The Sunny B Livestock Company. He's going out with a flock in a couple months."

"He didn't go home?" Mr. Reese said.

Ander shook his head. "It's strange what I heard. Supposedly he hasn't been home in thirty years. I was talking with a guy who knows him, and he said all those times Pedro told you he was going back to his wife and kids he was staying in Winnemucca and waiting it out in a camping trailer."

"In Winnemucca?"

"That's what I heard."

"Does he even have a wife and kids?"

Ander shrugged his shoulders.

"Why would he go back to the mountains when it causes him so much pain?"

"Who knows," said Ander.

Mr. Reese took a drink of coffee and looked down at the table.

"Some guys just can't do anything else," said Ander. "And some guys you just can't help. Anyway, what have you been doing with your free time?"

"I rebuilt the log splitter. I also rebuilt my Weed eater and tuned up the chain saw. Been working on the baler now. I still got most of the dogs and the horses. Someone dumped a donkey out near the Barley Creek Ranch. Lonnie Dixon found her, called me, and I went and picked her up. So now we have another donkey."

"I've never liked donkeys," Ander said. "The little bastards never shut up and they never die."

Mr. Reese laughed.

"I'm going down to Palm Desert to play golf next month. You should come. I've made friends with some people there."

"I don't know how to play golf."

"You just take a couple lessons. It's not hard to be bad at it. Louise is used to you being gone. Why not come down and see how other people live? You can't spend your life rebuilding all the broke-down shit you have."

"The problem is I almost already have. Once the parts for the generator come in I'll have that running again, too."

Ander laughed and finished his wine. "You know my daughter's been planning a trip to San Sebastián. We're going in the spring. You should come with us."

Mr. Reese sighed and shook his head. "I'd feel too guilty leaving Louise. Plus, I have three horses, three donkeys, and five dogs to take care of."

"Five?"

"I sold Whitey and Jip to a ranch in Idaho."

Ander nodded. "So what are you going to do?"

Mr. Reese shrugged his shoulders.

The blond waitress brought out two plates of steak, eggs, potatoes, and toast. She came back with the pot of coffee and a glass of red wine.

"The point of not working is having fun," said Ander.

Mr. Reese nodded.

"But you don't know how to have fun 'cause you ain't ever been able to go anywhere. And even now with all those bleating sons of bitches out of your hair you still have no freedom."

Mr. Reese again nodded and cut into his steak.

"This is an interesting case," said Ander and smiled. They ate in silence while Ander followed his keno numbers on the screen behind Mr. Reese. There was no one else in the restaurant. The waitress came out once more with the coffeepot and then sat on a stool and read a magazine.

Ander pushed his empty plate to the side of the table. "You know Eddie Morton still has fifty head. I bet he'd give you a deal. If I remember right, you got Eddie out of that jam when he had a falling-out with Rollins. And then there was that time you took your tractor all the way up Keystone Canyon to pull his rig out after he got drunk and rolled it. I'd personally shoot him if he didn't cut you a deal. He says he's gonna buy another place out here but won't. The cows are just sitting while he tries to make up his mind. And cows are less of a headache in some ways. I'll give you my four-wheeler. You could get by with one part-time man."

Mr. Reese set down his knife and fork. "You drive me crazy. You mail me brochures on cruises and fishing trips and you want me to go to Spain." He reached over and took the pack of cigarettes from Ander's shirt pocket. He took a cigarette and lit it with a plastic lighter on the table. "You want me to take up golf and sell my place. And then you want to give me your four-wheeler and run cattle even though you hate cattle as much as sheep. . . . You're crazy."

"Maybe," said Ander and smiled. "I'm just throwing things out there. I know you, one of the things I say will stick. Until then come down to Palm Desert and play golf with me. No women, just a couple drunk ex-ranchers. They have good food there. It's warm. There's palm trees and hot tubs. You ever been in a hot tub?"

Mr. Reese shook his head and slowly smoked the cigarette.

"We're going to die soon, Reese. Why live your last days out on two thousand acres of sagebrush when you can sit in a hot tub?" Ander looked to the keno screen as his numbers came up. He took a drink and smiled. "I just hit all four of my numbers."

"You would," said Mr. Reese.

Ander took a drink of wine and lit a cigarette. "You heard from your wayward son?"

Mr. Reese shook his head. "That's another problem that I can't understand and I don't know what to do about. Horace has disappeared. From what I've pieced together he had a boxing match at a casino north of Tucson. He didn't tell me about it, never mentioned it when I spoke with him. Only later when I looked online did I see that it had taken place. Turns out he got hurt. Broke his hand, hurt his eye, and went to the hospital. After that he got a ride from his trainer, Alberto Ruiz, who took him back to his house in Tucson. He was too hurt to work so he called his boss and quit his job. His boss hasn't seen him since, and neither has Ruiz. Maybe a week after that his aunt received a note saying he had moved out. She checked the guesthouse and he was gone even though he had two months left paid on the place. She said the house had no trace of him. There was nothing except in the trash, where she found his pictures of the Mexican boxers. During this whole time he has never once answered his phone. I've called him dozens and dozens of times. For a month his voice mail said 'box full,' but now the phone has been disconnected."

"Disconnected?" Ander said, suddenly worried.

Mr. Reese nodded. "A few weeks ago I drove down to Tucson and looked around. I met his aunt, his boss, and his boxing trainer. No one has seen him. So I went to the police and put a missing persons out on him."

Ander took a drink of wine, and tears suddenly welled in his eyes. "He's always been such a sensitive kid. You have any idea where he might be?"

"No."

"What about his folks?"

"His mom still lives in Las Vegas. Horace hasn't had much contact with her since he was twelve or so. A little bit here and there, during the holidays and things like that, but I don't think he'd confide in her. Horace always told me that he never forgave her for leaving him."

"It was a pretty mean thing to do," said Ander.

Mr. Reese nodded. "When I spoke to her she seemed worried but didn't have much to say about it or give me any ideas. I called his father, who lives in Seattle, but he's never had a relationship with Horace. The father said he sent a check for Horace's birthday but Horace didn't cash it. But then he never cashed those or his dad's Christmas checks."

"What's his dad do again?"

"He's some sorta higher-up at Costco. But he was gone by the time Horace was three. From what I've heard it was a bad breakup between him and Horace's mom and he moved on. Forgot about Horace." Mr. Reese sighed. "I just can't stop thinking about him. He's always been such a lost and confused kid."

"Who wouldn't be?" Ander said.

"What do I do now?"

"I don't know," said Ander softly. He wiped his eyes with a napkin and took a drink of wine. "But he's tough. I bet he's all right." Ander tried to smile. "Mr. Zubiri," the old man said, trying to talk like Horace. "You have to build the bricks that build the boat. And the boat will protect you and bring you to the next level. And each level will take you closer until you're your own champion. Until you're the best. *Building the Champion Inside of You: Believe, Overcome, Aspire, Triumph—B.O.A.T.*"

Mr. Reese smiled. "For a drunk you have a good memory."

"I lived with him for a fucking month in the mountains. All he talked about was that book he found at his grandmother's. I think he must have been sixteen or seventeen."

Mr. Reese nodded.

"How can you build a boat out of bricks? That's what I never understood. But I have to say it sorta inspired me. It's how I decided to finally quit working and have some fun. Being up there with that kid, I started lying awake at night thinking about my future. Thinking about who I wanted to be." Ander laughed and finished his wine. He called to the waitress, and she got up off her stool and went to the bar and got him another glass.

Mr. Reese knocked the ash from his cigarette onto his breakfast plate. "I read it 'cause he asked me to. I guess it says some good things, but it's just a self-published book from some guy in Florida."

Ander laughed. "Horace will be all right. He's a good kid."

Mr. Reese nodded. "I hope so."

"I liked his grandmother. She was mean but she sure was good in the sack. I went over there a half dozen times with a bottle of gin and . . ."

"Jesus, if I have to hear about you and her I'll throw up." Mr. Reese put his hat on. "And since you won, you're buying."

"Where you going?"

"I got things to do."

"Like what?"

Mr. Reese knocked on the table lightly with his knuckles. "Cattle, huh?"

Ander laughed.

"Have fun golfing."

Ander nodded and refocused his eyes on the keno screen, where new numbers were appearing. Mr. Reese put on his coat and left.

He drove to the Super 7 gas station, filled his tank, and then parked in front of the Clubhouse Saloon and walked up the street. He looked in the window of the A Bar L Western Store, but it was closed. He walked to the next block and picked up his mail from the post office. He thumbed through it, finding nothing but catalogs and a single bill. He threw away the tack and livestock catalogs, rolled up Mrs. Reese's catalogs, and put them in his coat pocket.

He walked farther up past Western Auto and crossed the street. He stopped at Nevada State Bank and used the ATM to check the balances in their checking and saving accounts. He continued on. He looked in the window of Whitney's Bookshelf but it, too, was closed. In Wolfe's Hardware he paced up and down the aisles, but there was nothing he could think of to buy.

Outside the sun was breaking and he walked back across the street, got into his truck, and drove to Scolari's grocery store. He got a cart and did the shopping, and then went to the pharmacy and got refills on their medications. He put the groceries in the toolbox in the back of the pickup. It was eight-forty-five in the morning and he had nothing to do.

25

Horace bought a small TV and a sleeping bag from Goodwill but nothing else for his new apartment. He spent his days aimlessly drifting about the city, walking through the maze of casinos. With his arm in a cast, the patch over his eye, and his ribs still hurt, he walked the entire Las Vegas Strip. He went in and out of Circus Circus, Encore Casino, Caesars Palace, Wynn, Treasure Island, the Palazzo, the Venetian, the Flamingo, New York-New York, MGM Grand, The Mirage, Harrah's, O'Sheas, Bally's, Paris Las Vegas, Tuscany Suites, and the Silver Sevens casino. Thousands and thousands of people in the flashy and extravagant buildings. Rivers of people everywhere but none of them he related to, and in that regard he was completely alone.

When he got back to his room each evening he crawled into bed, paralyzed with anxiety and shame. Why did he have to tell Mr. Reese everything? Why couldn't he have just kept to himself that he wanted to be Mexican and wanted to be a world champion boxer? The nights crawled by. Hours seemed like days. He would get lost in thoughts of Mr. and Mrs. Reese, the ranch, and the horses and dogs, and when he did his stomach would give out and he would feel like he was falling. He wanted more than anything to go back to them, to the comfort of them, but always something inside forced him not to.

One evening as he walked toward a casino for dinner he saw
an ad on a telephone pole for day labor. He took the flyer with
him and ate at a casino coffee shop. When the waitress wasn't
looking he stole a steak knife and put it in his coat pocket. Back
at his apartment, even though his hand was still too weak and
not fully healed, he cut the cast off his arm with the knife. In
the bathroom he took the patch and bandage off his eye to find
he could see only streaks of light. His eye looked normal, but
the doctor had been right, his vision was ruined.

The next morning Horace got up at five and walked two
miles in the desert cold to the state day labor office, a small,
nondescript, cream-colored building near the highway. Dozens
of men and a handful of women stood in a plain, square room
and took numbers from a machine in the corner. When Horace's number came up he was helped by a short Mexican lady
behind a counter. She found him a weeklong job doing cleanup
on a construction site in North Las Vegas. She handed him a
slip of paper to give to the site boss, and told him he could get
a ride with a man named Felix, who stood in the corner of the
room holding an unlit cigarette.

Felix, a thin, bald black man, had a rusted-out white Econo-
line van with Michigan plates. He drove Horace and two Mexican men to the site, where they met the boss. The boss took the
Mexicans to a corner of the building and had them sweep the
concrete floor. Felix and Horace were told to clean up the scraps
and debris that littered the job site. They moved broken and
discarded cinder blocks, scraps of wood and metal, and pieces
of Sheetrock to an industrial-size Dumpster.

Throughout the day Felix worked lethargically and spent
long breaks in a Sani-Hut. When he thought Horace was working too hard he'd say, "Slow down, motherfucker" or "Relax."
"The point of these jobs," he said finally, "is to go just enough
to get paid and not a bit harder. If you work hard then I'll have

to work hard and there ain't no point to that. These assholes make twice as much as we do. Let them bust their asses and kill themselves for the dough, we're sure as hell not gonna."

Horace forced himself to slow down even though he hated to and it made the day grind by even slower. At quitting time, the supervisor gave each of the men a sixty-five-dollar check, and Felix drove them to a liquor store that would cash them. Felix bought a twelve-pack of beer and pint of gin, and Horace bought a liter of Coke, and they went their separate ways. The next morning Felix picked up Horace and two different men at the labor office and drove them to the same site. They worked like that for three days, until Friday, when Felix didn't show up and Horace had to walk the three miles to the job site on his own.

On the weekend, Horace barely left his bed. He watched TV and ordered a pizza from Domino's on both Saturday and Sunday. There were moments when he'd almost run out the door to get a bus ticket home, but he never did. He just lay on the bed, watching TV, his mind racing and falling apart. He was stuck.

On Monday, he got a swing-shift job with two men at a warehouse in South Las Vegas. One of the men, Stew, had a car, a mid-eighties, yellow Chevy Cavalier, and drove them. The car had been hit from behind and the trunk was dented and bent. The signal cases were broken and covered in red plastic and held on with duct tape. Stew was white and middle aged with a small, flat nose and eyes that were set too far apart. He had a smoker's skin and a mustache yellowed from tobacco. Each day he wore faded black pants, a denim coat, and a green Fitzgeralds Casino baseball cap. The other man, Gene, was lanky and hollow faced with rotten teeth and greased-back black hair. Each day he wore stained work overalls and a shiny gold coat that read "Gold Dust West" in black ink. They worked together five days straight. The last shift of the week ended at ten o'clock, Friday night. As he did each evening Stew drove them to the same liquor store Felix had to cash their checks.

"So what are you doing now, Horace?" Stew asked as they got out of the car.

"I'm not sure," replied Horace. His black hair had begun to grow out and his face looked gaunt. He was having a harder and harder time sleeping and he had begun to lose weight. He figured he slept three hours a night, most in twenty-minute fits and starts. And food seemed to mean less and less to him as the days passed. Where he used to crave lunch and eat early, he would now forget to eat at all.

"It's Friday night," Stew said and smiled.

Horace just nodded.

"We're having a little party at my place. Why don't you use some of that check and get a bottle and then you can come over, too."

Horace looked at them. He didn't like either of the men, they didn't work hard and Stew had stolen a shovel and a pair of gloves, and like Felix they both spent long periods of time in the bathroom when they were supposed to be working. But the idea of going back to his apartment alone seemed worse than spending time with them. "All right," he said weakly.

Stew clapped his hands together and smiled. "Well, okay! You get a fifth of Old Crow and a twelve-pack of Keystone and you're in."

Horace nodded and they went inside. He cashed his check and bought the whiskey and beer. Stew cashed his and bought a twelve-pack and cigarettes. Gene bought three packages of Skittles and another twelve-pack.

They drove to the El Cortez Casino and parked in the lot. Stew seemed to be waiting for someone. He left the engine running and Gene got in the backseat with Horace. They all began drinking beer. After twenty minutes a Native American woman with long black hair came from the casino and got in the passenger seat. She wore fake fur–lined boots, blue sweatpants, and a black and orange Giants baseball jacket.

"How long did you think we were going to wait?" said Stew.

"I got out here as soon as you texted me," she said.

"My ass you did," Stew said.

"I did," the woman moaned.

"And you're already shit-faced."

"I am not."

"I can tell." Stew coughed, looked in the rearview, and lit a cigarette. "Horace, this here is War Hoop."

The woman sighed as he said it, he laughed, and they left. He drove them two miles and parked in front of a single-story 1960s tract house. There were two Cavaliers parked in the carport. Both were on blocks with no tires. The house itself was dark, and only a single streetlamp gave off any light.

A plastic flashlight sat on a cardboard box near the front door. Stew turned it on, took the house key from his pocket, opened the door, and they walked into a dark living room. He went to a lamp and turned it on. There were two couches facing an old TV. There were stacks of cardboard boxes in the corner and a table covered with empty beer cans and two ashtrays full of cigarette butts. Stew turned on an electric space heater and stood near it. The window behind him had a broken pane, and a series of orange extension cords ran through it leading outside.

"Horace, what you're looking at is my breaker box. The next-door neighbor goes out of town for months at a time. I keep an eye on his house for him and make sure nothing funny goes on. In return he gives me free electric." He pulled Horace's twelve-pack from the bag, took three beers from it and handed one to the woman, one to Gene, and one to Horace. He then grabbed one for himself and opened it. The woman went to the kitchen. She took a large pot, filled it three-quarters full of water, and set it on a hot plate that ran off another extension cord. They drank two more beers each while the woman made macaroni and cheese. They ate on paper plates with plastic forks and huddled around the glow of the box heater. When they'd finished, they threw the plates in a large black sack in the middle of the room.

"Now listen," Stew announced as he grabbed the fifth of Old Crow. "This here is for Horace, Gene, and me. War Hoop is to keep her goddamn mitts off it."

"I don't want that shit anyway," the woman said as she tried to open a pack of cigarettes. Her fingers couldn't manage the plastic wrapper, and she dropped it on the floor and nearly fell trying to pick it up.

"Watch out for her, Horace." Stew grinned. "You can't leave a goddamn drop in this house without her slugging it down. You Indians can sure put it away."

The woman opened the cigarettes. She put one in her mouth and lit it. "I hate when you get drunk," she said.

"I'm not drunk," said Stew.

"You only call me War Hoop when you're drunk and mean and trying to brag in front of new people."

Stew took the pack of cigarettes from her, lit one, and shook his head. "If you'd listen to me for a change, you'd see I was trying to help you. Is that so goddamn hard for you to understand? You'll be in bed for three days crying like a little girl if you start messing with this bottle."

"I know."

"Remember what happened last week?"

"Okay!" she yelled and looked at him. "I already said I won't touch it, so leave me alone."

Stew let out a short laugh and opened the bottle. "You want any, Horace?"

"I'll have a little, I guess," he replied.

"That's the spirit," Stew said and went to the kitchen. He came back with three small glasses and poured himself, Gene, and Horace a drink.

"To Friday night," he said, and they drank their shots. He poured them another and cleared his throat. "You know, Horace, I was a baker for thirteen years. Now I'm out of work or taking these bullshit day labor jobs. All because of the government and the way things are. I'm telling you there ain't no real jobs for real Americans anymore. And I'm afraid there ain't ever gonna be again."

"That's a laugh," the woman said. "You hate working. You always tell me how working's for fatheads and morons."

"I wish for once you'd shut your hole," Stew yelled at her. "Goddamn it. How many times do I have to ask you?" He picked up the glass and looked at Gene and Horace. "Let's forget about her and drink to being out of that warehouse."

The three men clinked their glasses together and drank the whiskey. Stew poured each of them another drink. He took a drag off his cigarette and sighed. "Before I was a baker I ran a roofing crew. This was back when I was married and living in Bullhead City. Roofing in a town like that is hard work. It's hot as a Mexican tamale down there by seven a.m. Imagine being on a roof all day in that sorta heat."

Stew stared at Horace as he spoke, but Horace was already drunk and his mind drifted. He tried to remember where they were but he couldn't. He hadn't paid attention. Stew handed him another beer, but the whiskey and beer mixed with the macaroni and cheese felt wrong in his stomach. And even in the cold, the room smelled like piss and rotten food.

The woman opened a bag of Skittles and hummed a tune while putting them in her mouth.

Stew looked at her but continued talking. "I made a lot of money on roofs over the years. Had three trucks and two full crews. Running a crew of roofers is like being a warden in prison. You gotta be twice as tough as any of them. And you have to ride them just to get a decent day's work out of them. You ride them hard but not too hard or they quit. You have to get that balance right."

The woman laughed.

Stew turned to her. "What are you laughing at, you fat-ass War Hoop?" He took an empty beer can and threw it at her. "Can't three grown men have a conversation without you ruining it?" He shook his head and took a drink of beer. He stared at the glass of whiskey for nearly a minute, drank it down, and then looked at Gene. "Tomorrow we'll put in the radiator. I think those hoses will hold and then we'll swap out the alternator. We'll put her back together and damn it if we don't have a car to sell. I bet we could make three or four hundred off her at least. And you're sure you still have the title?"

"It's in my suitcase," said Gene.

Stew nodded and leaned his head back, looked at the ceiling, and rubbed his chin. He blew out a plume of smoke and refilled his glass. "Boys, let's drink to the car. Tomorrow we'll get it running and by next week we'll have it sold." The three clinked their glasses together and drank while the woman reached into the twelve-pack, took another beer, and opened it.

"That car will never start," she mumbled.

Stew stared at her for a long time after that, his eyes flat and cold, and then he got up from the couch and went to a back room and came out with a pint glass and a half gallon of VO whiskey. "How about another round?" he said and poured Gene, Horace, and himself a drink from the Old Crow bottle. He then filled the pint glass three-quarters full with VO.

"War Hoop," he said to the woman. "Do your duty."

"Why should I?" she cried and looked at the glass.

"Because I'm telling you to. You think you're so goddamn

smart. Well, we'll see how smart you really are. Watch this, Horace. She can drink the whole thing in one swallow. Like apple juice."

"I'm not going to do it," she said, her voice suddenly weak. It became a little girl's voice. "I've had too many already."

"Then leave."

"Leave?"

"Yes."

"Where am I going to go?"

"I don't give two shits," Stew said.

"Why do you have to be so mean when you're drunk?" she said, nearly crying.

"Down the glass or I'm cutting you off. I'll take the beer from you. I'll take the pint of Jägermeister you have in your purse. I'll throw you out in the street like a shot dog."

Horace looked at the floor in front of him. He thought he might be sick.

"Drink it down," Stew yelled, and then he began making Indian sounds. He moved his hand over his mouth. "Woo, woo, woo, woo . . ."

"Stop it!" the woman cried. "Please stop it. Please. I'm begging. Is that what you want?"

Stew laughed.

"Why do you have to be so mean?"

Stew stood up and danced like an Indian off a TV western and again moved his hand over his mouth. "Woo, woo, woo, woo, woo, woo, woo, woo . . ."

Gene took a drink from his glass and stared sadly at the box heater. He said nothing.

The woman looked at Stew, flipped him off, took the pint glass of VO from the table, and drank all of it. The entire glass. Her eyes watered, she gagged, and spit drooled down the sides of her mouth, but she didn't vomit.

"I told you she can shotgun whiskey!" Stew yelled. He hit his hand against his leg and laughed. He looked at her and again danced. He moved his knees up and down. He bent over and moved his hand over his mouth and sang, "Woo, woo, woo, woo, woo, woo, woo."

"Please, goddamn it, stop," she whispered, her voice fading.

Stew kept going, "Woo, woo, woo, woo, woo, woo . . ."

Horace got up from the couch, unsteady and drunk, and grabbed the woman's arm and pulled her to her feet. "Let's go," he said. "That guy's an asshole." She could barely walk but nodded. She took her purse, and together they headed for the door.

"Where the fuck do you think you two Injuns are going?" Stew yelled and walked over to Horace and grabbed his arm. Horace turned around and hit him as hard as he could in the face. Stew stumbled back, his nose suddenly broken and shooting out blood, and fell into the coffee table. He didn't get up, he didn't even move. After that Horace opened the door, and when he did Gene took a thick metal pipe that was on the floor near the couch and swung it as hard as he could and hit Horace on the left side of his torso. Horace fell to the floor instantly, but Gene didn't hit him again. He could have killed him but he didn't. He just moved back and dropped the pipe. Horace got to his feet. Pain shot through his side and he thought he might be sick. He looked back at Gene in shock. Gene stood motionless, and Horace and the woman got out the door and stumbled down the road away from the house.

With each breath Horace's chest hurt worse and his left shoulder began to ache. He was light-headed and his vision grew hazy. They kept walking and were nearly a half mile from the house when the woman threw up on the side of the road. She was half crying as they continued to walk, and finally they came to a closed plumbing store and stopped. They sat down in front of it, and the woman began crying in earnest.

"Why are you with a guy like that?" asked Horace.

"I don't know," she muttered.

"He's really mean to you."

She nodded.

"You don't deserve that," he said.

She again nodded and spit bile on the ground.

"You have to build your own boat," Horace whispered to her. "You have to build it so you can move to the next level, away from here. So you can become the best person you can be. So you can be a champion. And a champion never lets things like that happen."

The woman laughed and then began crying again. She covered her face with her hands.

"Don't worry," Horace told her. "I'll help you out. I live on a ranch and I'm going to head back there soon and you can come with me if you want." He felt the warmth of her. Her hair smelled like lemon, and when she quit crying she held his hand and he held hers. It was warm and very soft, and even though his side hurt worse and worse, it felt good to be next to her and they both fell asleep against the building.

26

When Horace woke it was morning and the woman was gone and employees were arriving at the plumbing store to begin their workday. He got up, shaky and hungover, and his side, where he'd been hit with the pipe, pierced in pain as he stood. His left shoulder ached, and he lifted his shirt to see his whole side was black and blue and swollen. He barely made it back to his apartment. Once inside he ate a bowl of cereal and collapsed in bed. When he woke it was night and his side hurt so bad he could barely get up. But even so he walked downtown and ate a hot dog from a casino. After that he went to a mini-mart and bought a bottle of ibuprofen and a Coke. He took five pills.

It was past midnight and he was walking along North Las Vegas Boulevard toward his apartment when he saw a white Ford pickup pulling a three-horse slant-load trailer stopped on the side of the road. Its flashers were on and a man in a cowboy hat was looking at a blown tire on the left side of the trailer.

Horace went across the street to find the man was just a high school–age boy.

"Where you heading?" Horace called out. He stood bent toward his left to ease the pain in his side. He looked rough, his face sweaty and ill, his hair disheveled.

The kid, who was crouched, stood up, startled. "Reno," he replied nervously and stepped back away from Horace.

"Don't worry about me. I just want to help if I can. How did you end up here?"

"I was coming from St. George, Utah," the kid said. "I could have gone around Las Vegas, but I've never been here. I wanted to see it, but I wasn't really gonna stop. Then the tire blew. I can't believe it blew right then, but I have the worst luck ever. I only wanted to drive by the casinos and see the Strip, and now I'm in a world of shit. If my uncle knows I was driving around Las Vegas, he'll fire me and call my dad. And the poor horses are probably having a meltdown with all these lights and noise everywhere."

"They'll be okay," Horace said and leaned into the side of the truck to ease his pain. "They been on the road long enough that they're probably too tired to do much of anything except worry. I can help you out if you want."

The boy looked at Horace and shook his head.

"I know I don't look like it now, but I used to work on a ranch and I can change tires in my sleep. I really can."

The boy glanced around and then said, "Okay. I appreciate it. I'm having a hard time getting the lugs off and I got to get the hell out of here."

Horace nodded and they went to work. Together they got the rim off and put on the spare. The pressure held when the boy let the jack down, and then together they got the blown tire and the jack in the bed of the truck. Horace's side hurt so bad that he nearly collapsed.

Under the streetlights they shook hands and the boy tried to give Horace money but Horace wouldn't take it. He just asked if he could pet one of the horses. The boy opened the escape door and a chestnut quarter horse leaned his head out and looked at the bright lights and the people of Old Town Las Vegas. Horace ran his hand over the horse's neck three times and smelled him. Tears filled his eyes and he shut the door.

"You think I could get a ride with you?" he asked in a broken voice. "I'll stay in the bed of the truck if you want. I won't be any trouble. I'm an all right person. I swear I am. I just want to get out of here and you're heading through Tonopah anyway. I'll get out there. I promise I will, it's where the ranch is that I used to work."

"I don't know," the boy said, nervous again. "I don't think my uncle would want me to."

"I can pay for gas," Horace added. "I'll pay you extra, too. I won't be any problem."

The boy looked at the ground. "Well," he said, "I guess you can, but I gotta go right now."

"I just have to get my money and my clothes. It'll take me less than ten minutes to get it. I'd go faster but I hurt my side and I can't run. Will you wait?"

"I can wait a couple minutes," the boy said, and Horace nodded and began jogging the best he could to his apartment. When he got there his side hurt so bad he could hardly breathe, but he took the money he had hidden in the bottom of a cereal box and his new clothes and ran as fast as he could back to the kid and the truck. His side was on fire by the time he got there. He could barely stand as he reached the street to see the truck and trailer weren't there. The kid had gone.

He sat down between two buildings and began to cry. His side ached and he had trouble getting himself up, but eventually he walked to a mini-mart and bought a pint of Old Crow and mixed it with Coke and forced himself to drink it. He took five more ibuprofens. At two in the morning, with the pint gone, he began walking again. He found a pay phone in the Fremont Casino and called Mr. Reese collect.

"I'm sorry," he whispered into the phone.

"You don't have anything to be sorry about," said Mr. Reese as he sat up in bed. Mrs. Reese turned on the bedside lamp, suddenly wide awake. "Where are you, Horace?"

"In Las Vegas," he said.

"Have you been there the entire time?"

Horace paused and looked out onto the casino floor. "I hadn't seen horses in a long time, Mr. Reese. I miss being around horses. Horses make everything seem all right."

"I still have ours. They're waiting for you."

Horace fell silent, and Mr. Reese looked worriedly at his wife.

"Can I come see you?" he asked and shrugged his shoulders to her.

"No," Horace whispered. "You should just forget about me, Mr. Reese. I've always been trouble."

"That's not true. You've been nothing but a help to us. You have to remember how much we've leaned on you these last years. Maybe we leaned too hard and I'm sorry if we did. . . . But we love you, Horace. We feel so lucky to have met you. What part of the city do you live in?"

"In the old part," he said, his voice trailing off.

"Old Town?" Mr. Reese said and again looked at his wife. "Do you have a regular place you live?"

Horace sighed.

"I'll come find you and we can talk."

"Don't, Mr. Reese. I shouldn't have called. I'm just sorry, that's all I wanted to say. I just wanted to say I'm sorry. I wanted to come home. I did, but then I just couldn't. No matter how hard I tried, I couldn't." And then he hung up.

27

Mrs. Reese was already up when Mr. Reese got off the phone. She remained silent, put on her bathrobe, and went to the kitchen to make coffee. Mr. Reese used the toilet, put heat lotion on his back, and dressed. He pulled an old suitcase from under the bed and filled it quickly with two changes of clothes and his shaving kit. When he came out to the kitchen, Mrs. Reese had bacon frying and was making biscuits. Tears streamed down her face.

"You'll have to quit crying," he told her. He put his arms around her while she kneaded the dough. "If you don't quit then I'll start and I won't have it in me to make the trip."

She nodded, and he went to the silverware drawer and opened it. From underneath the tray he took an envelope with an emergency five hundred dollars and a credit card. He put them both in his wallet, poured a cup of coffee, and watched as Mrs. Reese put the biscuits in the oven and made him three turkey, Swiss, and lettuce sandwiches. He took a drink of coffee and his hands shook as he did.

The sun rose across the sagebrush and mountains and he drove his truck into Tonopah, filled the tank, and headed south. He listened to the radio and drank coffee from a thermos and pushed the old truck down the empty highway.

The hours passed, and it was midmorning when he came to Las Vegas and found his way to Old Town. He parked the truck and started walking up and down Fremont Street carrying a picture of Horace with him. Any person working in a store or a casino with a view of the street he showed the picture to. But no one he talked to had seen Horace. He looked for three hours and then he went back to his truck, ate lunch, and called Mrs. Reese.

"I can't walk much more without my back giving out," he said. "What am I going to do?"

"You'll have to get a room and take breaks," she said. "You have to remember to put heat on your back and do your stretches. Use your pills. This might take awhile, so don't do too much at once."

"I don't like it here at all," he said in a near whisper, and his voice trailed off as he looked out the window.

"I know you don't. Just please bring him home, Eldon," she said. "Please find him." He got a room at the Four Queens Hotel and spent the afternoon resting. At five he went out for three hours and then came back. He put more lotion on his back, did his stretches, lay on the bed, and slept for an hour. When he woke he made coffee, ate another sandwich, and left. But the night grew more unsettling, and the people he came across more unpredictable, belligerent, and drunk, so he went back to his room.

He ate breakfast the next morning and set off again. He searched farther out and down alleys and side streets. He made stops at the God in Me Ministry, Las Vegas Rescue Mission, the Salvation Army, and Catholic Charities. He made photocopied pictures of Horace with his phone number on them and handed them out. He did this for two days straight and grew more hope-less as he walked up and down Fremont Street and the sur-rounding areas.

On the third day he passed the Kabob Korner, a tattoo parlor, and a bar called the Griffin. There was yelling across the street. He stopped to see two men arguing by a white van. To the left of them, against an alley wall, he saw a person who looked, from a distance, like Horace.

He made his way across the street. His heart raced. He took off his cowboy hat, ran his hand through his hair, and put the hat back on. As he grew closer he could see that the person in front of him was a boy, and the boy was Horace.

He was wearing dirty jeans, boots, and Mr. Reese's old can-vas work coat. There was a paper bag in front of him with a half-empty pint of Old Crow inside it and a can of Coke to the left of him. His eyes were closed and he was asleep. The old man bent down, stiff and sore, and put his hand on Horace's shoulder.

Horace opened his eyes and looked up.

"I've been so worried about you," he said gently, and with difficulty he sat down next to Horace. "An hour doesn't pass without me thinking about you. Mrs. Reese is the same."

"How did you find me?" Horace whispered drunkenly.

"You called the house and told me you were here."

"I called the house?"

Mr. Reese nodded. "I've been looking for you for a long time, Hector."

"I don't go by that name anymore, Mr. Reese. I wish you wouldn't call me that."

"I'll call you whatever name you want. Just tell me which name."

Horace shook his head. Around them the city toiled on. Cars passed, delivery trucks stopped, and people walked by in endless streams. "Don't be nice to me, Mr. Reese. It makes every-thing worse. Don't you see? . . . It would be easier if you just went away and never came back."

"You look sick," said Mr. Reese. "Have you been eating? Are you okay?"

"I'm okay."

"You don't look it."

"I'm still tough. I still am."

"I know you are."

Horace shook his head. "I can't fight anymore."

"I heard."

"I'll never be a champion of anything. I know that for sure now. I'll never be anything."

"You don't know that."

"I do, because I'm cursed, Mr. Reese."

"You're not cursed," the old man said.

"But I am." Horace took a heavy drink from the can of Coke and poured the rest of the Old Crow pint into it. "I mean why else would my mom just dump me off? That doesn't happen to normal kids. Why would she do that, Mr. Reese?"

The old man sighed. "I think your mom was having a hard time with her marriage and the new baby. Sometimes a baby can wear a couple out. Maybe she was just trying to please her husband, I don't know. But I do know none of that was your fault."

"You don't know that for sure."

"I'm pretty certain."

"What about my dad?"

"I don't know why he left. I never knew him. But I know it had nothing to do with you. You weren't the reason. I'd bet my life on that. You were just a baby."

Horace's head fell toward his chest and tears streamed down his cheeks. "He has a wife and two kids and a cabin on a lake and a speedboat. He has a fancy house in Seattle. He has season tickets to the Mariners, but he never invites me to come. Why doesn't he invite me, Mr. Reese?"

"I don't know," the old man said. "I just don't know. You were raised to be ashamed of yourself. For all the good things your grandmother did, she did some bad things, too. As did your father for abandoning you, and your mother for leaving you with your grandmother. We both know you've had it rough. But even so, look at the good things you've done, that have come from you just being you."

"But I haven't done anything," Horace whispered.

"That's not true."

"It is, Mr. Reese."

"You're wrong. You helped me get the ranch back in shape when my back went out the first time. I was laid up for a long time and you took over. You ran a whole ranch and you were hardly eighteen. And remember you helped Boss become one of the best horses I've ever had. And I was certain he didn't have it in him. What would his life be without you? And you inspired me to try to be my own champion. Even Mrs. Reese tried to be her own champion, and while you were there she was, in her own way. You have to remember things. You graduated from high school even though it was hard and lonely for you. You became a great horseman and a real sheepman and you helped me so much I can't even begin to repay you. And then you had the guts to move to Arizona by yourself. A ranch kid all by himself in a city. You got a job without anybody's help and became a Golden Gloves boxing state champion. You did that on your own. And then you went to Texas and won a pro fight and then won two more in Mexico. And you nearly beat Raymundo Figueroa, and he went to the Olympics." Mr. Reese paused and let out a long breath. "Maybe you could have been a championship boxer, maybe that's true. I just don't know enough about boxing to say for sure. But if you were a champion, you wouldn't be a Mexican champion no matter what you did. You would have been the champion. All parts of you."

"Why are you wasting your time, Mr. Reese?"

"Because you're my friend, Horace. Because I think of you as my son."

"I wish I was your son, but I'm not."

"You are to me and Mrs. Reese. You've always been that to us."

"But it's not true."

"It is to us."

"My life's over anyway."

"It's not, it's just starting."

"But I don't care anymore, Mr. Reese. Every night I'm here I hope I get run over or stabbed or shot or thrown in prison. That's how I feel."

"I'd be tired, too, if I were you," the old man said. "It's hard to hate yourself every single day, and it's hard to try and be something you're not. Both of those take their toll. I know it took a lot of effort for you to try with your boxing. It took a lot out of you."

Horace looked at the old man. "I'm just a drunk Indian now."

"I don't think you're a drunk."

"I am," he whispered.

Mr. Reese paused. "Maybe . . . Maybe you are now. I don't know. But even if you are, it's not just the Indian that's the drunk, it'll be the Irish in you that makes you a drunk just as much. So you can't even be a drunk Indian without trying to be someone you're not. Because every time you're a drunk Indian you're also a drunk Irishman, a drunk American, and a drunk Nevadan."

"You're wrong about all this, Mr. Reese."

"What you don't understand, Horace, is you don't have to be one thing. You can take all the best things you are and be them. I don't know how many times I've tried to tell you all the great things that come from being a Paiute and all the great things that come from being from a small town and all the great things that come from being part Irish and one hundred percent Nevadan."

"No one thinks like that," Horace said and shook his head.

"That's where you're wrong. That is how people think. That's how people are. You can be a cowboy and listen to Slayer, Horace. You can be a cowboy and have long hair. Just as you could have been a boxer from Tonopah who was part Indian. It's all just up to you to be you. You just have to be strong enough to be yourself."

"But I'm not strong enough, Mr. Reese. That's what I'm trying to say."

"I can help you."

"No one can help me with that." Horace finished the can of Coke and wiped his eyes with his hands. "Please just tell Mrs. Reese you couldn't find me and forget about me."

"What about the dogs and the horses?"

"I miss the horses more than anything," Horace said, and again tears streamed down his face and his voice became barely audible. "And Little Roy."

"They all miss you."

Horace shook his head.

"I have to tell you something," Mr. Reese said. "I sold the sheep."

"You sold them?" Horace wiped his eyes on his coat and looked at the old man.

"My back can't take it. I can't ride anymore and Pedro has moved on."

"You sold them?"

Mr. Reese nodded. "For a while after I did I was feeling sorry for myself. I was lost. I had trouble getting out of bed. But I had forgotten about '*the B.O.A.T.*'"

"I don't think like that anymore, Mr. Reese. That's how kids think. It's stupid to think that way."

"It's not stupid, Horace. It reminded me that I need, for who I am, to keep building. So I went out and bought fifty cows from Morton. Ander gave me his four-wheeler and I'm going to run a small-time cow-calf operation."

"Cattle?"

"The new well will make sure we have enough hay, and I have the tractor running better than ever. It's going to be a good thing for both of us. Why don't you come back and help me for a bit? We'll fix up the barn so you can have your own apartment. You can be your own man and do what you like. You could live in Tonopah if you wanted. We'll get you a good truck."

"I don't have it in me anymore," said Horace.

"Please," Mr. Reese said. "You don't look well, Horace. Why don't you come back and heal up and give it a try? If you don't like it you can come back here. I'll drive you myself."

"I just can't."

Mr. Reese looked out across the street and was silent for a long time before he cleared his throat. "Then I'm going to be honest with you, Horace. I told myself I wouldn't tell you this, but I feel I have to. . . . What I'm trying to say is that I have cancer, liver cancer, and that's an aggressive kind, an incurable kind. What that means is I don't have long to live. It might be a month, might be two. But the doctors say for certain that it's not much more than that. What I need is some help to get things in order before I pass. To help Mrs. Reese. She'll be all alone out there. I've never begged anything from you, but I'm begging now. As a friend, I need your help."

* * *

The sky was blue and cloudless as Mr. Reese and Horace walked together down Fremont Street. The sun warmed the cold winter day, and Mr. Reese took Horace to the truck and helped him into the cab and shut the door. He then walked across the parking lot and went inside the Four Queens Casino, ordered two ham and cheese sandwiches to go from the restaurant, and got his things from his room. He paid the bill, picked up the food, and went back to the truck to find the cab empty. He put his luggage in the truck bed toolbox, waited in the cab, and five minutes later Horace stumbled out from the Four Queens Casino hunched over to his left and moving slowly.

Mr. Reese got out of the truck and went to him.

"Are you okay? Why are you walking like that?"

Horace nodded. "It's nothing, Mr. Reese. I've been hurt worse. It's just drinking gives me the runs. I tried to wait so you wouldn't think I left, but I had to use the toilet pretty bad and once I got in there I couldn't get off. I guess I'm not feeling too good." He leaned against the truck.

"Drinking whiskey is hard on your body. Especially when you don't eat."

Horace nodded. "You think it would be okay if I just slept in the back? I feel like lying down and I don't know if I can sit up for much longer."

Mr. Reese nodded. "I was thinking we could stop by Ander's before we head home. He's out of town and I figure we can get you sober and washed up before Mrs. Reese sees you."

"That's a good idea," said Horace.

The old man went to the cab of the truck, and behind the bench seat was an old, thick canvas sleeping bag. He laid it out flat in the bed and helped Horace get inside. He gave him a sandwich, a bag of chips, and a bottle of water.

"Try to drink some water and eat a little bit," Mr. Reese said. "That will help you get going again. It will help soak up some of the booze."

Tears welled in Horace's eyes. "I'm sorry I let you down, Mr. Reese."

"You didn't let me down."

"I know earlier I said I wanted you to leave, but I'm glad you came and got me."

"I'm just so relieved to have found you, Horace."

"It's hard to be alone all the time."

"It is," Mr. Reese said.

"We'll be cattlemen, huh?"

"My dad was for a while, I don't see why we can't."

"I'm sure we can," Horace said and closed his eyes.

Mr. Reese moved the rearview mirror to show the bed of the truck, and he kept one eye on Horace and drove fifty miles an hour in the right lane and they left the city at dusk. When the last suburb passed and the traffic thinned, he called Mrs. Reese.

"I got him," he said.

"Where is he?"

"He's in the bed of the truck in a sleeping bag. He's in rough shape, but I think he'll be okay. He's been drinking."

"Drinking alcohol?"

"Yes," Mr. Reese said. "I don't think he's been eating either. I'm going to take him to Ander's for a couple days. I don't want you to see him like he is and I know he won't want you to see him in the shape he's in. First thing tomorrow I'm going to take him to the clinic and get him checked out."

Louise began to sob. "You really found him?"

"I did, but the only way I got him in the truck was to use

your cancer trick. You're so smart about people. You knew he
wouldn't come unless we forced him."

"It's a good kind of force," she said.

The night was cool but not cold and Mr. Reese stopped only
once to use the toilet and get coffee. When he checked, Horace
was on his stomach inside the sleeping bag with his eyes closed.
It was just past nine p.m. when they arrived at Ander's shack on
the outskirts of Tonopah, with its white siding and red trim, its
ramshackle roof, and his three old, nonrunning trucks in the
drive. Mr. Reese found the hidden key underneath a gas can,
unlocked the front door, and turned on the porch lights.

When he walked down to the truck and opened the bed,
he put his hand on Horace's foot and squeezed it through the
sleeping bag. But there was no response. He did it three times
and still there was nothing. With great difficulty he climbed
into the bed of the truck to find Horace not breathing. There
was no vomit, no signs of distress. He was just not breathing.
Mr. Reese rolled him over and pulled him from the bag as tears
leaked down his face. He held him in his arms and rocked him
back and forth and the night went along.

ACKNOWLEDGMENTS

I couldn't have let *Don't Skip Out on Me* go without the help of my gal, Lee. Same goes for Lesley Thorne. She can always see the cracks in my work and is kind enough and tough enough to tell me where they are. Thanks also to Amy Baker and Angus Cargill for reading the book again and again and again. I'd also like to thank Anna Stein for her tremendous help, as well as Helene Fournier, Francis Geffard, Jane Palfreyman, Lisa Baker, Chris Metzler, Silvia Crompton, Susan M. S. Brown, and everyone at Bakhall and Berlin Verlag.

THE STORY BEHIND THE
SOUNDTRACK TO THE NOVEL

Visit HC.com/dontskipoutonme
to download the soundtrack.

I had always imagined a soundtrack accompanying this novel.
Its landscape as well as its characters, particularly Horace Hopper and Mr. Reese, felt like music from the very first sentence.
Even when I was just sketching out ideas for the novel, the songs came. Richmond Fontaine's "Whitey and Me," "Don't Skip Out on Me," and "The Blind Horse" were a few that I wrote for a record called *You Can't Go Back If There's Nothing to Go Back To*.

As I worked on the first draft of the book I began to notice that I was taking breaks to write instrumentals for the characters. Songs like "Meeting Billy in El Paso," "Mr. Reese's Place in La Jolla," and "Night Out with Diego" began to show up.
With each draft of the book came more songs. After the novel was in working shape, I met with the guys in Richmond Fontaine, showed them the tunes, and we decided to make the album. And what a fun one to make. It was recorded in a two-day snowstorm at Flora Recording and Playback in Portland, Oregon. A desert record made in a Northwest blizzard.

I want to thank the guys in the band for reading early drafts of *Don't Skip Out on Me* and for being so damn kind to do the session and all the practices that went along with developing the songs. Richmond Fontaine are the coolest guys I know: Paul Brainard, Dan Eccles, Sean Oldham, and Freddy Trujillo.

I'd also like to thank John Morgan Askew, who engineered and produced the record, Joe Powers for his great harmonica playing, and Cory Gray for his keyboard work.

It's not my intent that you listen while you read. I wrote the music so that when you hear it you might, for a few minutes, be transported to the Little Reese ranch, to Tonopah, Tucson, El Paso, Tijuana, Monterrey, and into the world of *Don't Skip Out on Me.*

Don't Skip Out on Me Track Listing

1. Horace Hopper

An introduction into the world of *Don't Skip Out on Me* and to Horace Hopper, a ranch hand on the isolated high-desert Little Reese ranch in central Nevada. Horace is lonely and scarred but also hopeful and ambitious. We wanted to capture all those emotions as well as the landscape of the ranch in this song.

2. Víctor Gets on the Bus

Horace is watching the failed sheepherder, Víctor, get on a bus to Las Vegas. It's early morning in Tonopah, the sun is just coming up, and no one is on the streets. Víctor, who speaks no real English or Spanish, is leaving by himself hoping, eventually, to get to Los Angeles. Such a bleak and rough situation.

A lost and troubled man alone in a country where he doesn't understand the language.

3. The Dream of the City and the City Itself

Part One: The Dream of the City

On the ranch, in the safety of isolation, Horace fantasizes about what he'll be when he gets to Tucson: first a Golden Gloves champion, then a world-champion professional boxer, and then, finally, he'll come back to the Little Reese ranch a savior. The song is fast and upbeat because in the privacy of his own mind Horace is full of swagger and success and ambition.

Part Two: The City Itself

Reality. Horace arrives by bus and sees, from the outskirts, the size and sprawl of Tucson. He's overwhelmed, and his confidence quickly fades.

4. Living Where You're Not Wanted

Horace stays in his aunt's guesthouse, an aunt who is, at best, indifferent toward him. He has moved from the ranch and the love of Mr. and Mrs. Reese to a city he doesn't know and a home where he knows he's not wanted.

5. Horace and the Trophy

The image that inspired this song was that of Horace leaning against the back wall of the Mesa

Convention Center after he becomes the Arizona Golden Gloves state champion. The trophy is next to him. He's won! He closes his eyes and feels his old life fading. He's no longer a failure or an outcast. Finally, after so many years, he's leaving Horace Hopper and his old identity behind him. He's becoming his dream, the future Mexican boxing champion, Hector Hidalgo.

6. **Rescue and Defeat in Salt Lake City**

Horace arrives at the Golden Gloves national tournament in Salt Lake City. As he goes to the Salt Palace to check in, all his ambition and confidence crumble. He sits by himself looking at the other boxers from all over the country, and he knows he's nothing. He knows he'll lose. Mr. Reese arrives unannounced and finds him. A friend to the rescue.

7. **Horace Decides to Go Pro**

In a motel room in Salt Lake City, Horace tells Mr. Reese he's turning pro, that he can't come back to the ranch until he's made something of himself, until he's proven to everyone that he is a somebody: a champion.

8. **Mr. Reese's Place in La Jolla**

We wanted a romantic feel. A melancholic beach tune, both in melody and tempo. A song that Mr. Reese could live inside and reminisce about a life and a woman he once had in La Jolla. A life and love that were taken from him when he was forced to go back to the Little Reese ranch after his father's death.

9. **Hector Hidalgo**

Hector is Horace's dream-self, a Mexican boxing champion. A man who is never frightened, who never backs down, and who never stops fighting. We made the song fast and tough and strong in tribute to Hector. Only toward the end, when the band breaks down, do you see hints of Horace's melancholy. But soon enough Hector is back and the song sprints to the finish.

10. **Meeting Billy in El Paso**

Horace meets the homeless man, Billy, late at night on the streets of El Paso. Billy's bleak situation goes alongside Horace's sadness that he'd been swindled by Ruiz. All around them the night carries on, and Billy tells him of his life and the story of Ernie "Indian Red" Lopez.

11. **Night Out with Diego**

Horace wins his fight in Tijuana, and Diego takes him out to celebrate. But Horace is unsettled by the city, unsure of the food, and unable to understand Spanish. The streets are wild and unruly. The song starts with the idea that Horace is seeing the city from the outside, an observer. The music is clean and upbeat and full of adrenaline. Slowly, however, the city seeps into him. He stops looking at it

from the outside and becomes a part of it. He eats
local food, gets drunk, and visits a prostitute. The
mariachi-influenced ending is drunken and a bit off,
and finally, collapsing, like Horace at the end of the
night.

12. Waking Up with Broken Ribs

The morning after Horace wins the fight in
Monterrey, Mexico, he wakes up at dawn in a small
hotel. The sun is coming through thin yellow
curtains. Horace is so beat-up he's unable to get out
of bed. He takes codeine tablets and tries to go back
to sleep. There's the yellow light, the dreaminess
of the codeine, the warmth of the early morning
sun, and again Horace's relief that he's won. But
that morning there is also a growing sense of
loneliness and confusion. Does he really want to
be a professional boxer? And why if he wants to be
Mexican, does Mexico scare him so much?

13. The Fight with Raymundo Figueroa

This is old-school Richmond Fontaine. The band,
in its early days, was faster and half-crazed, both
country and punk and full of odd and weird stops
and starts. That's what we have here. The first
section is the buildup to the fight and then into the
first rounds when Raymundo Figueroa overwhelms
Horace and lands dozens of brutal punches. The
following melody lines are when Horace comes
back—his resilience and toughness and strength—
maybe he could really win. The song goes back

and forth, the up and down of the fight. The end,
however, is when Horace loses and realizes he won't
fight again. His life as a boxer is over. The music,
like his life, is crumbling and in pain. It's angry and
brooding and lost.

14. **Horses in Las Vegas**

A young cowboy trailering horses to Reno gets off
the highway in Las Vegas to see the Strip. While he's
there, a tire on his horse trailer blows out. He's on
the side of the road in Old Town trying to put on a
spare when Horace sees him and helps. Afterward
the cowboy offers him money but Horace only asks
if he can pet one of the horses. While he does, the
horse looks out of the trailer door, both nervous and
curious, at the lights of the casinos and the people
walking by. A lonely and simple tune set to the image
of a ranch horse seeing the spectacle of Las Vegas.

15. **Finding Horace on the Street**

Mr. Reese sees Horace sitting against a wall. He's
found him! After months of looking and worrying he
walks across the street to him. The old man sits down
with Horace and tries desperately to get him to come
back to the ranch.

16. **We'll Be Cattlemen**

In a parking lot in Las Vegas, Horace is in a sleeping
bag in the back of the truck. He's beat-up, weak, and
hurt. He thanks Mr. Reese for coming to get him.

Horace says, "We'll be cattlemen, huh?" Mr. Reese and Horace will again run the ranch. Horace is coming home.

17. Back of the Pickup

Mr. Reese gets Horace back to Tonopah. It's night. No clouds are in the sky, only stars. The music reflects Horace's life, all its heartache and pain. His quest to become a champion is over, his dream of changing his identity has collapsed, leaving only himself and the old man in the back of the pickup.

ABOUT THE AUTHOR

Willy Vlautin is the author of *The Free*, *Lean on Pete*, *Northline*, and *The Motel Life*. He is the singer and songwriter of the band Richmond Fontaine and a member of the band The Delines. He lives outside Portland, Oregon.

ALSO BY WILLY VLAUTIN

THE FREE
A NOVEL
Available in Paperback, E-book, and Digital Audio

"A portrait of American life that is so hard and so
heartbreaking that it should be unbearable, but it isn't. The
straightforward beauty of Vlautin's writing, and the tender
care he shows his characters, turns a story of struggle into
indispensable reading. I couldn't recommend it more highly."
—Ann Patchett

LEAN ON PETE
A NOVEL
Available in Paperback, E-book, and Digital Audio

"Willy Vlautin writes novels about people all alone in the
wind. His prose is direct and complex in its simplicity, and
his stories are sturdy and bighearted and full of lives so
shattered they shimmer."
—Cheryl Strayed, *The Oregonian*

NORTHLINE
A NOVEL
Available in Paperback and E-book

"*Northline* shines with naked honesty and unsentimental
humanity. The character of Allison Johnson, and the
wounded-but-still-walking people she encounters on her
journey, will stay with me for a long while. Vlautin has
written the American novel that I've been hoping to find."
—George Pelecanos

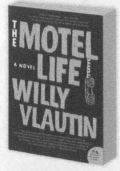

THE MOTEL LIFE
A NOVEL
Available in Paperback and E-book

"Slighter than Carver, less puerile than Bukowski,
Vlautin . . . manages to lay claim to the same blearyeyed
territory, and . . . to make it new."
—*New York Times Book Review*, Editor's Choice